GREEN ZONE JACK

I. JAMES BERTOLINA

EAST THIRD STREET PRESS, LLC

Published in the United States of America by
East Third Street Press, LLC

First Printing, 2018

Edition ISBNs

Trade Paperback: 978-1-7321409-0-5
Digital: 978-1-7321409-1-2

This is a work of fiction. Characters and events are either the product of the author's imagination or are used fictitiously. Any resemblance to actual persons, living or dead, or actual events, is purely coincidental. Although many of the settings and agencies involved in this story are real, the author has taken liberties to suit the needs of the story, and this book does not purport to provide an accurate, true depiction of either locales or organizations – though the author has done his best to be true to the spirit of both.

ACKNOWLEDGMENTS

THE AUTHOR would like to thank: Renni Browne, Ross Browne, Shannon Roberts, Amanda Clark, Leigh Westerfield, Colleen Sheehan, Monica Haynes, Jane Ryder, and Alan Bowen.

CHAPTER 01

"YOU'RE NEEDED back in the embassy, it's urgent."

"Wrong guy," Payton Ladd said. "I've a flight to catch."

"John Thornton called a few minutes ago to make sure you hadn't been waved through."

Payton glanced away from the Marine Embassy Security Guard who leaned down to his driver's open window. Irritated, he took a deep breath. What now?

Another MSG, on the other side of the embassy's main gate, circled a Citroen Coupe with a leashed Belgian Malinois security dog.

At the moment, Payton's only interest was his first run in months along the South Carolina shore in front of his Isle of Palms beach bungalow. After eight months undercover in Egypt and the botched operation that cost his team the lives of two good men with Egypt's State Security Investigations Service, he was through with the Middle East for what he hoped would be a long time. Before he'd left for the airport forty-five minutes ago, he'd stopped by Regional Security Officer John Thornton's office. John had assured him he'd be on vacation for the next month and to forget about any Diplomatic Security Service, DSS, business. They'd said their goodbyes and he left.

"Make it quick, Faheem," Payton said to his Palestinian driver.

Faheem drove the five blocks back to the embassy building and pulled his Volvo behind a line of military vehicles parked around the circular drive.

"Don't turn it off. I won't be long," Payton said.

Faheem nodded.

Urgent or not, he'd make sure John kept it short. His flight left in less than two hours from Queen Alia International Airport, and he planned to be on it.

Payton made his way up to the second-floor DSS offices.

John had his telephone hunched up between his shoulder and his bald head. He waved Payton to the chairs in front of his desk.

Payton sat with his long legs crossed at the ankles. He glanced at his watch. An hour and twenty minutes 'til wheels up.

"King Abdullah will be there and I want Queen Rania seated next to the ambassador's wife." John listened, then said, "No, the second table." He replaced the phone. "Glad I caught you."

"Caught me for what?"

"Your time off."

"Which I plan to enjoy."

John flipped open a folder, peered over his half-moon glasses, and handed Payton a piece of paper.

Payton saw the memo's letterhead, "Embassy of the United States of America, Baghdad, Iraq."

"We have a situation," John said.

Not my problem, Payton thought.

"I'm not going to miss my flight."

"Catherine McCabe asked for you."

Payton readjusted in his chair. He would never have expected to hear her name, especially after the way they'd ended their relationship.

"She's in Baghdad?"

"Been RSO for several months," John said.

"I heard she'd taken a position with a corporate security company."

"Didn't last. She's too ambitious to let a challenge the size of Baghdad slip by. Don't you two have a history?"

"We were together for almost two years in Mexico."

"One person in a relationship with an embassy security job is hard enough but two?" John shook his head.

"We knew the odds and had a great run of winning hands. Look, you need to find someone else. Remember, for the next month I'm not available."

"She asked for you because an American's disappeared outside the Green Zone. Ambassador Rhodes called Director Santiago in DC and requested your immediate transfer to Baghdad." He pointed with his glasses to the memo. "I received the request a few minutes ago."

Payton handed it back unread. He stood and walked over to the window.

"They need someone with your special talents. The situation's a top priority because the person who disappeared is Senator Miles Ater's nephew. *The* Senator Miles Ater."

Payton gazed down at the helicopter on the helipad behind the embassy. He could recommend any number of competent agents in embassies around the globe who'd be able to find a missing person. Why request someone she had a failed relationship with? Though scarred over, his soft spot for her had never disappeared. Catherine was special, someone he once thought he could spend the rest of his life with. Well, until she blindsided him and blew up what they had.

He turned back to John. "You and I both know kidnapping's a growth industry in the Middle East. Pay the ransom, end of story," Payton said.

"There hasn't been a ransom demand and they're not sure he's even still alive."

"If he went outside the Green Zone on his own, the odds are he's already dead," Payton said.

"We botched the transition to civilian rule when we let the Shiite-Sunni civil war rage on for so long after we took Saddam out. Now our military's concerned we only have one more opportunity to stabilize the country. Since Ambassador Rhodes was put in charge, real headway's been made to bring both sides together."

"After so many dead, it's about time."

"Ater disappeared in part of the city controlled by one of the principal militia leaders involved with the truce talks. There's no indication he's involved with Ater's disappearance, but if he or any of his people are implicated, then the entire negotiation process could be derailed."

"And the killing starts all over again," Payton said.

"The military, Ambassador Rhodes, and the White House want him found without delay to minimize any chance the talks could collapse."

"Then throw several agents already in the embassy on the case. Why me?"

"They don't want just anybody. They want the top man hunter in the service."

If it was anyone other than Catherine, he'd push back harder. There'd be no South Carolina beach. He moved away from the window and leaned with both hands on John's desk. "After I find him, I want an additional two weeks off."

"I'll make it another month," John said.

Payton sat back down. "What do we know?"

"Not much. He disappeared after midnight."

"Why's the chairman of the Appropriations Committee's nephew in Iraq?"

"Audit work of some kind." John folded his hands on his stomach paunch. "Ambassador Rhodes was appalled when he arrived to take over for the Coalition Provincial Authority, CPA, and saw how lousy the situation on the ground was. The military knew they invaded with too few troops, and when the CPA took charge, the manpower fiasco worsened. To fill the void, our military's gone outsource mad with private contractors."

"The whole debacle could've been prevented," Payton said.

"Well, now we own it." His desk telephone started to ring. "Your flight leaves at four."

CHAPTER 02

BAGHDAD

THE EIGHT-SEAT State Department Cessna Citation jet banked hard in the late afternoon sun. Payton was the only passenger. He looked down at the Tigris River and saw several small fishing boats and a barge. To the west, beyond the river and city sprawl, were the terminal and runways of Baghdad's International Airport, BGW.

Fifteen years ago he'd led an extraction team to exfiltrate Brigadier General Abdul Matin, commander of all Saddam's forces in southern Iraq. From that game of hide-and-seek, he knew Baghdad was a city of fatal illusions, where truth was a desert mirage. The United States might be in charge now, but nothing would be different.

Saddam contained the centuries-old blood feud between the Sunni and Shiite populations with an iron fist. The US-led invasion unleashed those furies, and now every terrorist and financial opportunist in the world would stream into Iraq for a piece of the action.

If any RSO could handle such a volatile situation, it'd be Catherine. Of all places for her to turn up. Was Mexico six years ago already?

She'd been the assistant regional security officer at the Mexico City embassy when they first met. He was a member of an elite team of Diplomatic Security special agents sent to embassies around the globe to handle crisis situations, and had been sent to Mexico to assist the DEA with the capture of a drug cartel leader. The case grew to include high-level members of the Mexican government, and with Catherine's assistance, he saved Mexican president Antonio Cruz's presidency. In the process, they fell in love.

In the end, the job came first—for both of them—but his bitterness after she broke off their relationship took years to diminish. John Thornton was right: embassy security jobs are relationship killers, but theirs lasted far longer than the sell-by date. Payton wondered if all the career ambition was worth it.

They passed over the ten-story-tall turquoise split dome Al-Shaheed Monument east of the river, one of many structures the monument-obsessed Saddam spent hundreds of millions of dinars to construct all over Baghdad.

"Two minutes," the pilot said over the intercom. Payton snapped on his seat belt.

An hour ago, right after takeoff, the copilot came back to tell him their final approach into BGW would be in a tight corkscrew to avoid surface-to-air missiles.

He waited but nothing happened. Three minutes went by and they still hadn't started their descent. Maybe airport ground controllers told the pilots to pass and circle back.

The nose dipped, he grabbed the edge of the table between him and the opposite seat, then the left wing dropped and several city blocks of packed residential neighborhoods filled his window. Blue sky blazed through the right side cabin windows. They twisted skyward, and through the opposite windows, he saw rooftops along a wide street with heavy traffic. Pressed into his seat, they accelerated, leveled, and roared onto the runway.

In the open cockpit door, the pilot grinned. "Sorry, I waited too long to start our approach," he said.

Payton stood in the aisle behind the copilot, who chuckled and pushed the door out and open.

"Thanks for the baptism," Payton said and stepped out into a wall of heat. On the tarmac, in front of black armored Toyota Land Cruisers with tinted bulletproof windows, stood several MSGs armed with M4 carbines.

A wiry, dark-skinned, dark-haired young corporal stepped forward. Latino or American Indian, Payton wasn't sure. He had a Marine Embassy Security Guard Battalion patch on his uniform with the "In Every Clime and Place" motto.

"Special Agent Payton Ladd?" he asked. "Lance Corporal Thomas Blacknife."

Payton stepped off the air stairs onto the tarmac and gestured to the men behind Blacknife. "You expect trouble?"

"Route Irish is the main road into the city and the deadliest road in the country. Our orders are to get you to the embassy alive and without delay."

"The alive part works for me," Payton said.

Blacknife gave him an easy smile.

Two marines got into the first vehicle. Blacknife went to the second. Payton climbed in behind him and put his go-bag on the middle seat. He unzipped the bag, removed his Glock semiautomatic handgun, and set it on top of the bag. The rear window was open, and a marine sat in the reversed third-row seat with his carbine ready.

The rest of the marines followed in the last Land Cruiser.

"Meet Private First Class Carl Nez. We'll be your security detail." Blacknife thumped the driver's shoulder.

"Special Agent," Carl said and reached back and shook Payton's hand.

He appeared younger than Blacknife, and Payton could see from his gray eyes he was the more serious of the two. If Senator Ater's nephew disappeared outside the Green Zone, he'd have to search for him in the city's most violent neighborhoods and would need a team who'd be able to handle themselves. He knew he could trust these men. Only a select few marines are chosen for the intense training at Marine Security Battalion headquarters in Quantico to become embassy guards.

"Do I call you Thomas or Tom?" Payton asked.

"Most people call me Blacknife."

"Where're you boys from?"

"Snowflake, Arizona," Blacknife said.

"Navajo?"

"Yes, sir, how'd you know?"

"I spent time in Northern Arizona."

"Navajo are our people," Carl said.

"Glad you're with me," Payton said.

"Ever been to Baghdad?" Blacknife asked.

"Once and it wasn't a vacation."

"Nothing's changed," Carl said.

Blacknife handed a Mini Uzi submachine gun with several clips of ammunition over the seat to Payton. "Courtesy of RSO McCabe."

Catherine hadn't forgotten the Israeli weapon was one of his favorites. With expert ease, he popped a clip into place. It wasn't new but was well oiled and in excellent condition.

"I thought DSS agents used Colt SMG 9 mm submachine guns or Colt M4 carbines," Blacknife said.

"An Israeli loaned me one of these years ago. They're reliable, easy to use, and get the job done."

"You'll need it in this city," Carl said. He and Blacknife put on helmets. Blacknife handed one back to Payton. In tight formation, the black vehicles sped toward the main airport entrance and exited onto a four-lane expressway.

Payton watched the speedometer over Carl's shoulder: 50, 55, then settled on 62.

"Ten kilometers to the Green Zone," Blacknife said.

Open spaces gave way to periodic buildings and every so often a stand of palm trees.

Up ahead black smoke billowed skyward in front of stalled traffic.

"Don't stop," Blacknife said into his radio.

They merged onto the left shoulder and sped past dozens of vehicles until they came to a Humvee on its side next to a crater.

"A Bongo truck. They're used to move supplies from the airport to the Green Zone," Blacknife said.

Through angry orange flames and smoke Payton saw an overturned flatbed city truck inside the crater. A charred form was draped over the driver's side door and another was sprawled on the pavement. Cases and reams of paper burned and littered the crater and road.

"Scumbags used an IED," Carl said.

"The Humvee belongs to a security contractor. Dozens of companies are hired to provide security for airport Route Irish runs," Blacknife said.

"Contractors call it IED Alley," Carl said.

They accelerated and the city loomed in front of them.

"Won't be long, sir," Blacknife said.

Low, sand-colored buildings lined the expressway. Saddam's picture was plastered on a few of them. Payton noticed one difference from his last visit when Saddam ruled with his boot on the throat of every Iraqi: bullet holes now stitched across his face.

Five minutes later.

"There," Blacknife said.

Ahead was a seventeen-foot-high wall of reinforced concrete slabs crowned with thick coils of razor-sharp concertina wire. Behind the wall was the Green Zone.

"Where's the moat?" Payton asked.

"The siege mentality is nowhere near the level it was when we first arrived," Blacknife said.

"Thanks to the fast-action response teams," Carl said.

"Months ago, twice, sometimes three times a week rocket or mortar rounds would land inside the four square miles behind the wall," Blacknife said.

"They came from the Red Zone across the river," Carl said.

"The military put in place fast-action response teams to swarm the launch sites, which all but stopped the incoming," Blacknife said.

The wall sliced across the expressway and created a three-way intersection. They slowed and turned left onto a four-lane road with a dirt median, and the wall to their immediate right.

Blacknife pointed out Carl's side of the Humvee. A few hundred yards beyond an irrigation canal were stadium bleachers beside a paved area the size of several football fields.

"The festival and parade grounds where Saddam watched his military parades. The Baghdad Zoo's farther back, closer to those buildings. We still don't have the neighborhoods behind the zoo secured."

"And never will," Carl said.

"Half the zoo animals were killed during the war," Blacknife said.

To avoid slower traffic, they sped along the hard-packed shoulder. When a vehicle drifted toward them, Carl laid on his horn.

"*Get back*," the marine behind Payton yelled.

Payton turned around. The marine had his carbine aimed at two boys on a motorcycle. The boy on the back in rapid motion tapped the driver and with his other hand pointed toward the marine's machine gun. They dropped back.

"Here's the July 14 Bridge checkpoint, the main entrance into the Green Zone," Blacknife said.

Several Bradley Fighting Vehicles were parked in the center of a wide roundabout. Past the Bradleys, car-sized cement blocks had been placed in front of yard-high concrete Jersey barrier walls along with rock-filled Hesco bastions. Machine gun barrels poked out from under the sandbag-laden roof of a pillbox.

Blacknife motioned to the wall opening and four cement trucks faced nose-to-nose on either side of a narrow strip.

"Those trucks are in case a suicide bomber gets lucky and makes it past the Bradleys and machine guns."

Vehicles snaked back into the roundabout, while guards with mirrors on long poles scanned underneath a battered jeep. Another guard followed them with a black Lab. The jeep's owner, an Iraqi man, stood with his wife and two small children off to the side.

They bumped over tank track treads spread at close intervals across the road and pulled to a stop. One of the marines climbed out of the first Land Cruiser and spoke with several guards clustered at the entryway.

"When the wall was put in place, suicide car bombers made several attempts to get inside. There they are." Blacknife pointed to a stack of what was left of the ruined vehicles behind the cement trucks. "Hasn't been another attempt in months."

"What about those three who tried with the school bus?" Carl asked.

"They were taken out before they entered the round-about," Blacknife said.

A second pillbox stood beside the open space that led inside the Green Zone. A black scorch mark ran up the concrete wall behind a tower with more guards who scanned the cars with binoculars.

Was the war even over? Payton thought. He was reminded of a castle wall siege from the Middle Ages.

They rolled into the Green Zone and turned at the first intersection.

He expected soldiers everywhere, but instead saw civilians. Most were in their twenties and thirties. They strolled along sidewalks and in and out of buildings set back from the street. If you discounted the wall and guards with machine guns, they could've been in any city in the United States.

"Republican Guard barracks, one of the first buildings we bombed," Blacknife said. They were in front of a half-destroyed domed-roof granite building. Several young men threw Frisbees on the expansive lawn of brown grass.

They drove for several more blocks. Through his open window, Payton heard the faint loudspeaker muezzin chant the call to worship.

"Where's the new embassy being built?" Payton asked.

"Over by the river," Blacknife said.

"The largest US Embassy in the world," Carl said.

"Wars are always good to construction companies," Payton said.

Payton had heard through the DSS grapevine the new embassy complex cost was millions over budget, and the number of employees now slated to work there had morphed into the thousands. He wondered how Iraqi lives would be improved with a fortune being poured into the construction of a building larger than an American suburban shopping mall.

"Here's the convention center, the embassy's temporary home. RSO McCabe's office is on the third floor," Blacknife said.

They stopped in front of a massive building with rounded concrete slabs along the roof line.

"Thanks for the lift," Payton said.

"Call when you need us," Blacknife said.

Payton stepped out and walked up several marble steps toward Post One, the MSG-guarded main embassy entrance.

CHAPTER 03

PAYTON WATCHED Catherine come out from behind her desk. Her auburn hair still accentuated those determined green eyes. A brief smile appeared, then she was all business.

"It's been way too long," she said and gave him a stiff hug.

"Thanks for the Mini Uzi."

"I wasn't sure you still used one."

"Surprised you even remembered." He waved around her expansive office. "You've come a long way from an assistant RSO in Mexico City."

"No one else wanted the job, so Ambassador Rhodes offered it to me."

"I'm sure you're the only RSO he wanted." If he were Rhodes and needed an efficient embassy security operation, Catherine would be at the top of his list too. Organizational skills were part of her DNA.

She motioned to chairs by double glass doors that opened onto a narrow balcony with panoramic views of the Green Zone. "Did you hear what happened to Delgado?" she asked.

"He's not much of a swimmer."

"Thanks to you, Mexican federal police caught him when he tried to swim away from his Lake Cuitzeo houseboat in the middle of the night. He gave up his entire organization. President Cruz's finance minister was behind the whole plot," she said.

He sat across from her and could tell by the look in her eyes that she was preoccupied.

"They should've let him drown," he said.

"You never seem to change," she said. "Unlike some of us."

"Everyone changes."

"How've you changed?" she asked. She always did get to the point.

"I'm older and no longer married to the job."

"Eight months undercover in Egypt sounds like a marriage to me," she said.

He smiled. "Egypt doesn't count."

She stood, moved over to the doors, and gazed out.

"After what happened between us in Mexico, I wasn't sure you'd even come."

"Did I have a choice?" he asked.

She turned back to him. "John Thornton brought you up to speed?"

"You've got a politically charged problem on your hands with the disappearance of Senator Ater's nephew. But why me? Agents are already here who can handle the case."

"Most are assigned to protective security details. The rest are inexperienced hump agents on temporary duty assignments who cycle through every sixty days and have never been in a war zone. I told Ambassador Rhodes you were the only person I wanted because you won't be deterred by embassy politics, so he called Director Santiago. We need someone with your experience—someone who doesn't care who gets in the way of your investigation."

"You going to be okay with those complications?" he asked.

"We don't have time to soothe egos. I needed the best investigator, not the most politically correct one. I'm dealing with hundreds of US government employees who expect the short time they spend in the Green Zone to juice up their résumés so they can vault over their peers when they get back to Washington."

"I shredded my résumé years ago."

She looked out to the Green Zone. "Besides, I can trust you."

He joined her. "Ater was outside the wall?" he asked. Several blocks away he saw the checkpoint guard tower.

"I don't know what the fool was up to."

"John said he disappeared in part of the city controlled by one of the militia leaders involved with Ambassador Rhodes's peace talks," he said.

"We've heard the same rumor, but no one knows anything for sure. Bottom line, he has to be found in a hurry. We're at a critical juncture. Ambassador Rhodes and the military have made significant gains with their militia cease-fire agreement. The future of Iraq hangs in the balance. We don't need the distraction or have the time to waste finding an American who thought it was a brilliant idea to leave the Green Zone."

She went to a city wall map with a clear plastic cover and put her finger on an X across the river in the shaded red area. "He disappeared in Ishbiliya, the Red Zone's bloodiest neighborhood." She slid her finger down to another X on the shore, close to the wall. "A security contractor saw him here when a group of armed men in a boat snatched both of them at gunpoint. The contractor managed to escape and make his way back. We have no idea what happened to Ben or if he's even still alive."

Payton stood next to her. He saw, nestled against a curve in the Tigris River, "International Zone" scrawled in black grease pencil over the green-shaded area inside the wall. "The International Zone?"

"Once the CPA left, the geniuses in Washington thought the Green Zone should be renamed the International Zone. With the number of countries involved in the rebuilding effort, they wanted a more inclusive name. Everyone here still uses Green Zone."

"Who had the brilliant idea to send Senator Ater's nephew to Iraq?"

"The senator's sister heard our military needed accountants with audit experience, so she badgered him to pull a few strings. Her boy, two years out of Ohio State, arrived with a degree in accounting and a substance abuse problem."

"Did she hope the Green Zone would be his rehab?"

"I guess she thought he needed a change of scenery. I told Ambassador Rhodes he shouldn't be here, but the White House wants to do whatever they can to placate Senator Ater because war funds requests go through his committee. I was instructed to find Ben a job. Something light and secure."

"Right, light and secure in Baghdad."

"Security's improved, but we still get an occasional mortar or Katyusha rocket sent our way. Thanks to the army, they've cut them down to a trickle. The Red Zone's another story. Can you believe after all the lives and money the United States invested, we've had to carve Baghdad up into ridiculous board game colors?" Her cell phone trilled. She looked at the screen and tossed it on her desk.

"What work did you find for Ben?" he asked.

"Auditing military contracts with a team of British accountants."

"Doesn't our government have their own people to fill those positions?"

"Tell the Department of Defense. Iraq's their show now. They attempted to pull off the occupation the same way they fought the war … with the fewest people possible. When Ambassador Rhodes arrived and saw how dire the situation was, he demanded more people be sent over."

"Of course the military welcomed suggestions from an ambassador," he said.

"Imagine common sense from the State Department." She leaned back on her desk and crossed her arms. "You can make omelets with the amount of egg military commanders have on their faces because they botched the number of people required to fill thousands of positions to administer the country. The brilliant solution proposed by Defense Secretary Ordway was to use private contractors to fill the void. Every jackleg contractor in the world has beelined their way to the Green Zone with their hand out. Of course, proper controls weren't in place to account for the obscene amount of cash we fly in by the cargo plane-load to pay them."

"In most cases, cash beats bullets, but in the Middle East it usually comes down to bullets," he said.

"The main reason we've finally gained traction are the C-notes fresh off the Treasury Department's presses we flood the country with. Since we invaded, our top priority's been to jump-start the economy."

"All contractors are paid in cash?"

"Can't print it fast enough to pay them with. DOD's solution for how to keep track of where all the money goes was to contract with outside auditors. Ben was on one of those audit teams."

She reached over, hit #, and pressed the speaker button on her desk telephone.

Click.

"Ms. McCabe, Ben Ater. I have to speak with you. I found something you need to know about. Please call 202-41—."
Click.

"202?" Payton asked.

"Telephone companies gave the Green Zone a DC area code. When my staff called his office to get the rest of his cell number, he'd already disappeared."

"Why call you?"

"Maybe because I found him a job."

"Has there been a ransom demand?"

"We've heard nothing."

"Not good."

"I agree, and the longer we go without one, the more worried I become. The DS/CC will alert me if there's any Internet or cell phone chatter," she said.

DS/CC computer analysts monitor embassy and consulate computer systems along with terrorist websites around the globe 24/7. Payton knew they'd be the first to know if a terrorist organization took credit for Ben's disappearance.

"Of course," Payton said, "no one mentioned you were right. He never should've been here in the first place."

"Being right doesn't always matter, but I'm still bothered I didn't stand my ground, uncle or no uncle."

"You know these operations can turn ugly!" Getting Ben back would be difficult, and with a hurry-up offense came more pressure and the likelihood of mistakes that could get someone killed.

"Do what you do best and locate him. You'll find the DSS offices in the basement. Pick one of the rooms on the fifth floor that we've turned into apartments."

"I need to speak with the security contractor who was taken with Ben."

"He works for a company called Titan United. I'll arrange a meeting. I asked the military police to pinch-hit until you arrived. Lieutenant Quinn Wiley's done some preliminary work—you can check in with him."

He got up to leave, and she ruffled through several pieces of paper on her desk.

"By the way … I'm sorry," she said.

He paused near the door. "About?"

"The way I ended things in Mexico."

"I should've tried harder," he said.

"Our jobs didn't leave—" she stopped with the paper. "Maybe I should've tried harder, too."

"Sometimes mistakes involve other people who also have to live with the consequences."

"My quote unquote mistake you've had to live with?"

"It took awhile, but I finally realized, job or no job, you wanted to be with someone else. Someone who wouldn't get in the way of your career trajectory."

"Do you really think there was someone else or my career was the reason—?"

He held up his hands for her to stop. "Let's forget the past. You wanted me in the Green Zone. Here I am."

"We don't have the luxury of time and you won't play politics. Besides you're the best at what you do. That's why I brought you in."

"Once I find the accountant, I'll be back on my South Carolina beach."

He opened the door.

"Payton …"

"I'll let you know if Lieutenant Wiley found anything we can use," he said and left.

CHAPTER 04

MILITARY POLICE HEADQUARTERS

HE DIDN'T KNOW why Catherine felt the need to dredge up their past. Landing the most sought-after RSO job in the world, she'd gotten what she wanted, a superstar career. He wouldn't be burned twice and get in the way of her ambition again. Once he found the senator's nephew, he'd be on the next flight out.

It was after 8 p.m., but he decided not to wait until morning to speak with Lieutenant Wiley. He needed to know if the military police found anything he could use.

He called the MSG office and found Blacknife and Carl were still there.

Carl drove the Humvee parallel to the river along a palm tree-lined boulevard with villas sprawled on either side.

"Saddam wanted his generals close to his command headquarters, so he kept them in all these villas," Blacknife said.

"Every one of them's crammed with Western amenities," Carl said.

"Have either of you been across the river?" Payton said.

"Once," Carl said. "I don't recommend it."

"What happened?"

"UN administrators had the inspired idea to bring Sunni and Shiite militias together somewhere in the Red Zone for a joint project."

He turned left at an intersection.

"Why didn't they meet in the safety of the Green Zone?" Payton asked.

"They said it would be a show of good faith to meet on the militias' side of the river," Carl said.

"Look where it got them," Blacknife said.

Carl went on, "Under pressure from Washington, the CPA OK'd the UN's request for an initial meeting with one of these so-called Sunni leaders to get the project rolling. The UN guy in charge was a Venezuelan college professor who specialized in sewer and clean water management and had never been in a conflict environment. The Sunni was Bakru Zobgy, an Al Capone look-alike, only shorter and with a hundred more pounds. No more a Sunni leader than I am."

They passed a military bulldozer and dump truck parked on the side of the road.

"Now for the best part," Blacknife said.

"Zobgy operated out of a butcher shop he owned in Fadhil. A neighborhood with thousands of Sunnis packed in like sardines in the Rusafa administrative district, where some of the heaviest house-to-house combat with our troops occurred. Like all the other self-styled freedom fighters, Zobgy's Sunni militia was a glorified gang."

"With a penchant for dead Shiites," Blacknife said.

"Every time one of his men killed a Shiite militia member, Zobgy gave them a rack of lamb. Kill more than one a day, he'd toss in the loin," Carl said.

He turned into a crushed-stone driveway. Payton saw what appeared to be a four-story stone donjon in the middle of a massive villa at the end of the drive.

"I worked security for the meeting," Carl said. "We met in the back of Zobgy's butcher shop. He wore a blood-smeared apron and perched himself on a cutting table. The Venezuelan told Zobgy how they planned to purify water in his neighborhood and wanted to bring Shiite and Sunni contractors together to help with the construction project. Once work started, they intended to open a day care run by women from both sides. He needed Zobgy's word there wouldn't be any trouble. For ten grand, Zobgy said he could guarantee everyone's safety."

"The UN sap didn't recognize a shakedown when he saw one," Blacknife said.

"The professor said he was concerned Zobgy asked for money when all they wanted to do was help his people," Carl said.

"They're in the middle of the Red Zone, and the UN bureaucrat has a concern," Blacknife said.

"Zogby waved his hand, cut off the professor, and said in perfect English, 'Ten large or no project.' That's when gunfire erupted a few streets away, and Zogby said, 'Bullets fly every day after lunch.' We had Army Rangers on guard around the shop, and when they opened up with their grenade launchers, Zogby disappeared through the back door with several of his men," Carl said.

"Two months later a car bomb destroys the UN mission. The Venezuelan and several UN staffers were killed. Soon after, the UN pulled out of Iraq," Blacknife said.

"Hello, Baghdad," Carl said.

"I heard Ben was taken into Ishbiliya," Payton said.

"For his sake, I hope not. Nassar al-Dori and his militia rule Ishbiliya. Zogby's a Boy Scout compared to al-Dori," Carl said.

Payton climbed out and walked over to the villa's MP-guarded entrance.

Military Police Commander Lieutenant Quinn Wiley stood in the expansive lobby, a husky black guy with close-cropped silver-tinged hair who Payton figured in his younger days lifted weights.

"Quinn Wiley," he said and shook Payton's hand. "Let's go to my office." He turned and limped through an open door. "I was on my way out when you called."

"Glad I caught you," Payton said.

Quinn saw him glance at several police pictures on the wall behind his desk. "Civilian life, Newark PD commander. Got the hobble there."

"Shot?"

"Chased a crack dealer over one too many rooftops. After a nasty fall and a long stint in rehab, doctors said they couldn't set it straight."

Payton sat down. "Catherine appreciates the help you've given her."

"I'm partial to RSO McCabe. She's got a tough job with her embassy security operation. We're all short-staffed. I take it you're the help she said was on the way?"

Payton nodded.

"My opinion, Ater got what he deserved if he snuck out in the middle of the night." Quinn shook his head. "Dumb, real dumb. Every contract worker knows to stay out of the Red Zone."

"She said a security contractor was with him?" Payton asked.

"The contractor told my investigator a boat full of men took them at gunpoint. He said Ben was expecting them."

"The guys in the boat?"

"Imagine that."

"Did he leave the Green Zone with Ben?" Payton asked.

"He saw Ben disappear down a manhole behind bombed-out buildings over by the river wall and followed him through a sewer tunnel to the shore. When he told Ben to get back inside, the boat came ashore. Ben said he'd handle them, which didn't work out too well."

"What can you tell me about Ben?"

"Graduated a year ago with honors from Ohio State. Gets along with his coworkers, though a few said he can be cocky. Has a reputation for being a sharp auditor who enjoys a good party."

"The Red Zone's no place for honor students. I'll get over to the manhole and tunnel in the morning," Payton said.

"My people will be waiting for you," Quinn said. He pulled open a drawer and tossed over a clear, ziplock baggie with an inch of purple-tinged dark weed.

Payton picked it up.

"Afghan Kush, premium quality weed we found in the tunnel. The contractor said Ater might've dropped it. Fits with his party boy reputation and why he might pull a stunt like going to the river in the middle of the night."

"Catherine said he has a substance abuse problem," Payton said.

"Recreational drugs are everywhere inside the wall. If you have a problem with drugs, the Green Zone's the last place you need to be."

"The contractor believes he was at the river to meet these guys?"

"That's his story. After they were put on the boat at gunpoint, the kidnappers took them upriver where a van with Nassar al-Dori's men waited."

"How'd he know who they were?"

"They wore desert camo. al-Dori's a militia leader with a brigade of several hundred men who operates out of a slice of the Red Zone called Ishbiliya. All his men wear desert camo. The guys who have Ben and the contractor drove through several neighborhoods before they ended up in Ishbiliya and were taken inside a tea shop, where Ben spoke with a guy the contractor said he knew. It was the last thing the contractor remembers before an explosion blew him through a window into an alley behind the shop. When he regained consciousness, he made his way back to the Green Zone. One thing he's sure of, Ben knew what he was doing."

Payton fingered the weed and wondered if drugs were Ben's motivation to go into the bloodiest neighborhood in the country.

"Have you been to the tea shop?"

"Not yet. We're stretched pretty thin with our current caseload. Ben has a roommate we planned to speak with, a guy named Thierry Rousseau. He might have more information about why Ben was outside the wall."

"Where can I find him?"

"I'd start with a club in the lobby of Hotel Q over by the conference center. He and Rousseau hang out there most nights. One of the people Ben works with said he partied with both of them at the club the night Ben disappeared. Ben was with two Hungarian nurses. The fellow accountant and Rousseau left Ben with the nurses around 11:30. He never showed up for work the next day—the coworker figured he'd gotten lucky. It wasn't unusual for Ben to drag into the office late morning. By lunch, the rumor mill's in full swing that he disappeared across the river."

"How do I get to the hotel?"

"Take a left at the arch across from the embassy. Go two blocks to the first light. You'll see Hotel Q on the other side of the intersection."

"Have you looked into his work?"

"We know he works with auditors who review military contracts. His last assignment was an MWR audit—a Morale, Welfare, and Recreation facility in a forward operating base near Fallujah. These accountants are after contractor fraud."

A fraud auditor with a drug problem … no wonder Iraq's a money pit.

"The military's brought in dozens of accountants to review the mountain of contracts we've put in place. Inflated invoices, ghost employees, work not performed being billed for. Name the scam, they find it. Multiply by a hundred and you get the picture of what they're up against. If you're anybody in the private military contractor world, Iraq's the big leagues, and they all want a piece of the action."

Payton thought, were they military contractors or financial mercenaries?

"What're the chances his work motivated him to leave the Green Zone?"

"We haven't found a work connection." Quinn pointed to the Kush. "My opinion, drugs are the reason and he's way out of his league."

"Why leave for drugs if he could get whatever he needed inside the walls?"

"Ohio State might not teach Common Sense 101," Quinn said.

If drugs were involved, Payton wouldn't discount Ben might leave the Green Zone for them.

"Who do I speak with about his work?" Payton asked.

"His boss, Dale Lowsley." Quinn stood and held his hand out. "If you need any help, ask, and I'll try to free up one of my people. I'm glad you're here."

CHAPTER 05

TRICKS

CARL DROVE back to the embassy.

"The military police found a bag of weed in the tunnel Ben used to travel outside the Green Zone. Quinn figures Ben for the weed, which fits his reputation for being a party boy," Payton said.

"He has a lot of company. Half these contractors live in glorified fraternity houses," Carl said.

"For most of them, the good times start midafternoon," Blacknife said.

"Pick any night of the week and go over to the emergency room at Ibn Sina Hospital and watch the fools who come in wasted from too much booze or freaked out on drugs," Carl said.

"Young Americans overseas for the first time," Blacknife said.

"Pills, coke, heroin … name the drug and you'll find it in the Green Zone," Carl said.

"Quinn said the weed was Afghan Kush," Payton said.

"Kush is up there with the best weed in the world," Blacknife said.

"What do you know about ganja?" Carl asked.

"I wasn't born yesterday," Blacknife said.

"Any theories on how drugs are brought inside?" Payton asked.

"If the smugglers use the three-gate entrances, then they've figured out how to get past the dogs," Carl said.

"Every vehicle can't be checked," Payton said.

"If Ben found a tunnel, there might be others," Blacknife said.

"He didn't need to leave to buy a bag of weed," Carl said.

"Unless he went for some other reason," Payton said.

"It wasn't for night fishing," Blacknife said.

"He might be selling dope and went to meet his supplier," Payton said.

"Use a tunnel and you don't run the risk of being caught," Carl said. He pulled to a stop in front of the embassy.

"Midmorning, I'm going to the tea shop," Payton said.

"We'll bring some help," Blacknife said.

Payton decided to walk the few blocks over to Hotel Q and see if he could find the roommate, Thierry Rousseau. Quinn said Rousseau and Ben hung out there most nights. If Quinn was right and the Kush belonged to Ben, then Rousseau might have some idea if he dealt drugs and would risk going to the river to meet his supplier.

In less than ten minutes he found Hotel Q, a narrow eight-story hotel, tight against an apartment building at a busy five-way intersection.

On the other side of the ornate lobby, "Love's Divine" by Seal pulsed through frosted glass doors, with "Tricks" scripted on each door.

Payton scanned the dark club. Quinn said the roommate was French-Algerian, medium height, and well groomed.

He moved through the cocktail tables, past the circular bar to the few couples on the dance floor.

No Rousseau.

Payton didn't see him in the low lounge chairs and couches beside the sushi bar in the rear of the place either. He worked his way back to the bar and motioned to a bartender. "One of your regulars is a guy named Thierry Rousseau. He comes in here with another man named Ben Ater."

The bartender wore a creased white long-sleeved shirt buttoned at the wrists and a purple bowtie. "Yeah, I know them," he said and continued to turn a towel inside a highball glass. "Too bad what happened to Ben. Should've been the Frenchman. He's the cheap one, never tips." He gestured with the glass toward the low lounge chairs. "Over by the window."

"The guy with the woman?" Payton asked.

"She's the wife of an African diplomat he's hit on all night."

Rousseau, on the edge of a lounge chair with his back to the club, was deep in conversation with a black woman whose beauty reminded Payton of a runway model.

When he approached, he heard Rousseau speaking French to the woman.

"Thierry Rousseau?" Payton asked.

Rousseau turned, irritated for the interruption.

"I need to ask you a few questions about Ben Ater."

The woman unfolded her long toned legs and stood. "Thank you for drinks. I have an early meeting," she said.

Rousseau followed her with his eyes while she made her way past the bar.

Poof, he went with his hands. "You cost me two hours and four drinks," he said with a heavy French accent.

"Better luck next time," Payton said.

Rousseau shook his head and drained the rest of his margarita. "Who're you?" he asked.

"Diplomatic Security." Payton reached for his shield and ID, but Rousseau waved him off.

"Go ahead, ask your questions."

Payton sat down on the couch. "How long've you and Ben been roommates?"

"Eight months. A mutual friend who works in the US embassy knew I needed a roommate and introduced us."

"What can you tell me about the night he disappeared?"

"I was about to leave our apartment when he came in from work. He'd been over in Fallujah for an audit and found another company stealing from the government. He said this one was different and he wanted to get my opinion how to handle it. I had a date and was rushed and said we'd talk in the morning. My date didn't work out, so I came here and found him with one of his coworkers and two nurses. When I left, he was on the dance floor with both nurses."

He lifted a pack of Gauloises off the table and jiggled one out. He offered one, but Payton shook his head. Rousseau's face lit up when he used his lighter.

"By the time I left for work the next morning, he still hadn't returned. I figured he'd gotten lucky with one of the nurses."

The cocktail waitress stopped by the table, and Rousseau held up his empty glass. Payton waved no.

"Is there anyone else he might've gone to see?'

"Maybe Leah, a girl he works with he's close to. After lunch, I heard an American disappeared in the Red Zone. Someone told me the guy was an auditor. I called his office, and the receptionist said it was Ben. When I tried his cell, his voicemail kept answering."

"A bag of Afghan Kush was found in the tunnel he used. Could it be his?"

He took another pull on his cigarette and avoided Payton's gaze. "How would I know?"

"You're his roommate."

"The only time I ever saw him use drugs was at a party where he offered me a joint. I don't do drugs and I can't afford to lose my job by being connected with someone who does. The company I work for has a zero-tolerance policy."

"Then why is he still your roommate?"

"He said it was a one-time thing and wouldn't happen again. Ben's a smart guy. He knew terrorists operate in the Red Zone and would jump at the chance to get their hands on an American with an influential uncle. It doesn't make any sense he'd sneak out."

"How about his work? Any problems there?"

"He works with ESM, Englewood, Schnabel, and Murrari, an accounting firm from England. They're one of four companies that review military contracts. He gets along with everyone he works with. One of them told me he's an excellent auditor."

"Did he say what else he found in Fallujah?"

"He only said he wanted my opinion and we'd talk in the morning. Have his kidnappers asked for a ransom?"

"Who said he was kidnapped?"

Rousseau didn't need to know there'd been no ransom demand and the lack of one concerned Payton.

"I hear rumors."

"He's considered a missing person until we know more." Payton wrote his cell number on a cocktail napkin and slid it over. "Call me if you remember anything else."

CHAPTER 06

THE EMBASSY

IT WAS 11:10 P.M., and the restaurant, a converted ballroom on the second floor, was still humming with embassy staff.

Payton sat at a corner table, ate the last of his chicken salad sandwich, and considered what Rousseau said: he only saw Ben use weed once. He might not have any idea if Ben was more involved with drugs. Ben could be a heavy user or even a dealer and keep his secret from everyone close to him.

He finished his coffee, went to the elevators, and took one to the fifth floor. Catherine said to pick any room. He opened a random door.

The renovated room smelled of fresh paint and was dorm room chic with a desk and chair beside a single bed. He set the Mini Uzi and Glock on the bed with his bag.

Cheap laminated wood bookshelves hung on the wall next to the bathroom door. A window faced east toward the river, where a boat bow light motored downriver.

He looked at lights twinkling in the Red Zone where Ben disappeared over twenty-four hours ago. Why hadn't they heard from the people who'd taken him? Most kidnappers were in business to make money. If they killed him, the payoff goes bye-bye—unless he wasn't snatched for money.

If Quinn's right, then he was at the river to smoke weed, meet a buyer, or pick up a delivery of drugs. What troubled Payton was the easy availability of drugs inside the wall … why would Ben need to leave?

He went into the tiny bathroom. If he stooped, he could make do with the shower. He waited for the water to heat up, then stripped and stepped in.

With a towel wrapped around his waist, he went into the room and heard a gentle tap on the door. He was surprised to see Catherine. She held a bottle by the neck in one hand and two glasses in the other and glanced at his towel and bare broad chest.

"Sorry, I'll come back later," she said and started to turn.

"Give me a minute," he said and held the door open while she came in.

He went into the bathroom. "Five-star accommodations," he said from behind the half-closed door.

"We do the best we can."

Barefoot, he padded out in jeans and a T-shirt and pulled over the desk chair.

She sat on the bed. "I wanted to apologize," she said.

"For what?"

She handed him one of the glasses. "Being a jerk."

"I don't follow you."

"When I heard you were in Jordan, I knew there was no one else I wanted on Ben's case. I called in a favor with Director Santiago. He told me you were due time off, but I insisted I needed you."

"I didn't know I was in such high demand."

"Part of me wanted you here because of how we parted ways in Mexico."

"We buried the past earlier."

"At the time I didn't believe we could give a hundred percent to each other and our jobs." She shook her head. "You really wanted our lives to be, 'Honey, how was your day? I worked a car bomb case that killed a dozen people.' Or how about, 'You take the kids to soccer. I have a conference call with the FBI about a fugitive rapist.'"

"Kids are several bounces of the ball further along than I ever considered. I wanted us to enjoy each other," he said.

"We can't deny we hurt each—"

"We?"

"I thought the only way up the glorious Department of State ladder was to keep our relationship—keep anything— from distracting me," she said.

"I was a distraction?"

"Believe me, I've regretted being so naive."

"Is there someone now?" he asked. For some reason, the thought of her being alone all these years bothered him.

"Until last Christmas when he realized he didn't want two relationships, one with me and one with the Diplomatic Security Service."

"At least you gave yourself permission to have a personal life."

She laughed. "Some personal life. I've wondered over the years what would happen if I saw you again. Would you hate me? Would you ever speak with me again?"

"I never hated you, but you blew the call. We had something special," he said.

She'd always been a work-comes-first person. He tried to convince her in Mexico to lean on coworkers more and step back from the eighty- to one-hundred-hour workweeks. The few times she did let go, she enjoyed herself but soon reverted back to serious mode. He told her the guilt she felt for brief periods of downtime was pointless because an assistant RSO's to-do list never ended.

"If I knew in Mexico what I know now I'd"—

He put his hand on her shoulder. "My job's to find people. Your request wasn't out of line."

She looked at him for a few long seconds. "You were right. We all make mistakes," she said.

He doubted she'd changed. You don't get the Baghdad RSO job, a twenty-four-hour-a-day grinder with responsibility for a horde of people in one of the most hostile environments the State Department operates in, without being married to it. To change the subject, he pointed with his glass to the bottle. "What're we having?"

She glanced at the label. "Remy Black Pearl something."

"Black Pearl? Let's see."

She handed him an exquisite magnum with curved ribbed edges. He saw "Black Pearl Louis XIII" etched in elaborate script around the narrow neck.

"When embassy staff first arrived, our temporary offices were in one of Saddam's private villas. In a liquor room attached to the villa's wine cellar, I saw the bottle and thought it'd be an interesting conversation piece to have on my office shelf."

He tapped the bottle. "Baccarat crystal. A full bottle retails for over fifty grand."

He poured a half-finger width into each of their glasses and set the bottle on the desk. They clinked glasses. He tasted the slightest hint of wood and ginger.

"Not bad. I met with Quinn. His people found a bag of weed in the tunnel Ben used. His opinion, the bag belonged to Ben. The contractor with Ben told Quinn's investigator they were grabbed at the river by several men in a boat and delivered downriver, where Nassar al-Dori's men brought them into Ishbiliya."

"The contractor confirmed al-Dori's people were involved?" she asked.

"His camo-uniformed men transported them in a van from the river to the tea shop."

"al-Dori's the last person Ben needs to come in contact with. He's killed scores of Sunnis, many of them women and children," she said.

"I won't discount if Ben's mixed up with drugs, he might be associated with the wrong people. His roommate told me he only drank with Ben and they never used drugs. He did say he saw Ben smoke weed at a party."

"His drug history's another reason I didn't want him. We already have too many young people here with an appetite for getting loaded," she said.

"Something about the drug lead bothers me. With easy access to dope inside, why leave?"

"Ambassador Rhodes will go ballistic if he was in the Red Zone to buy drugs," she said.

"I'm more concerned about the absence of a ransom demand," he said.

"His kidnappers might think the price increases if they wait to contact us," she said. She took the last sip of her cognac and held her glass out for a refill. "I've had one of those days."

He poured another quarter of an inch.

"Ben disappearing couldn't have come at a worse time. Ambassador Rhodes has pulled off a miracle with the tentative cease-fire agreement he's stitched together between these militia leaders."

"And the possibility one of them might be involved with Ben's disappearance could blow away the peace pipe smoke," he said.

"The whole process would be at risk," she said and finished the cognac.

"Tomorrow, after I talk with the security contractor taken with Ben, I want to hear what his boss and coworkers have to say, but first I need to get over to the tea shop. Can you arrange a drop-off?"

"I'll go with you."

"Your plate's full. I'll handle it," he said. He had no idea what they'd run into. She was needed here, not in a part of the city where firefights were a daily occurrence.

"I'm going, end of discussion, but first, meet me in the lobby at eight. I want to show you the type of companies Ben audited and how Iraq's being run now we're in charge."

"Eight then."

She held her glass out again. "A little more."

"I guess it has been a rough day," he said.

She tilted her head to one side and smiled. "I won't get drunk and ask to spend the night."

"You had me worried."

He splashed more cognac into her glass. She still had a sense of humor. "I'll need a competent SEO if I'm going to find Ben," he said.

Payton had worked with the finest security engineering officers, SEOs, in the service. Skilled engineers who assist with technical analysis, SEOs are crucial to embassy Diplomatic Security operations. Their tiny fraternity knows more about counterfeiters and bomb makers than any intelligence service in the world. They develop networks of contacts outside the embassy that can be crucial to an investigation. No way he'd find Ben without a top-notch SEO.

"I recruited Cleveland Pinnix."

"He's still around?"

"When I heard he hadn't been fired, I jumped at the chance to bring him on board. He had ninety days left on his Halifax TDA, so I pulled a few strings."

"Did you tell him to behave himself?"

"You know Cleveland?"

"We go way back."

"He understands if he's not a good boy, Baghdad will be his last job."

"Is the booze under control?"

"He said it is."

"Keep him on a tight leash," he said. At one time Cleveland was one of the best SEOs he'd worked with, until his drinking got the better of him. If he hadn't dried out, he'd be worthless.

He joined her at the door and looked into those beautiful green eyes. The thought flickered through his mind to give her a hug, but then he remembered, she was now the boss.

"Will you take care of my bottle?"

"I'm not sure I can handle the responsibility," he said.

She hesitated with the door open. "I'm glad you're here," she said and left.

He wondered if her being in his room meant she wanted a second chance. She'd closed that door years ago, and he didn't know if he wanted to open it again.

CHAPTER 07

THE SEO

PAYTON STEPPED into the cramped embassy basement office. "You haven't been fired yet?" he asked.

Through black-framed glasses, Cleveland Pinnix studied a piece of fabric he held up with a pair of tweezers under an intense desk lamp light. Hunched forward, he appraised Payton for a few seconds, then a sly smile appeared. Payton knew even when he drank, Cleveland was at his desk by 5:00 a.m.

His flattop was more salt than pepper now and his complexion ruddier than the last time Payton had seen him four years ago in Kazakhstan. Toes poked through a flesh-colored elastic bandage wrapped around his left foot, which was encased in a plastic boot. He had propped the boot on a wastebasket.

Cleveland slid the tiny piece of cloth back into a sandwich-sized ziplock bag, set it and the tweezers on his junk-strewn desk, and reached across to shake Payton's hand. "I heard you might turn up. Good to see a familiar face. Not many of us old-timers around anymore," he said.

"What happened?" Payton pointed to the foot.

"Tripped. Balance isn't what it should be." He tossed his glasses on the desk, "Coffee?"

"Black," Payton said and moved a stack of paperback romance novels from the only chair to the floor and sat down. Tripped or he's drinking again. Payton knew if Cleveland wasn't the best SEO in the entire service, he'd have been bounced out long ago.

Cleveland reached over and took a silver coffee pot from a side table, poured coffee into a chipped white cup with a picture of Batman on it, and passed it over.

"I'm glad they sent you and not some knuckle dragger," Cleveland said. He leaned back in his chair, lit a cigarette, and blew a perfect smoke ring.

"How was Canada?" Payton asked.

"Boring and cold. Besides, Baghdad's where all the action is."

"I heard Nova Scotia was your last chance. Let me guess, booze or cards?"

Cleveland picked a piece of tobacco off the tip of his tongue. "Still blunt, aren't you? I guess that's why I always enjoy your company." With the heels of both hands, he pushed up to readjust his propped foot. "Had one too many Gran Old Parrs, an excellent blended Scotch by the way, at a Rome reception where I told a pope joke within earshot of the undersecretary of state and several cardinals. Ambassador Bannick wanted me fired. Santiago said no more screwups and hid me away in Halifax. Out of the blue Catherine called. Now, here I am in sunny Baghdad."

"Can I count on you?" Payton asked.

Cleveland's cigarette glowed from another long drag. He blew smoke up and away. "I won't botch my last chance. Now, what was the bean counter up to?"

"With your help, I plan to find some answers. I'm going into the Red Zone where he was last seen. Can you join me?" He pointed to the propped foot.

"You don't want me to slow you down with these." He grabbed one of his metal crutches. "I have someone who'll fill in for me. Rammer!" he yelled.

Payton heard a chair scrape and feet jog in the hallway.

"Yes, sir?" A middle-linebacker-sized young man appeared in the doorway. His short blond hair was clipped close to his head, and he appeared to be in his early twenties.

"Philip 'Rammer' Fulkins, meet legendary Special Agent Payton Ladd," Cleveland said.

"Sir," Rammer said.

Payton half rose, shook Rammer's powerful grip, and sat back down.

"Mr. Fulkins is our newest addition from Silicon Valley. He's adroit with a wide range of electronics, a useful skill if he's to become a proficient SEO."

"Agent Pinnix's a great teacher," Rammer said with enthusiasm.

"Do you have any field experience?" Payton asked.

"I transferred from San Francisco, where I assisted SFPD with a GPS-based, suspect-tracking software program I helped develop."

"A desk job?" Payton asked.

"I worked with software engineers in department headquarters and went on several ride-alongs."

"Being in a critical threat post will do wonders for his experience," Cleveland said.

"Iraq's your first field assignment?" Payton asked.

"And I look forward to the experience."

Payton agreed with the DSS's approach. Young agents didn't have their hands held: they had to sink or swim. The sooner they were weeded out, the better, because lives were on the line. If Rammer with his ride-along experience wasn't up to the job, he wouldn't hesitate to send him back to Northern California to play video games with the San Francisco Police Department.

Payton gestured with his chin toward Cleveland. "Listen to what he tells you. It might save your life."

"We've been asked to assist with Ben Ater's disappearance," Cleveland said.

"I was surprised to hear he left the Green Zone," Rammer said.

"We all are," Payton said. "The military police found a bag of Afghan Kush in a tunnel he used."

"Kush is premium weed," Cleveland said.

"Was it his?" Rammer asked.

"We don't know yet," Payton said.

"He could have gone out to smoke?" Cleveland asked.

"We won't discount any possibility," Payton said.

"Has there been a ransom demand?" Cleveland asked.

"We haven't heard a word," Payton said. "And nobody's taken responsibility."

"Baghdad's full of gangs. Is it possible one of them, and not a terrorist group, might have him?" Rammer asked.

"Finding answers is what we do. Now we'll see if you're worth the big money the US government pays you," Cleveland said.

The newbie asked the right questions. He might've been a good hire. Still, Payton always reserved judgment until he'd seen how a rookie acted under stress.

"A security contractor saw Ben access the tunnel and followed him out to the river, where both of them were taken at gunpoint by several men in a boat. The contractor made it back." Payton stood. "Can I borrow him?" He pointed to Rammer with his thumb.

"He's all yours," Cleveland said.

CHAPTER 08

TIGRIS RIVER

PAYTON RETRIEVED a Humvee from the embassy vehicle lot and drove over to the security wall with Rammer.

A military policewoman stood with a carbine rifle where the wall curved close to several bombed-out buildings. Payton showed her his ID.

"Lieutenant Wiley said to expect you," she said. They walked along a narrow footpath between the buildings and the wall and approached her male counterpart, who showed them a destroyed house with one cinder-block wall still intact.

Among several scorched ceiling timbers Payton saw crushed rock and stone piled around a manhole. The dislodged metal cover leaned against the iron base of the hole.

"Ben had to know the tunnel access was back here. Otherwise, he wouldn't have seen it hidden in the rubble," Rammer said.

Payton motioned to Rammer to hand over his flashlight, then started down the ladder.

"We've marked where the weed was found," the MP said.

He stepped off the last rung, and his head was several inches from the tunnel ceiling. Rammer followed him down. Sunlight streamed through a metal grate a dozen yards toward the river. He walked over to a miniature orange construction cone.

"The Kush was here."

"He might've been too wasted to even realize he'd lost his weed," Rammer said.

"Check the grate," Payton said.

Rammer went over and examined the wall mount screws that held the grate in place.

Payton moved the light around. From the accumulation of gravel and other debris, the tunnel didn't appear to be still in use. He aimed the beam deeper into the tunnel to an iron bar barrier no one could get past without welding equipment.

"These are rusted out," Rammer said.

Payton went to Rammer at the grate.

Rammer pushed with his foot. A gap opened. "He got out through here."

They both stepped down through the opening and stood on several oversized boulders on the sloped riverbank. The river lapped ashore thirty yards away. Industrial buildings bordered cliffs across the wide river in the Red Zone. Off to the right, eroded wood pilings from a long-gone dock marched into the water and disappeared. They left the boulders and walked over the pebble-covered hard sand toward the pilings.

"With these stones we won't find any footprints," Rammer said.

Payton stopped at the first piling. "The contractor told Quinn the boat came in somewhere along here. Do you have any idea what the tides were?" Payton asked.

"Low, which, best guess, would be past the third one." Rammer pointed to a brown rotted stump fifteen feet from shore.

"It was dark, so how'd the guys on the boat avoid these pilings when they brought the boat in?"

"They had a light?" Rammer asked.

"Or Ben did, to guide them in," Payton said.

He surveyed the wall that towered over the embankment and ran downriver, then disappeared around a curve. In the opposite direction, a few hundred yards upriver, the wall turned at a busy bridge. Anyone inside the Green Zone could not have seen what happened out here to Ben and the contractor.

Payton realized what time it was. He had to get to his meeting with Catherine.

CHAPTER 09

CONTRACTOR JOB FAIR

PAYTON MET Catherine in front of Post One and they started down the steps.

"Feel okay?"

"How should I feel?" she asked. She held a to-go cup of coffee.

"For fifty grand a bottle, you shouldn't need any hair of the dog."

She was quiet, then stopped at the bottom of the steps.

He could see something was on her mind.

"Last night might've been a mistake. You're right. I should leave the past in the rearview mirror."

"What we said was long overdue."

"It always bothered me how I treated you."

"You're older, I'm older. Though you're probably wiser than I am. How about no more regrets?" he asked.

She looked up at him.

He moved his hands in a what-can-you-say? gesture.

"Okay," she said and started across the delivery driveway between the embassy and the tilt-up concrete auxiliary building.

They pushed through a revolving door into an open multistory air-conditioned lobby and stepped behind several people with identification documents out at a security checkpoint manned by MSGs.

"Except for his broken foot, Cleveland seems up to the job," he said.

"Did you meet Rammer?" Catherine asked.

"Not much experience to be in Baghdad."

"When I interviewed him, I sensed he could take care of himself."

"With his size he better be able to," Payton said.

"Of the three candidates for the job, he was the only one Cleveland signed off on."

"You know better than anyone that it's impossible to tell if new hires will cave when the shooting starts. The last place I want to be is in the Red Zone with an inexperienced agent who can't handle the pressure," he said.

"I believe Rammer has what it takes." She handed her ID to a young marine and motioned to Payton. "He's with me." The marine saw the badge and waved them around the metal detector.

"Rammer and I got back from the tunnel thirty minutes ago. With the destroyed buildings around the manhole, Ben had to know where to find it."

"What about the boat with the men who took them?"

"High tide erased any sign they were there."

"Ben knew better than to go outside," she said.

"If he's involved with drugs, I won't discount anything."

They crossed the crowded lobby and went into an exhibit hall.

To his left, Payton saw booths—a Peruvian personal security company, beside a French armored car company, next to an Italian aircraft leasing outfit, and on they went. The same on the other side, one company after another.

"What you have here is a Defense Department–sponsored contractor job fair."

"Business looks good," he said.

"A hundred-plus companies from around the world. Ben's accounting firm is one of four engaged to keep an eye on all the private contractors hired to help with the rebuilding effort. I've heard the accountants can't keep up with the avalanche of work."

"What about them?" Payton pointed to open doors in the back of the hall to more booths in a smaller room.

"Those are the ones that can't afford the twenty-five grand set-up fee to be in here."

Payton thought he recognized someone in the cheaper room.

"Whose idea was the twenty-five grand?" he asked.

"Hers." She pointed to a diminutive Asian-American woman in an army officer uniform with two Iraqi men and a tall dapper guy, who stood behind them. They'd gathered beside a kiosk stocked with Romanian cell phones.

"Colonel Dara Mifflin, with the Defense Department's Army Materiel Command, AMC. She's in charge of the contractor program. Has an MBA from Dartmouth's Tuck School of Business. Her specialty's supply chain management. Something to do with logistic transportation cost analysis."

"An army can't have enough MBAs," he said.

"With the volume of money being shoveled out to these contractors, Pentagon administrators sent her over to manage the program from inside the Green Zone." Catherine motioned to several booths. "They've all been vetted, but several hundred more are on the wait-list. Every job in Iraq has contractors involved in some capacity. Ambassador Rhodes even uses private security contractors on his security team."

"Along with our people?"

"Contractors make up half his security detail, and the rest are DSS agents. The ambassador said the contractors are nonnegotiable. He doesn't want to get sideways with Colonel Mifflin because she's a favorite of Defense Secretary Ordway."

Payton saw the tall guy bend forward and say something to Mifflin. All four shared a laugh. "Who're the men with her?"

"No idea about the one in the suit, but the other two are Zaki and Marco al-Dulaimi, Iraqi businessmen with diverse interests who have connections the colonel uses to help with our rebuilding efforts. They're into everything from real estate to shipping. They inherited one of Iraq's largest hawala broker systems from their father and grandfather, who were smugglers in Anbar Province."

Payton knew from past money-laundering investigations, hawala systems were trust-based money transfer systems used in the Muslim world where hawala brokers lent money to be repaid based on a borrower's word. The informality of the system meant detailed transaction records weren't always kept.

Several contractors mingled around Mifflin to compete for her attention.

"Zaki and Marco are close advisers to prime minister candidate Wafiyi Khleifat. If Khleifat comes out on top, Zaki will be his finance minister. They'll be the first al-Dulaimis to go legitimate."

"You don't sound convinced," he said.

"The apple doesn't fall far from the tree. They're hoods, like their father and grandfather, only these two are better educated. Of all the candidates, Defense Secretary Ordway feels Khleifat is the only one with the skill set and political savvy to run Iraq. He wants Khleifat provided with whatever help he needs to win, so he told the colonel to assist his campaign however she can."

"She appears to enjoy her rock star status," he said.

Mifflin shook several hands. She saw Catherine and started toward them with her retinue.

"Hello, RSO McCabe." She approached and held her hand out.

"Congratulations on another successful job fair," Catherine said. They shook hands.

"Eighty-six companies have been turned away. Even with the back room filled to capacity, we can't accommodate all of them," Mifflin said.

She spoke with authority, and Payton sensed she relished being in charge.

Catherine motioned to Payton. "I want you to meet Special Agent Payton Ladd," she said.

"Special Agent," Mifflin said.

Payton shook her tiny firm hand and saw her confident dark eyes.

She introduced the brothers. More handshakes.

Zaki had a head of wispy thin hair and a weak beard. Marco, a bruiser, was a head taller than his brother and several inches wider at the shoulders. Part of his left earlobe was gone.

"Have you met Graham Vicar?" Mifflin asked and half-turned to the tall guy. "Graham's country manager for Titan United, one of the more active contractor firms we've engaged to help put Iraq back on track."

The contractor who had been taken with Ben also worked for Titan United. With lanky arms and legs, Vicar appeared to be in his mid-fifties. His gold-framed round glasses, pinstripe double-breasted suit, and fluffed white pocket handkerchief projected more City of London banker than military contractor. Even the maroon bow tie fit right in. Payton couldn't tell if his sandy blond helmet of tight curls was permed or a rug.

Vicar tilted his head back and peered through the bottom of the thick bifocal lenses, which exaggerated his sloped chin.

"Pleasure's mine," he said. The refined British accent went with the suit. He proffered Payton his hand.

How could a guy with such a weak handshake claw his way over the legions of contractors here to feed at the Defense Department's trough?

Vicar glanced over Payton's shoulder and with a politician's wave acknowledged a group of Chinese business executives.

He even had a sappy smile to go with the wave. How much money did Mifflin pay the pompous fool's company?

"Special Agent Ladd's the lead investigator on Ben Ater's case," Catherine said.

"What did he think he was doing? Our military doesn't even go into the Red Zone at night," Mifflin said.

"Americans should stay out of Ishbiliya," Zaki said. His deep voice didn't go with his size.

"Shia scum everywhere," Marco grunted and turned his meaty head to look at the entrance lobby.

"I heard one of your security people was with Ben," Payton said to Vicar.

"Wade Loft, and he told the military police everything he knows," Vicar said.

"I'll still want to speak with him," Payton said.

"When you call our office, the receptionist will put you through to the right person to arrange a time," Vicar said. He leaned over and whispered to Mifflin.

"RSO McCabe, Special Agent, good to see you," she said.

Mifflin and her groupies trooped toward the entrance.

"See the one with white hair?" A guy with a short white ponytail was the center of attention in the lobby. "Wafiyi Khleifat, Zaki and Marco's Sunni meal ticket."

"It doesn't hurt to have DS Ordway in your corner," he said.

"If those brothers are any indication of the type of people Khleifat will surround himself with, then Ordway's picked the wrong guy." She motioned around the hall. "I wanted you to see how the military's dealt with the situation they created by going to war with too few people."

"The American way—throw money at a problem," he said.

She glanced at her watch. "I've a meeting in fifteen minutes," she said.

"I'll catch up with you later," he said.

He watched her leave. Mifflin came back inside with Khleifat's group. She glanced his way. Her gaze lingered on him for a few brief seconds before she pointed to an Italian helicopter manufacturer booth and spoke with Khleifat.

Payton wondered if the al-Dulaimis were close to her because she could help their guy get elected or because they knew she controlled the contractor program checkbook.

He made his way to the rear of the hall and walked into the back room. At one of the booths, an attractive young woman wearing a short tight camo skirt with matching high heels handed out brochures. BearHug Security was scrawled in blocky letters on her T-shirt across her ample chest. Another woman in the same getup stacked a pyramid of Koozies on a display table.

"Jack around?" he asked.

"Went to the bathroom," the one with the brochures said. "He should be back any minute." She flung her dark hair over her shoulder.

He chuckled to himself. Jack Underhill the ladies man would never change.

"Ladd?"

Payton turned around.

"Of all places," Jack said and gave him a bear hug.

A retired MSG, Jack Underhill worked with Payton years ago at the US embassy in Managua. He still had a runner's build.

"These girls full-time employees?" Payton asked.

"Cindy and Holly are freelancers. Help me whenever I need a hand. Come on." He went behind the booth. "Welcome to my office. Have a seat."

Payton sat down on one of the metal folding chairs next to the cardboard box Jack used for a table.

"You after a piece of the contractor action?"

"Why not? All my competitors are here," Jack said.

He pulled disposable cups from another box. Before Payton could wave him off, he had a bottle of Jim Beam up and poured some into both cups.

"A little early, isn't it?" Payton asked.

"You being here's a special occasion."

He touched Payton's cup with his, then drank it in one gulp. Payton twisted his on the box with his fingertips.

"BearHug your idea?" Payton asked.

"Made it up myself."

"Who does your security work?"

"Retired Gurkhas. We specialize in personal security details. Transport business executives to and from BGW."

"Dangerous work. I saw a truck blown up on the airport road yesterday."

"Every airport run's a crapshoot. Insurgents have gotten better with their targeted IEDs. They now use cell phones for detonators. My boys rely on speed because I can't afford six-figure blast-resistant South African Mamba vehicles. In forty-two BGW runs, I haven't lost one client or Gurkha."

Jack knocked on the box, realized it wasn't wood, then used his head. He half-filled his cup and threw it back.

"How long've you been posted to the embassy?"

"Flew in from Amman yesterday," Payton said.

"You here for the AWOL accountant?"

"Know where I can find him?"

Jack tossed his empty cup behind him into a paper grocery bag he used for a trash can. "Auditors only snoop around companies that pull down a quarter million a month. I'm way under their radar. Is the rumor true he had a security contractor with him?"

"I haven't confirmed the contractor's story," Payton said.

"Who does the security man work for?"

"Titan United."

"Figures. Graham Vicar's the company's top guy in the Green Zone."

"I met him a few minutes ago."

"Something about Titan United doesn't smell right."

"How so?"

"Someone should be fired at the Defense Department if they vetted Vicar's director of operations, Otto Van Heerden."

"What have you heard?"

"He's ex-Recces, South African special forces who specialized in underwater demolition and sabotage."

"All these Green Zone contractors employ guys who did their time in the special forces," Payton said.

"How many were sent packing because a unit under their command destroyed a village where two dozen women and children were killed?"

"Vicar was with two Iraqi businessmen and Colonel Dara Mifflin," Payton said.

"Doesn't surprise me. You know me. I'm not into gossip but the scuttlebutt I hear is, they're an item."

"Who?"

"Vicar and the colonel. Might be the reason he scored so many contracts."

If Mifflin funnels contracts to Vicar and she's caught, she'll need more than a good lawyer.

"Have you gotten any work from her?"

"Penny-ante stuff. Nowhere near the millions Titan United pulls down."

"They haul in that much dough?"

"On a slow month. Titan United's her go-to contractor."

"She appears to be all business," Payton said.

"I figured it was sour grapes when I heard from other contractors she played favorites. Once I saw Titan United's workload, I knew something wasn't right with the amount of work she spoon-feeds them when dozens of capable contractors bid for the same jobs."

Jack screwed the Jim Beam top back on.

Holly stuck her head around the corner. "Time to go," she said.

"Do you mind?" Jack motioned to Payton's untouched cup. Payton slid it over. Jack drank it, then crumpled and tossed the cup into the garbage bag. "I've got to meet someone. If they need any extra help over at the embassy, tell RSO McCabe BearHug's always available."

CHAPTER 10

THE TRAILER PARK

BACK IN THE embassy, Payton rounded up Carl, Blacknife, and Rammer. They drove several blocks to an enormous trailer park used for contractor housing behind the General Federation of Labor Union complex.

"Did his roommate know what Ben was doing at the river?" Blacknife asked.

"Has no idea," Payton said.

Carl rolled through row after row of trailers.

"Turn right at the next row. His number is 118A," Rammer said.

Carl turned and drove past dozens of trailers.

"There," Blacknife said.

They pulled up to a trailer where American and French flags fluttered on a flagpole next to the walkway. Payton saw Italian, Japanese, Polish, and Bulgarian flags in front of other trailers. "You two are drafted," he said to Carl and Blacknife. "If you see anything of interest or out of the ordinary, let me know."

Carl and Blacknife nodded.

"I'm going to want any electronics or computer storage devices you find," Rammer said.

"Why electronics?" Blacknife asked.

"He might've stored information we can use to piece together what happened to him," Rammer said.

Payton knocked on the flimsy locked door.

No answer.

He pounded harder. When no one answered, he gestured to Rammer, who, with the blade of his pocketknife, had the door open in less than a minute.

They stood on the kitchen's linoleum floor. The place smelled of stale Chinese food.

Through an open door next to the dishwasher was a hallway. A Ping-Pong table occupied half the living room.

"Take the hallway," Payton said to Rammer and Carl.

He and Blacknife walked over to the Ping-Pong table. Blacknife went through the door beyond the table where Payton motioned.

Half the table hung down toward the floor. On the other half lay several well-read *Sports Illustrated* magazines addressed to Benjamin Ater at his Englewood, Schnabel, and Murrari Green Zone address.

"Nothing back there except a pile of dirty laundry," Blacknife said from the doorway.

"Check the clothes for pocket litter," Payton said.

Blacknife stepped back into the room.

Next to the magazines on the Ping-Pong table were pencils, pens, sticky note cubes, and a cord with earbuds beside an Ohio State Buckeye saucer filled with red and white paper clips.

Beside the Ping-Pong table, a sofa faced a wall-mounted wide-screen television. Two wireless video game remote controls were tossed on the sofa.

A cantaloupe-sized fish bowl with two Beta fish separated by a clear partition sat on a low glass table between the television and sofa.

Staples, a few beer bottle tops, and crushed potato chips littered the industrial carpet.

Payton picked up an empty beer bottle from the floor, La Bavaisienne Blonde Ale. French, must be Rousseau's.

"Only some loose change," Blacknife said.

"Check the kitchen," Payton said.

Blacknife went over and started to pull drawers and cabinet doors open.

Payton lifted a shoebox from under the table. Inside were a new pair of penny loafers with a week-old receipt from a Columbus, Ohio, men's store. Ben's mother apparently making sure her boy had the right Green Zone footwear.

Carl came back out, followed by Rammer.

"The Frenchman's room is a pigsty. I counted eighteen rubbers in his nightstand drawer. I didn't see anything you can use," Carl said.

"Nothing in Ben's room either," Rammer said.

Blacknife closed the refrigerator door. "French beer, Pepsi, bread, and eggs. Paper plates and cups in the cupboards, and plastic utensils in one of the drawers."

"Let's go," Payton said.

Blacknife and Carl were already out the door when Payton asked, "Did you check the freezer?"

Blacknife stopped on the walkway and shook his head.

Rammer went to the freezer and pulled open the door. He moved a few items around, then came out with a loaf-of-bread-sized package wrapped in newspaper bound with twine.

Payton walked over. Rammer slit the twine with his pocketknife, pulled apart the paper, and started to count out rolled baggies of weed.

"Thirty-eight," he said.

"Take them to Cleveland. See if it's the same weed Quinn found in the tunnel. When we get back from the Red Zone, I want to know where I can find Rousseau," Payton said.

The Frenchman lied to him. He knew about the freezer stash.

CHAPTER 11

TITAN UNITED

AFTER CARL LET Rammer and Blacknife out at the embassy, Payton had him drive over to Titan United's office building.

A monument clock that stood in front of the building read 12:15. He had an hour and forty-five minutes before he met Catherine at the helicopter landing pad behind the embassy to fly over to the tea shop. He wanted to hear what the security contractor with Ben had to say before they left.

The receptionist showed him into a conference room. Floor-to-ceiling windows spanned the entire side of the room and showcased views of the security wall and the city beyond the river. Located in a choice river curve, the twenty-story office building was one of only a few that were not destroyed in the air war. Every floor except sixteen, Titan United's floor, was occupied by the military.

His anger started to rise when he thought about the weed they'd found in Ben's trailer. Rousseau would soon discover how he handled people who lied to him.

Titan United's logo, a hawk with outstretched wings and a globe clutched in powerful talons, was etched on the double glass conference room doors. Beyond the doors, he saw men and women milling about in a cubical farm. Catherine said the company had ten times more employees in the field than they had administrators.

Two men stopped and talked outside the doors. By their ramrod straight posture, Payton figured them for ex-military.

One had a shaved head and a Fu Manchu mustache and was beefy rugby forward big. He wore his cargo pants tucked into brown laced-up military boots.

The other guy glanced toward the conference room. Payton saw his cauliflower ear before he turned back and nodded at something the tucked-in-pants guy said.

Graham Vicar joined them, then—to Payton's surprise—followed the Fu Manchu guy into the conference room.

"Hello again, Special Agent. You should've called first," Vicar said with another flimsy handshake.

"I had a few minutes and figured I'd see if your guy was available," Payton said.

"He'll be here shortly. Meet Otto Van Heerden, my director of operations."

Acne scars covered Otto's thick neck and cheeks. His Fu Manchu was trimmed to perfection. With dark hooded eyes he gave Payton a sharp nod.

He was the guy Jack Underhill said should not have been cleared by the contractor vetting process to work in the Green Zone.

They all rolled back ergonomic chairs at the massive granite-topped conference table to take seats. Vicar set his

Blackberry down. His monogrammed gold cufflinks poked out of his suit coat sleeves.

Payton wondered if he ever unbuttoned the double-breasted coat.

"We've told the military police all we know," Vicar said.

"I want to go over what happened again. Make sure we haven't missed any details," Payton said.

Otto shook his head in disgust. "Do-overs are a waste of time," he said with a South African accent.

Payton ignored him. "I'm curious," he said to Vicar. "How'd your company get access to a building where every floor's occupied by the military?"

"Being close to Central Command Headquarters is imperative with our workload," Vicar said.

Payton motioned to all the employees beyond the glass doors. "Iraq's been good for business."

"The glass is always half full at Titan United."

"How did millions worth of contracts end up in your half of the glass?"

"We've been successful for two reasons." He held up his index finger to emphasize his point. "One, I've worked with militaries in the Middle East for twenty years, and the Pentagon values my extensive contacts." He popped up another finger. "Two, our people work hard and are the best at what they do." He lifted his weak chin to adjust his bow-tied collar and peered across the table. "Titan United's one of your military's most valued partners." He folded his hands next to the Blackberry.

Payton guessed he was through with the finger counts.

"We provide a full range of services, from the management of your embassy's day care to Route Irish dignitary transport. We even protect money the US Treasury flies into the country and stores at BGW. Otto, how much was the last delivery?"

"Four hundred and seventy-three million," the South African said.

A loose-limbed guy in his early twenties shuffled through the doors. Flesh-tone butterfly bandages stretched over a nasty gash on his right cheek. He had a purple and black left eye.

Vicar pointed to Payton with his Blackberry. "Wade Loft, Special Agent Ladd."

"Special Agent," Wade said. He winced and held his side when he reached across to shake Payton's hand, then eased down between Vicar and Otto. Wade twisted the lid off a plastic water bottle with Titan United's logo that he'd brought in with him. He took a sip and set it on a coaster, which also bore a company logo.

"Broken rib?" Payton asked.

"Bruised."

"How can we help—" Vicar's Blackberry vibration interrupted him and he peeked at the screen.

"You were with Ben?" Payton asked.

"You know he was," Otto said.

"I want to hear it from him." Payton gestured to Wade. "Tell me what happened."

Wade glanced sideways to Otto, who moved his hand to go on, then sat stone-faced, eyes on Payton. Vicar slow typed with his thumbs on the Blackberry.

"We drove four British business executives back from BGW to the Al-Rashid hotel," Wade said. He had a Southie accent—he was definitely from Boston.

"We?"

"Me and five other company security guards in three vehicles. I drove the lead vehicle."

"What time?" Payton asked.

"Two a.m. Their flight arrived several hours late. After we dropped them off, we drove over to the company's Haifa Street parking lot. Drivers two and three took the last parking slots. My shooter got out, and I drove over to the Al-Jumhuriya Bridge lot behind the asphalt plant. I left my vehicle and was on my way back here to check in when I saw someone walk behind several demolished buildings near the security wall. No one should be back there, so I followed him. I went through a narrow space between the wall and buildings and saw a light flicker down a manhole."

Wade took another drink and his eyes darted over to Otto. "The metal cover had been moved and I saw a ladder. I climbed down to a tunnel that empties through a grate out on the river. At the grate, I saw the light near the water. A corner of the grate was loose and I shimmied through it. A guy had a flashlight beam pointed out over the water. I surprised him when I came up behind him."

Ben had the flashlight to guide the boat clear of the pilings.

"I asked, 'Why're you out here?' That's when I saw the boat. A rowboat with armed men slid ashore."

"Weren't you armed?"

"All my people carry weapons," Otto said.

"Why didn't you use your gun?"

With his hands flat on the table, Otto said, "Because the accountant was between him and the boat."

Wade turned his head toward Otto and nodded in agreement.

Otto continued, "If he moved for his gun, you'd be here to discuss two dead men, not a missing person. He made the right call."

Wade took two quick sips from the bottle and came back to Payton. "I tried to stop him but he climbed into the boat. One of the men hopped out and put a handgun to my head. He took my gun and nudged me to get in."

"You're a security contractor and now you're unarmed?" Payton asked.

"He's alive, isn't he? My people are trained to make the right decisions," Otto said.

Vicar glanced up and said, "We spent two point three million dollars in the last fiscal year on weapons training for all of our security staff. I want my people to know how to handle themselves in difficult situations. Go on."

BBs of sweat glistened on Wade's forehead while he continued. "They rowed out to more men in a bigger boat. One of them started to yell and jab his AK at me. The rowers had to back him off."

After more water for his dry mouth, Wade continued. "Ben said under his breath, 'Be cool, man, be cool.' We got into the other boat and, with the rowboat tied to the back, they took us upriver to a landing beyond the Al-Sinak Bridge, where more armed men made us get into the back of a van. Two of them, the driver and the guy in the front passenger seat, wore camo uniforms. We were driven through Ishbiliya to a tea shop, where several more men with the same camo stood guard."

"Nasser al-Dori's army brigade members wear camo fatigues," Otto said.

"They left us alone in a back room. I could see Ben was on something. He had bloodshot eyes and his pupils were way too small. He said he'd handle whatever happened."

Wade finished the water. "A dude with a lit cigarette and dark sunglasses came into the room and sat across from us. I'll never forget him."

"Why?"

"He had one ear. Ben said, 'Yusuf, I can explain. I—'"

Otto cut in, "Yusuf al-Dawud's a top commander in al-Dori's organization. He's responsible for the majority of illegal drugs brought into the Green Zone."

"Ben went to meet Yusuf in the Red Zone because of drugs?" Payton asked.

"Give us another reason," Otto said.

"The military police found a bag of weed in the tunnel," Payton said.

"Ben must've dropped it," Wade said.

"I can assure you, if any drugs were found they do not belong to Wade. All our employees are drug tested on a regular basis. I'll not tolerate drug use," Vicar said.

Wade crinkled the empty water bottle.

Why was he so edgy?

"With all the security, how would Yusuf smuggle dope into the Green Zone?" Payton asked.

"The tunnel's a start. You're the investigator, you tell us," Otto said.

"If Yusuf moves dope inside, why would Ben need to go across the river to meet him?" Payton asked.

"I believe you Americans would call what Ben's up to a sixty-four-thousand-dollar question," Vicar said.

Otto flipped his hand for Wade to go on.

"Yusuf said to Ben, 'I told you to come alone.'"

Otto didn't take his basilisk eyes off Payton. Vicar scrolled through his e-mails.

"Yusuf told Ben to follow him into the front room. I can't tell you what happened after that because an explosion ripped through the front of the shop. All I remember, I'm on my back in the alley." He pointed to his black eye. "I got the eye when I hit my head on the pavement. Screams came from inside the shop. When I managed to get up, I didn't see Ben, and the shop was on fire. Three hours later, I was back at the river and swam out to a boat where a man and his grandson were fishing. They dropped me back near the tunnel."

"Nothing new here. The military police know all about what happened," Otto said.

What didn't make sense to Payton was for an auditor from Ohio to be in business with Yusuf al-Dawud. Yusuf would have his own men take care of drug deliveries inside the Green Zone.

Payton asked Wade, "Then you don't know if Ben's alive or dead?"

"Maybe you missed what he said. He didn't see him after the shop was hit," Otto said.

"Is there a problem?" Payton asked.

Otto leaned forward. "You waste our time with questions the military police already have answers to." He pointed toward the windows with his thumb. "Iraq's not a place for amateurs. You should be across the river, not in our offices. The accountant's probably dead by now anyway. The fool should've known the risks if you go into the Red Zone."

Vicar motioned in front of Wade for Otto to sit back, then said, "Ishbiliya's a slum and not a pleasant place."

"Yusuf and Ben died in the tea shop?" Payton asked.

"We have no idea," Vicar said. He glanced at his watch. "I'm afraid I have another meeting. I hope you find the young man. Please don't hesitate to call my office if you need anything further."

He loped out.

"I might need to speak with you again," Payton said to Wade.

Wade turned to Otto for his approval. "Arrange any meetings through me," Otto said and jerked his thumb again toward the windows. "Your answers are over there, not inside the Green Zone."

Wade shuffled out with Otto.

Payton believed that Wade was too uptight. Could it be because he was stressed and didn't want to fumble his side of the story in front of his superiors? Or was he over-coached? What would he have to say if Otto and Vicar weren't around?

Payton planned to find out.

CHAPTER 12

RED ZONE

"WE FOUND THIRTY-EIGHT bags of weed in Ben's trailer," Payton said to Catherine. They stood beside a helicopter gunship on the embassy helipad while the pilot went over his checklist.

"Are they Ben's? I thought the roommate told you he only saw him smoke once," she said.

"When we get back, I plan to jar his memory."

Blacknife, Carl, and two MSGs, each with an M249 light machine gun, jogged over and climbed in. An airman readied a mounted M134 mini gun in the open door.

"If the stash turns out to be Ben's, then Quinn might be right … drugs are the reason he went into the Red Zone. Did you speak with the security contractor?" she asked.

"Young guy from Boston named Wade Loft. Said he saw Ben go down the manhole and followed him. When he confronted him at the river, armed men in a rowboat came ashore and took them at gunpoint to another boat. They motored upriver to a van and were driven to the tea shop where Wade said he saw several guys in camo. Inside the shop, Ben spoke with a guy named Yusuf al-Dawud. Ever hear of him?"

She shook her head.

"He's one of al-Dori's commanders. Wade said Ben knew the guy."

"What did he say happened?"

"No idea, because an explosion blew him into the alley behind the shop. The shop's on fire and he doesn't see Ben again. Despite his injuries, he made it back to the river. A fisherman dropped him near the tunnel. The problem I have, how would Ben know a commander in al-Dori's organization?"

"He might be more than a party boy," she said.

"Graham Vicar and his director of operations, an ex-South African Special Forces tough guy named Otto Van Heerden, sat in on our meeting. Their opinion, Ben's involved with drugs."

"Why was Graham in the meeting?"

"Said he wanted to assist if he could."

"Did he?"

"He and Otto were there to make sure Wade didn't muff his story."

"Wade lied to you?"

"Don't know yet, but I thought he was too keyed up. You said Titan United has Ambassador Rhodes's security detail contract?"

"They have an exclusive. No other company gets a piece of the work."

"How much is the contract worth?"

"Seventy-five grand a week plus bonuses."

"Bonuses for what?" Payton asked.

"If no one's killed. They get another twenty percent of the seventy-five grand."

"Ninety grand a week adds up. Who cuts their checks?"

"All payments are handled out of Colonel Mifflin's office," she said.

"She should split the contract between different companies."

"No one questions her. Defense Secretary Ordway gave Mifflin carte blanche. She's queen of the Green Zone."

"I ran into an old acquaintance who said he heard there's more going on than business between her and Vicar."

Catherine arched her eyebrows. "Sex?" she asked.

The door gunner glanced down at her.

"Mifflin would never be that stupid," she said.

"Pay to play. The oldest trick in the book," Payton said.

"I've heard Mifflin favors companies with administrative staffs who can keep up with all the reports she requires. I can't imagine her and Graham together on a personal level," she said.

"My contact's a one-man shop. Handles all the admin himself." Jack's girls wouldn't be the secretarial type.

"Then he doesn't have the in-house paper-shufflers Mifflin demands for bigger contracts," she said.

The pilot gave them a thumbs-up. After he lifted off, they joined another gunship and flew upriver before both machines banked hard over a Tigris River bridge clogged with stalled traffic. The Red Zone's dense neighborhoods passed under them. Minutes later they started to descend.

A cloud of dust whirled away when the gunship set down in a gravel car lot. They hustled out, and seconds later the machine rose to join the other one. Both circled overhead while the group made their way to the tea shop.

Blacknife took the lead. Catherine pulled her SIG from its thigh holster and followed him. Carl came next with another marine, then Rammer, who carried a Remington 870 shotgun. Payton with the Mini Uzi brought up the rear behind the last marine. Each wore a bulletproof vest with their blood type identified on a plastic-covered patch.

Payton stressed before they left to move with speed. He didn't want to be exposed deep inside the Red Zone. They jogged along a narrow lane bordered by low cinder-block buildings. A few Iraqis stopped and watched them pass.

Blacknife turned into a short alley where a mechanic worked under a car suspended on a hydraulic lift in a service garage.

"Move … move," Payton said from the rear.

They picked up their pace and emerged into a tight round-about bordered by more low buildings, then slipped in between warehouse structures with dock-high truck doors. Once past the warehouses, they jogged along a one-way street toward the tea shop.

Payton saw several men holding machine guns across their chests, arrayed in a semicircle next to SUVs with tinted windows in front of the tea shop.

"Who're these guys?" Rammer asked.

"With those sunglasses, I'd say private security contrac-tors," Catherine said.

The helicopters thundered above them. Both of the M134s were aimed in their direction.

Payton and Catherine approached the nearest contractor. Blacknife and Carl stood behind them while the other marines took up positions across the street. Rammer went to the shop's front door and waited.

"Diplomatic Security agents, we're going in," Payton said.

The gunships flew in tighter circles.

Catherine showed the contractor her gold shield. He glanced at it, then nodded them toward the shop.

Payton stopped a few feet inside the doorway and surveyed the damage. The place smelled of burned wet wood. Half the roof hung down into the destroyed front room.

Rammer motioned across from the only window to a crater in a load-bearing wall between the front and back room.

"My guess, someone put a bazooka or RPG round through the window," he said.

Catherine pointed to the doorway next to the crater. "Ben and Wade must've met Yusuf back there," she said.

"Look around outside," Payton said. Rammer and Blacknife left.

Catherine went to the opposite side of the room to check out a mound of debris between a table with high-back chairs and a cabinet with several broken porcelain containers of tea.

Payton crunched his way over broken glass to the back-room's doorway. Carl stayed at the front door.

He stepped into the rear room.

Two men were on the other side of the debris-littered room in front of a shattered window. One crouched and peered under a piece of door. When he saw Payton, he dropped it and stood.

"Payton Ladd, what a surprise."

"Gabe," Payton said.

Gabe Kuttic still carried the extra stomach weight. His brown hair was several shades lighter than the last time Payton saw him—and much thinner.

Kuttic motioned for his man to leave.

"What interest does the CIA have in Ben Ater?" Payton asked.

"Sorry, can't say."

"I'm not surprised."

Kuttic pulled a black comb out of his shirt pocket and in one movement smoothed what was left of his hair over. He slid the comb back into his pocket.

"Listen," Kuttic said. "We can work together or not. Your choice." He tipped over a blackened section of sheetrock with his shoe.

"Work what together?"

"If Ater was here to meet with Yusuf al-Dawud, my people in Langley want to know why."

Payton was curious as to how Kuttic came about his information. Other than the military police and his Diplomatic Security team, the only people who knew that Ben might've been in the tea shop were Vicar, Otto, and Wade. None of his people or the military police would share information about an active investigation. That left Titan United. Why would anyone at Titan United speak with Kuttic?

"How'd you know who he met?" Payton asked.

"I decided to see for myself if the Green Zone gossip is true and Yusuf might be involved," Kuttic said.

Payton stepped closer, the Mini Uzi pointed to the floor.

"Since when does a missing person investigation register on the CIA's radar?"

"We don't care about Ben Ater. Yusuf's another story."

"I'm all ears."

"Some other time." He started past Payton to the door. "Good to see an old friend after all these years."

Kuttic left and Payton heard the SUVs speed away.

Catherine joined him. Rammer and Blacknife stood in the alley on the other side of the window.

"Did you know Gabe Kuttic was in Baghdad?" Payton asked.

"He's been in the Green Zone for several weeks. You know him?" she asked.

"Met him in the early nineties when both of us were posted to the Istanbul embassy. He's old school. Spent years in Moscow and Soviet Bloc countries where he learned to survive. Translation: Don't trust him," Payton said.

"Why's he here?" Rammer asked.

"He wants to know if Ben came to meet Yusuf."

"I would too," Catherine said.

"Someone told him Ben came here," Payton said.

"Did he say how he got his information?" she asked.

"Best guess, someone at Titan United," Payton said.

"What connection would they have with the CIA?" she asked.

"The Green Zone's a competitive place," Payton said. "If Titan United has access to the right piece of intel, it could be the difference between winning or losing a contract."

"Quid pro quo," Rammer said.

"Titan United shares information with the CIA, and the CIA reciprocates," she said.

"Bring Wade in by himself," Payton said to Rammer. "Let's see if his story changes without Vicar or Otto in the same room."

"Any theories on who destroyed the building?" Rammer asked.

"Otto said Ben came to meet Yusuf al-Dawud, one of al-Dori's commanders," Payton said.

"Could be he was the target and not Ben?" Blacknife asked.

Catherine looked at Blacknife with a smile. "You may have another investigator on your team," she said to Payton.

"Tell Cleveland I want everything he can turn up on Yusuf." Rammer nodded. "If Kuttic has interest in him, I want to know why," Payton said.

"I know someone over at the Defense Intelligence Agency, DIA, I can speak with who doesn't carry any water for the CIA. I'll see what she's heard," Catherine said.

Was Kuttic's interest only Yusuf, or was Ben on his radar too? His smoke and mirrors were a complication Payton didn't need.

"Time's up," the gunship copilot's voice came through their earpieces.

They jogged along the same route back to the car lot.

CHAPTER 13

THE ROOMMATE

ON THEIR APPROACH to the landing zone, Payton saw Rammer have a brief conversation on his cell phone. "Cleveland said Rousseau's on lunch break behind his office building," he said and put the phone back into his jacket pocket.

"You pull Wade in and I'll take Rousseau," Payton said.

If Ben was more than a casual user and did sell drugs, then being at the river to receive a delivery of weed, though a stretch, might make sense. What bothered him was the Yusuf connection. Yusuf would have his own network inside the wall. Why would he meet with Ben?

When they landed, Catherine left for the embassy with Rammer. Payton and Blacknife waited while Carl retrieved a vehicle. He drove back ten minutes later in a Humvee, picked them up, and maneuvered into midday traffic on a wide boulevard parallel to the embassy.

"Did you get the package?" Payton asked.

"Rammer brought it out," Carl said.

"Someone went to a lot of trouble if Ben was taken into the Red Zone," Blacknife said.

"He might be deeper into drugs than a bag here and there," Carl said.

"If he owed someone money, they might be motivated to kidnap him," Blacknife said.

"I can name half a dozen Green Zone security contractors who'd off him for the right fee," Carl said.

"He's worth more alive than dead," Blacknife said.

"The problem with a ransom play is, we won't know if they killed him until we show up with the money," Payton said.

Carl followed the boulevard, then turned toward a block-long abandoned construction pit. Five streets over, he drove into a circular paved driveway and pulled between bongo trucks parked in front of a concrete multistory office building.

Several people entered and left through glass front doors. Next to wide marble entry steps, the reader board listed eight tenant companies.

"Cleveland said he's around back," Payton said.

They followed the stone walkway and emerged into an expansive square.

In the square's center, brown grass edged a scum-covered wading pool. People sat on benches or blankets spread on the grass. Lines formed at two food trucks.

Payton scanned a group of young men who kicked a soccer ball beyond the trucks. He came back to a guy and girl who sat on a short wall along one side of the pool.

"Got him," he said.

When they approached, the red-haired girl tossed her head back with a cackle at something Rousseau said. He had a burrito in both hands and was about to take a bite when Payton tossed one of the Kush baggies from the package Rammer had given Carl onto the wax paper in his lap.

Rousseau stopped with the burrito at his mouth and glanced down at the bag.

"Let's talk," Payton said.

The redhead saw the Kush, gathered up her lunch, and hurried away.

"Wait," Rousseau said after her. The burrito dripped on the Kush.

He shielded his eyes from the sun with one hand and looked up to Payton. "Twice you've blown my chances," he said.

"We found your freezer stash. Is the weed yours or Ben's?"

Rousseau tossed the Kush on the wall next to him, rewrapped the burrito, and shoved it and an orange juice into a brown paper bag. He stood. "I told you what I know already. I don't have to—"

He dropped the bag when Payton grabbed him by the front of his pink dress shirt. One of the collar buttons popped off. With half a step Payton was over the wall and had Rousseau under the water. A few seconds later he pulled the Frenchman up, let him gulp some air, then pushed him back under the scummy water. When he let go again, Rousseau gasped and on all fours scrambled and slid over the slick bottom to the wall.

"Don't play games with me," Payton said.

"You can't do—" His feet slipped out from under him when he tried to stand.

Payton reached down and had him by the shirt again.

"It's Ben's. Now let me go," Rousseau said.

"The whole story … now."

"I told you I don't have anything to do with drugs."

"Right, employer zero tolerance."

Payton hauled him up.

"He said Kush was hard to come by and if I ever changed my mind, to let him know." Rousseau was unsteady on his feet.

"Did he go to the river because of drugs?"

"I have no idea, but when baggies turned up in the freezer, I knew he'd been to see his supplier."

Payton let go of his shirt.

Carl and Blacknife moved the crowd back.

"Who's his connection?"

"Several days ago we were in an Italian restaurant off Haifa Street, close to where the new embassy's being built. Ben came back from the bathroom and said his supplier, the Kurd, was in a private party room near the bathrooms. When I went to the bathroom, the party room door was closed. I never saw her."

"His supplier's a woman?"

Rousseau nodded.

"She have a name?"

"He only said she's an NGO attorney."

If Rousseau was being truthful and she worked inside the Green Zone, he was back to the same question, why would Ben go outside the wall?

"Is he still alive?" Rousseau said.

"His odds diminish the longer I have to play games with people like you. Did he have problems with anyone, maybe someone he sold weed to?"

"How could hundred-dollar party bags of Kush get him kidnapped?"

"Not my question."

"He never mentioned any trouble."

"Who buys from him?"

"Other accountants, a few people we know in the residential trailer park, and security contractors."

"Which contractors?"

"He said Titan United has a security division with ex-Special Forces soldiers. Adrenaline junkies who accompany ESM auditors on their assignments when they leave the Green Zone. I told him to be careful. Every security contractor I've met is amped up on steroids."

Payton wondered if Vicar or Otto knew Ben sold weed to one of their security people and hadn't told him.

"He give you the security contractor's name?"

Rousseau shrugged his shoulders no.

"If you've lied again, you'll wish you'd been in the Red Zone with Ben."

CHAPTER 14

ENGLEWOOD, SCHNABEL,
AND MURRARI

PAYTON DECIDED to change his damp shoes and pants after he met Cleveland. Carl drove through heavy traffic and followed Rousseau's directions to Ben's office building.

"The Frenchman didn't appreciate his bath," Blacknife said from the back seat. He'd picked up three pastrami on rye sandwiches from one of the food trucks, and handed one up to Payton. "I hope you like lots of mustard."

Payton unwrapped the sandwich. "If we don't find a female Kurdish attorney, Rousseau will wish he had never heard of the Green Zone," he said.

Several minutes later Carl turned into a side street behind the old Ministry of Justice building. Cleveland was on the sidewalk, where he leaned on his crutches under the shade of a date tree.

Carl pulled over.

"Good work at the tea shop. I'll make investigators out of you two yet," Payton said. He left the half-eaten sandwich on the seat and climbed out.

"How'd Rammer do?" Cleveland asked.

"Not bad for his first time out of the Green Zone," Payton said.

"When the shooting starts, he'll hold his own." Cleveland pointed to a block of buildings with one of his crutches. "The pink windows."

They started toward a multistory office building with a row of second- and third-floor pink-tinged windows.

"The roommate confirmed the weed belongs to Ben," Payton said.

"He lied about Ben's drug involvement?"

"Let's say we've come to an understanding."

"Did he have any idea where he gets the weed from?"

"A Kurdish woman attorney who works for a Green Zone-based NGO. Which means him being near the river to bring weed back in might not be true."

"Then what's he doing out there in the middle of the night?" Cleveland asked.

"I'm still not convinced drugs are involved. If we find the Kurd, she might know if the dope lead is a dead end," Payton said.

"She shouldn't be hard to track down," Cleveland said.

"Rousseau said one of Ben's customers was a Titan United security contractor."

"He give you a name?"

"Has no idea."

"What about Wade Loft?"

"I've considered the possibility."

"For him to see Ben disappear by the wall in the middle of the night was a lucky break," Cleveland said.

"It might not be a reach that he and Ben were more involved."

"They left together?" Cleveland asked.

"The weed Quinn's people found is our only evidence that anyone was in the tunnel. Rammer and I found no indication either of them was at the river. Did Rammer connect with Wade?"

"He sent him an e-mail and left a message on his cell to come over to our offices. I'll let you know when he's there," Cleveland said.

Payton held open the glass door. "If I'm not available, good cop/bad cop him with Rammer. Put pressure on his story."

"With pleasure," Cleveland said. "I heard Gabe Kuttic was in the tea shop."

Payton stopped at the elevator. "Kuttic is not someone we need near the investigation."

"He replaced the previous CIA station chief. I don't agree with his methods, but he produces."

"Never trust him. Did Rammer tell you Kuttic wants to know if Ben was in the tea shop to meet with a guy name Yusuf al-Dawud?"

"He did, and he said you wanted more information on Yusuf. I called Police Chief Inspector Raheem Akrawi, one of the few police commanders who stayed in place after we invaded. He rules a slice of the Mansour administrative district—a violent place west of the Green Zone. I helped his daughter get an embassy translator job. He knows all about

Yusuf al-Dawud. Says he's the only Kurd in al-Dori's organization and is one bad actor." The elevator door opened. Cleveland pressed the fourth-floor button. "Raheem said Yusuf's connected to Kurdish gangs who control the city's drug rackets. Iranians are his main supplier. Not just any Iranians, but the Quds Force, a unit inside the Revolutionary Guards who handle special operations outside Iran. They transport drugs across Iran from Afghanistan into Iraq."

The doors opened. Cleveland went out first.

"Kuttic's not convinced Ben was in the tea shop," Payton said.

"Akamai hasn't heard any rumors about what happened with Ben, but he reiterated if Yusuf's involved, anything's possible," Cleveland said.

They stepped into the muted lobby of Englewood, Schnabel, and Murrari. A young man sat behind a desk and played a game of solitaire on his computer screen. He X'd out of the game when they approached him.

Payton showed his badge. "We're Diplomatic Security investigators and need access to Ben Ater's office."

"We can't believe he went outside the Green Zone," the young man said.

"Which door?" Payton motioned to doors on either side of the lobby.

"I'll have to call my supervisor."

"Dale Lowsley?" Payton wanted to speak with him, too.

"Mr. Lowsley's out of the office, but his assistant's here." He picked up his phone, pressed a button, and spoke in a low tone. "She'll be out in a moment," he said and replaced the receiver.

Payton stepped over to Cleveland, who tossed a copy of *CPA Journal* back on the side table between two chairs.

A middle-aged woman all of five feet came through one of the doors. She spoke with the guy behind the desk, who pointed to Payton.

"How can I help you?" The plastic ID card attached to an orange cord around her neck said "Brin" in bold black letters.

Payton explained why they were there.

"Do you have any idea what happened to him?" she asked.

Payton picked up on her Welsh accent. "Besides being in the wrong place at the wrong time, no," he said.

She held her ID card to a square black wall-mounted pad next to the doorknob. A red light turned green and she pushed open the door. They walked down a hushed corridor past offices with accountants who read documents or studied spreadsheets on computer screens.

Near the end of the hall, next to a copy/mail room, she opened a door. "Ben's office," she said.

Cleveland went over to his desk, sat down, and lifted the lid of a notebook computer attached to a docking station.

"If we need anything else, where can I find you?" Payton asked.

"My office is next to the lobby."

She started back up the hall and he closed the door.

While the notebook booted up, Cleveland went through the desk drawers.

The desk had a telephone, the docking station, the notebook computer, and a monitor screen. Payton didn't see any personal items.

"Pencils, staples, tape, stamps … otherwise it's empty. Check those file drawers." Cleveland motioned to four metal drawers in the corner.

Payton pulled out the top drawer.

Empty.

So were the others.

"All empty."

"We have a problem," Cleveland said and leaned back. "The hard drive's corrupted."

"Can you fix it?"

"I'm not sure." He pulled open the desk drawers again and felt all the way to the back. "He might have a backup drive."

Payton left and brought Brin back.

"He never said he had a problem with his computer," she said when she entered the office.

"Where are all his files?" Payton pointed to the file drawers.

"Ben doesn't care for clutter. He does all his work on the computer."

"How about a backup drive?" Cleveland asked.

"Our people are issued external hard drives and we encourage them to back up their work daily. We have a strict company policy: no external hard drives are to leave the office. Have you checked each desk drawer?"

"If the hard drive was in here, it's gone now," Cleveland said.

"A main server does automatic backups of everyone's computer once a day. One moment." She went back into the hallway.

"We didn't find a hard drive in his trailer," Payton said.

A few minutes later she reappeared. Next to her was a guy with a slight stoop who wore a maroon button-down sweater. He looked to Payton to be Pakistani or Indian.

"Kailash is our IT manager. He can answer any of your questions," she said.

"Did Ben say anything about his computer to you?" Payton asked.

"No. Is there a problem?" Kailash said with a British refined Indian accent.

"The hard drive's corrupted," Cleveland said.

Cleveland pushed back and motioned Kailash to the computer.

He came over and hit several keys. "Strange," he said under his breath and typed some more, then shook his head.

"Can you access your main server?" Cleveland asked.

Kailash looked to Brin, who nodded. "Come to my office," he said.

"Take the computer," Payton said.

"I'm afraid I'll need to get approval from my superior for you to remove his computer," Brin said.

"Dale Lowsley?" Payton asked.

"He should be back in a few hours."

"Tell him to call me," Payton said.

Cleveland popped the notebook off the station and handed it to Payton.

Kailash's office was the exact opposite of Ben's. Stacks of file folders, computer magazines, and manuals piled on both chairs and the floor.

Kailash went to work on his computer keyboard.

After a few minutes, Payton saw his eyes widen and his forehead furrow.

"Someone has accessed Ben's account."

Cleveland moved behind Kailash's chair, pulled his glasses out of his shirt pocket, put them on, and peered at the screen.

"When?" he asked.

Kailash typed away. "Four days ago."

"The day he came back from Fallujah," Payton said.

Cleveland pointed to the screen. "Several of his e-mails have been deleted. Don't you have firewalls?"

"We have two and I designed both of them," Kailash said.

"Tell me you back up the server," Cleveland said.

"Every day."

"I'll need to see the backup."

"We keep backup tapes in another building. I will need time to retrieve them."

"You still use tape backups?"

"I have complained to our management in Manchester about the poor backup system we've been provided with."

Cleveland scribbled on a sticky notepad. "Here's my cell," he said.

"Today would be helpful," Payton said.

In the elevator, Cleveland pointed to Ben's notebook that Payton carried. "Don't get your hopes up."

"I thought you were a computer genius."

"Whoever got to the hard drive was no amateur. We need to find the external hard drive."

"Ben could have made the decision to take it out of his office if he thought someone might hack into his computer," Payton said.

Cleveland slowed his pace when they exited the building.

"Behind us, halfway up the block, opposite side of the street. Two guys in a dark four-door Peugeot. I saw them pull into the parking space when we entered the building. They're still in the car."

"The tobacco shop," Payton said.

They walked to the corner and stepped into a tobacco shop on the ground floor of an apartment building.

Inside, Payton peered back up the street through white script scrawled across the front window that advertised several brands of tobacco. He saw the Peugeot.

"I'll circle the block and come at them from their side of the street. Call my cell phone if they move."

Cleveland stepped to the window.

Payton disappeared through a side street door. He went to the corner behind the tobacco shop and circled over to an alley that ran parallel with the Peugeot. When he figured he was close, he tried the rear door of an apartment building. The door opened. At the end of the hallway was a vestibule. Through a side window he saw the two men several cars back.

The guy in the front passenger seat appeared to be Middle Eastern with straight black hair that hung over his ears. He couldn't make out the other one behind the wheel because of his low baseball cap.

He stepped out and went toward them, but the driver saw him and gunned the car into the middle of the street.

Payton rushed forward. The car shot back, half-turned, and then sped toward the tobacco shop.

Cleveland was on the sidewalk when Payton jogged up.

"Now why would we have a tail?" Cleveland asked.

"We're popular guys," Payton said.

"Got the license number, but I can guarantee you the car's stolen," Cleveland said.

CHAPTER 15

EMBASSY

PAYTON CAME into Catherine's office. She was on her cell phone.

"How many confirmed dead?" she asked, then paused. "Does the ambassador know?" Another pause. "I'll tell him." She set the phone down on a conference table where she stood with an assistant. "How many doors in the new wing?"

He pointed to the building plans rolled out in front of them.

"Forty-nine."

She picked up and examined a door lockset.

"Get fifty. We might need a spare."

The assistant nodded, put the lockset back into a box, rolled up the plans, and left.

She pulled out a chair and sat with a huff. Payton joined her.

"Here's today's other bad news," she said. "Marines were sent to Al Kut, a city southeast of Baghdad, to put down a riot at a Bank of United Iraq branch. When they arrived, dozens of Iraqis were gathered around a bonfire in front of the building. Several pieces of lumber pulled from the fire were thrown through broken windows at the barricaded bank employees. Someone took a potshot at the marines. When the shooting stopped we had four dead and eighteen wounded civilians."

"Why attack the bank?" he asked.

"Several people taken into custody said they were given counterfeit money. The marines confirmed they saw bills being thrown into the flames. A BBC crew filmed the confrontation. Now every major network will run the film clip of marines shooting into a crowd. Guess where the fortune in C-notes we fly over here is stored?"

"BUI?" he asked.

"With branches in a dozen cities, every Iraqi knows BUI's the only bank on solid financial ground because we're the money behind it. Know what happens if rumors spread that BUI's full of counterfeit money?"

"A mob of a few hundred grows into thousands," he said.

"If Iraqis lose confidence in our Hail Mary C-note game plan, we could lose the country. I had several of the burned bills delivered to Cleveland to see if they really are counterfeit. Did you find Ben's roommate?"

"He needed help with his memory," he said.

"Alright, what happened?"

"With some assistance he remembered the freezer weed was Ben's. He said his supplier's a woman attorney employed with an NGO."

"A woman?"

Payton nodded.

"If he'd told you who the supplier was when you first talked to him, we might already've found her," she said.

"We're looking for her now."

"With a supplier inside, why would he need to leave?" she asked.

"The Kurd woman may have some answers. Her being in the Green Zone could torch any theory he went out for drugs."

"What have you turned up on Yusuf al-Dawud?" she asked.

"Cleveland has a Baghdad police inspector source who said Yusuf's connected to Kurdish gangs that run the city's drug rackets. Iranians supply him with product they smuggle across Iran from Afghanistan. He said if Yusuf's involved, don't discount anything."

"The Kurds are a tight-knit ethnic group. If Ben's roommate is right about the woman supplier, it might not be a reach to consider she's involved with the same gangs mixed up with Yusuf," she said.

"Here's another possibility: Yusuf was the target, not Ben." he said.

"That might explain why we found the CIA in the shop," she said.

"Kuttic's interest might be Yusuf's Iranian connection," he said.

"If you're the CIA, wouldn't you want to recruit someone close to the Iranians?" she asked.

"Have you spoken to your DIA contact?"

"She said she'd get back to me. You know Ben will be collateral damage if the CIA's only interested in Yusuf," she said.

Her desk phone started to ring. She went over, checked the caller ID, and let it ring.

"I know from experience Kuttic destroys lives if you get in his way," Payton said.

"Didn't he tell you he's not sure Ben was even in the tea shop?"

"If we confirm Ben's supplier inside the Green Zone was the Kurd woman, then Kuttic might know more about what happened than he's told us."

"Which means Ben didn't go out for drugs and Titan United's contractor lied to you," she said.

"I told Cleveland and Rammer I want Wade reinterviewed without Vicar or Otto in the same room. Are you still coming?"

She looked at her watch and motioned to her phone. "Give me forty-five minutes to tell Ambassador Rhodes the bad news about Al Kut's BUI."

"Cleveland and I went over to Ben's office. We found his notebook computer with a corrupted hard drive, and someone hacked into ESM's server and deleted several of his e-mails."

"Didn't they have computer security in place?"

"Firewalls, but they were compromised. Cleveland said whoever's behind the breach is sophisticated and knew what they were after. He'll attempt to reconstitute the hard drive but he's not optimistic. We haven't found Ben's company-issued external backup hard drive either. If we can locate it, maybe we find what was hacked off his server account. When we left Ben's building, we saw two men in a car who Cleveland thought had his building under surveillance. I approached them and they took off."

"Ben's attracted a lot of attention," she said.

"He might not be the only one."

CHAPTER 16

CLIFFSIDE

PAYTON WAVED CARL and Blacknife over from the Humvee to the pub's entrance where he stood with Catherine.

"His roommate also said Ben sold weed to a Titan United security contractor," Payton said.

"Got a name?" Catherine said.

"We'd be over in Vicar's office right now if he gave us one. I'll start with Wade Loft."

"Graham might not know what all his people are involved in, but he'd certainly tell you if he knew an employee bought weed from Ben," Catherine said.

"If I uncover he or his South African director of operations knew, then Colonel Mifflin will have to rethink her Titan United strategy because I'll make sure they lose every contract she's awarded them."

"With all the government work they have, you'll need an act of Congress."

"I'll save Congress the effort. You two ready?" he asked.

Blacknife and Carl both nodded.

Payton pushed through the double doors and surveyed the early evening crowd in Cliffside, a British-operated pub on the edge of Ben's trailer park. Young office workers and a few Iraqis at tall tables were crowded in front of the bar. Several private security contractors stood around two pool tables. "Roxanne" by the Police pulsated from speakers hung from the plywood ceiling. He smelled stale beer mixed with sawdust and noticed the air conditioner couldn't handle the crush of sweaty bodies.

With Catherine beside him, he made his way across the sawdust-sprinkled floor to a cocktail waitress in short cut-off fatigues and a tight white T-shirt over a Union Jack bra who was taking glass beer mugs from one of the bartenders and setting them on a round tray.

Blacknife and Carl stepped to the side of the front door and stood next to the lone pinball machine.

"Where are ESM's people?" Payton asked.

"Who?" she asked. Light reflected off a round metal ball drilled through the center of her tongue.

"The accountants," he said.

She motioned with a full mug to the other side of the bar. Next to a dartboard sat two women and four men on bar stools clustered around cocktail tables.

He and Catherine wove through the dance floor mob.

"Dale Lowsley?" Payton asked at the tables.

"Who wants to know?" one of the young woman slurred with a Cockney accent. She had a streak of blue in her black-rooted blond hair and a self-important attitude.

He showed her his shield while she took another quaff from her almost-empty mug. "We need to speak with him about Ben Ater."

When he mentioned Ben's name, the smile disappeared from the face of the girl seated beside blue streak and she looked away from him.

Was she scared?

"He might be in the gym. What a joke," blue streak said. She laughed and so did the black guy with short dreadlocks to her right, who appeared to be more loaded than she was.

"Maggie, Dale's our boss. You've had too much to drink," the other girl said.

"Come on, Leah, we've only started to party," Maggie blue streak said. She raised her mug, tapped dreadlock's, and finished what was left.

Leah was the name of the girl Rousseau said Ben was close to.

Dreadlocks stood and leaned into Payton. The smell of beer followed his belch.

"Sit down," Payton said, but dreadlocks swayed there.

"We have a problem here?" Two security contractors appeared on the other side of Catherine. The one who spoke sounded Afrikaner and was well over six feet with a part shaved into his short brown hair. A Titan United logo spread across his maroon shirt.

He must be one of the special forces goons Otto brought with him from South Africa. Payton hadn't noticed these two with the other security contractors at the pool tables when they entered the pub. Were they already in here or had they followed them in?

Dreadlocks grabbed the back of his chair to steady himself. "Is Dale in trouble?" he asked.

Payton looked at Leah, who glanced away again.

The South African stepped in closer and towered over Catherine. His buddy, who had a nasty white scar along his jawline and a bowling ball for a head on a compressed, thick neck, came with him.

Blacknife and Carl appeared behind the contractors. They held pool cues with the heavy side down.

"They've ruined our party, Johannes," Maggie said with a fake whine to the tall one closest to Catherine.

Payton placed his left hand on the sticky round table's edge next to a full plastic pitcher of beer.

Johannes came in closer. "We can't have that—" he said.

"Back off," Catherine yelled up at him.

Johannes's fist roundhoused over Catherine's head toward Payton. He avoided the blow, palmed the pitcher, and smashed it into Johannes's blocky head.

Blacknife slammed his cue behind bowling ball head's knees, who folded back like a card table. On his way down, Carl twirled and cracked the cue above the guy's ear.

Payton stepped past Catherine and rammed his size fourteen foot between Johannes's legs. The South African hunched forward with both hands on his crotch. Blood and beer covered his face. Catherine shoved him, and he toppled backward over his unconscious buddy sprawled on the floor. Blacknife thwacked his cue on Johannes's head.

Payton touched Catherine's shoulder and nodded behind the bar where Leah slipped through a door. "Follow her," he said.

Catherine pushed past several onlookers and went after her.

With Carl close behind him, Payton followed her. Blacknife brought up the rear, moving his cue back and forth in case any more heroes followed them.

Payton went through the door into a storage room. The low-ceilinged space held boxes of bar glasses, plastic sleeves of napkins, oversized bottles of cherries, and miniature white bar onions crammed on floor-to-ceiling shelves. Light seeped under the dented metal door.

Outside, behind the bar, Payton saw Leah disappear around the corner of the building. "Stop," he said.

Trapped in a narrow space, Leah turned. "Leave me alone," she said.

"We need to talk about Ben," Catherine said.

"I have no idea what happened to him." She started to cry.

Payton held her thin shoulders when she tried to push past him. "Let's find somewhere we can talk," he said.

"Please leave."

"The longer it takes to find him, the higher the odds he dies," Catherine said.

"There's a pizza place down the street where we can talk," Payton said.

She hesitated, then with frightened eyes nodded.

CHAPTER 17

SHOOTER

THE PIZZA HUT occupied a low-slung concrete building with a warped corrugated metal roof.

Payton and Catherine sat across from Leah in one of the back booths.

In her early twenties, she had deep blue eyes and chocolate brown hair cut so that it curled back up around her collar. Her gaze was on a sugar packet she drummed.

A waitress came over.

"Coffee?" Payton asked.

Leah gave a slight nod. He held up three fingers.

"What's your last name?" he asked.

"Grisewood." She kept up with the sugar packet.

"Why'd you run?"

"I … who're you again?"

"Diplomatic investigators," he said.

Catherine slid her shield over.

Blacknife and Carl sat in a booth behind them.

"Why did those security men come over?" Payton asked.

"My company hired Titan United to provide security for all our auditors. We were told they're for our own protection."

"Even when you're inside the Green Zone?" Catherine asked.

"They hang around all the time. Johannes and Tau are friendlier than the other ones, who are creepy. You didn't need to smack them with those pool cues."

"Tell us how you ended up in Iraq," Catherine said.

"The British government sent requests to firms in the UK—they needed auditors to review military contracts from offices located inside the Green Zone. Several people from my Manchester office signed up. We thought coming here would be an adventure."

The waitress came back with their coffees. Leah sipped hers, black, no sugar.

"Ben joined our audit group a few weeks after we arrived. We were told the Green Zone would be safe. None of us expected to be in a war zone."

"Did ESM provide all the auditors?" he asked.

"Four other firms also sent people."

"Is Dale Lowsley your supervisor?" he asked.

"They put him in charge of the day-to-day contract oversight auditing group. He's a senior audit partner with a national firm in Atlanta and an air force reserve lieutenant colonel."

"Who does he report to?" Catherine asked.

"Colonel Dara Mifflin, who oversees the AMC office and manages the entire Iraqi contractor program. Her office hires and pays every contractor in the country. She requested we stay on two- to four-person audit teams to be more productive."

After he spoke with Dale, Payton would pay a visit to Colonel Mifflin. She might know if Ben had any problems with his work.

"Are you?" Catherine asked, "… more productive?"

"We do alright, but we're understaffed. The bigger issue is so much contractor work's performed in the Red Zone, we can't verify they've even completed what they were contracted to do."

"Why?" she asked.

"Too dangerous. Titan United has their security people with us on the rare occasions we leave."

"How do you get your job done without verifying work?" Catherine asked.

"We review their financials and conduct contractor interviews here in the Green Zone. These contractors aren't stupid. They know the likelihood of work being field audited is nil to none. You're aware we pay a large percentage of them with cash? New one-hundred-dollar bills flown in from your US Treasury."

"Cash is difficult to keep track of," he said.

"We look for any proof of payment we can find. I've seen receipts written on gum wrappers, matchbook covers, even toilet paper."

"Is your team responsible for a certain geographic area?" Catherine asked.

"Ben and I were paired up and given responsibility for Baghdad security work, MWRs in Anbar and Ninawa Provinces, any Tigris River bridge repair, and of course, all Titan United's work."

"You two audit Titan United?" he asked. He didn't know Vicar's people worked security for the same accountants who audited his financial statements.

"Dale put both of us on Titan United's account right after Ben arrived."

"Do any other audit teams review Titan United's work?" he asked.

She shook her head.

"What's the current value of their contracts?" he asked.

"Titan United's Iraq portfolio's valued around seventy-five million."

"Do you know of any reason why Ben might cross the river?" Catherine asked.

Leah emptied the sugar packet into her coffee. "I told him to stop but he wouldn't," she said.

Her eyes welled up again. Catherine moved the Parmesan cheese and red pepper shaker. She pulled a few white paper napkins out of the metal napkin holder and handed them to her.

"Stop what?" he asked.

"About Fallujah." Leah wiped her eyes. "He wouldn't leave what he found there alone."

"What did he find?" Catherine asked.

"Dale sent Ben to Fallujah to audit Titan United's FOB facility. He found out that a subcontractor sent inflated invoices to Colonel Mifflin's office for payment. We run across cheats everywhere."

Did Vicar or Otto know what Ben turned up? Payton wondered.

"I know Ben has his flaws. We all do, but he's working on them," she said.

"Is being a dope dealer one of them?" Payton asked.

"It was only marijuana."

"His roommate said he could get any drug he wanted," Catherine said.

"I've no idea what he could or couldn't get. He knew I wouldn't go out with him if he didn't stop."

"He ever mention where the drugs came from?" he asked.

"We never discussed drugs."

"How long've you two dated?" Catherine asked.

"We had a connection from the start." Her eyes were wet with tears.

"His notebook computer was in his office with a destroyed hard drive. Any idea where we can find his external backup drive?" he asked.

"Why do you want his hard drive?"

"For any information it might contain we can use to find him."

She avoided their eyes and asked, "Isn't that private?"

"Not when someone's life is in the balance," he said.

"Did any of his e-mails concern you?" Catherine asked.

"He sent me one from Fallujah about something else he found."

"Inflated invoices?" he asked.

She shook her head. "Another problem."

"Company," Carl said over his shoulder. "Near the door."

Above Leah, Payton saw reflected in the bottom edge of a Plexiglas wall-mounted Pizza Hut sign a guy in a booth with sunglasses pushed up on his military-cut dark hair. He peered their way, then went back to his menu. Payton recognized the cauliflower ear of Otto's man whom he'd seen outside Titan United's glass conference room doors. A waitress had her order pad and pen out next to him.

Two men outside Ben's office building, Recces in Cliffside, and now this guy. If they were being followed, he wanted to know now.

He touched Catherine's hand and nodded to the sign. "Let's go for a walk," he said and slid out.

Catherine motioned to Leah to follow.

Payton pushed through a door beside their booth that led to the bathrooms. Leah and Catherine were close behind him. When Blacknife and Carl came through, Payton opened an emergency exit door and stepped out into the evening heat.

"Take her behind the car," Payton said.

Catherine took Leah in between the security wall and a rusted, yellow, four-door Chevy Caprice mounted on cinder blocks with no tires.

Payton gestured to the marines, who moved to either side of the door. He stepped in front of the Chevy.

Three minutes passed. Blacknife moved toward the door and paused. He looked over to Payton, who shook his head to wait.

Another couple of minutes ticked by.

"He's not coming," Catherine said behind him.

Seconds after Payton whistled to Blacknife to go back inside, car tires ground and spun on the gravel service drive beside the Pizza Hut. The Peugeot with the same two guys he'd seen outside Ben's building slid to a stop in the open space yards to his left.

"Gun," Payton yelled and pulled the Glock.

In the rear driver's side seat the guy with straight black hair rested the blunt barrel of a pump shotgun on the open window frame. He fired. Dozens of shotgun pellets slammed into the Chevy's grill and hood. The shooter pumped and fired again. The windshield exploded and pellets smashed into the wall behind Catherine and Leah.

Payton fired low from behind the Chevy around one of the cinder blocks. Over the hood Catherine squeezed off several rounds with her SIG. Another shotgun blast and the Chevy's side and rear windows shattered. Splinters of glass rained down on Payton.

Blacknife and Carl lay prone in a shallow concrete grease trap pit and fired their handguns.

The driver, still with the baseball hat pulled low, threw the Peugeot into reverse and fishtailed back where they'd come from.

Payton sprinted after them and fired several times. The car's rear window disintegrated before they disappeared down the trailer-lined street.

"Leah's hit," Catherine yelled.

He rushed back. Blood covered the shredded white blouse on the left side of Leah's chest. He could tell from the wound they had to get her to Ibn Sina Hospital, a Combat Support Hospital, CSH, that was located several blocks away and featured the best triage doctors in the country.

"Get a medic," he called to Carl.

Catherine ripped the bottom of Leah's blouse, folded the torn fabric, and pressed it against the chest wound to stop the bleeding.

"No exit wound," Catherine said.

Not good.

Leah whimpered.

"Help will be here soon," Catherine said to her.

From her pale color Payton knew Leah was going into shock.

Blacknife came back out of the Pizza Hut. "The contractor's gone," he said.

It took fifteen long minutes for CSH's medical response team to arrive, load Leah into the ambulance, and speed back to the hospital.

"Did you see the shooter?" Catherine asked. She stood next to Payton where the gravel drive met the street.

"They were the same two guys from outside Ben's office," Payton said.

"Leah's closer to Ben than anyone else," Blacknife said.

"Which put a target on her," Carl said.

"Kill her and we may never know what Ben was involved with," Catherine said.

"I want security on her around the clock," Payton said to the marines.

"She was about to tell us what Ben e-mailed her about," she said.

"How could the guys in the car come at us so fast back here?" Blacknife asked.

"Someone in the Pizza Hut let them know where we were," Carl said.

"The Titan United guy?" Blacknife asked.

"He's the same Recces I saw in Titan United's office when I spoke with Wade Loft," Payton said.

"He might've wanted a pizza," she said.

"And two Titan United guys in Cliffside were there for a beer?" Payton asked.

"They followed us into the pub," Carl said.

"Graham wouldn't be that stupid to have his men tail us," she said.

"Maggie with the blue streak might still be in a talkative mood. I want to hear what she has to say about Ben and these Titan United security contractors," Payton said. Then he'd track down Vicar and Otto. He needed to get answers why their Recces were following them.

"I'll be with Leah," Catherine said.

CHAPTER 18

EMBASSY

PAYTON MET WITH Rammer and Cleveland in an oversized storage closet converted into a conference room next to Cleveland's office.

"Who called in the shooters?" Cleveland asked.

"I'll start with the Titan United guy I recognized in the Pizza Hut. Get me pictures of all their security people. I want to know who he is," Payton said.

"How's the girl?" Rammer asked.

"Her doctors won't know for twelve hours if she's out of the woods. Ben sent Leah an e-mail about something he found in Fallujah. Talk with ESM's IT guy. See if he's aware of any e-mail red flags Ben raised with his Fallujah audit. What about the notebook hard drive?" Payton asked.

"No luck," Cleveland said.

"Which brings us back to Ben's external hard drive," Payton said.

"We'll pick through his trailer again," Cleveland said.

"Where are we with Wade?" Payton asked Rammer.

"I've left him two more voice messages and sent him another e-mail he never responded to. I tried Otto and Graham, but they're out of the Green Zone at a meeting. I finally got in touch with Wade's dignitary protection unit shift manager. She said he'll be back from a BGW run later tonight. I'll intercept him in the lobby of his building when he checks in after his shift."

"Is he playing games with you?" Payton asked.

"I don't know yet," Rammer said.

"Was the girl aware of Ben's drug involvement?" Cleveland asked.

"Leah said she wouldn't have had anything to do with him if he sold drugs."

"Tell him about the Kurd," Cleveland motioned to Rammer.

"The only female Kurdish attorney employed by an NGO is Evette Azard. Raised in Diyarbakir, Turkey, she's worked for The Institute of Legal Affairs, a Paris-based NGO, since she graduated from the Sorbonne Law School six years ago. ILA offers free legal advice to France's sizable Kurdish population. She arrived in the Green Zone with four other ILA staffers thirteen months ago to coordinate humanitarian aid to Kurdish refugees."

"Any known drug involvement?" Payton asked.

"French law enforcement said she has no arrest record," Rammer said.

"Didn't your police inspector contact say Yusuf was the only Kurd in al-Dori's organization?" Payton asked.

"He did," Cleveland said.

"If she's plugged into the Kurdish community, maybe we can find a Kurd who can connect her to Yusuf," Rammer said.

"Let Quinn know we may've found Ben's supplier. See if he can help locate her. Tonight I'm going to speak with Ben's boss after I talk to one of his coworkers," Payton said.

CHAPTER 19

MAGGIE

CARL PULLED their Humvee to a stop in front of a sandstone apartment building's main entrance.

"Think she's sobered up?" Blacknife asked.

"Let's hope so," Payton said. His cell phone rang. It was Catherine.

"I'll see you in the lobby," he said to the marines.

"She's lost a lot of blood," Catherine said. Her cell signal was weak.

A few seconds went by and he didn't hear her. He thought they'd lost the connection.

"Catherine?" he asked.

"She should never have come to the Green Zone."

"Who's with her?"

"One of her coworkers arrived a few minutes ago."

"I'm on my way to see her friend Maggie from Cliffside," he said. She didn't answer. "You still there?"

"Sorry, have you had dinner?" she asked.

"I was going to grab something when I get back."

"Can I join you? I—"

"Is something bothering you?"

"Let's talk later."

"I'll see you around ten in the second-floor cafeteria."

Silence.

"Hello," he said. She didn't respond. The call must've dropped. What couldn't wait until morning?

THEY STEPPED OUT of the third-floor elevator, and Payton saw Maggie several doors down in front of her apartment.

With an overstuffed leather briefcase pinned under her arm, she held a scrunched-up brown paper bag by the neck and jostled several keys on a key ring. Her disheveled hair with its blue streak obscured her face.

"Need help?" Payton asked.

She jumped and dropped the keys. "What's wrong with you people? You don't come up behind someone like that."

She smelled of beer. He picked up the keys and held them out. "Which one?"

She looked at Blacknife and Carl behind Payton and then pointed with her bag hand. "The gold one."

He opened the door. She plucked her keys back, quick-stepped in, and turned. "Ben's Leah's friend, not mine."

"Leah's been shot. She's in Ibn Sina Hospital."

She looked at him for several long seconds, then asked, "When?"

"A few hours ago, after we left Cliffside."

Her eyes teared up, she dropped the brown bag and brief-case, and disappeared inside. He heard a door slam.

He gathered up her bag with an empty plastic lunch container still inside and several spilled papers from her briefcase. "Wait here," he said to the marines and closed the door behind him.

Sobs came from the bathroom down a hallway past her cramped kitchen. Her apartment was unkempt, with mag-azines and clothes strewn everywhere. In the kitchen, he filled her teapot with water, put it on a burner, and turned up the flame.

He heard the shower.

Ten minutes later she walked into the living room wrapped in a white terry cloth bathrobe with "A.F.C. Bournemouth" embroidered under a red, black, and white soccer ball. She'd combed her wet hair straight back, and the blue streak was no longer visible. Her eyes were red from crying.

He handed her a plastic mug of tea.

She tossed several copies of *The Sun* from a wicker love-seat to the floor and sat with her feet tucked under her, then wiped both eyes with an oversized sleeve. "What hap-pened?" she asked.

"Two guys came at us behind the Pizza Hut."

"They were after her because of Ben, weren't they?"

"We don't know," he said.

"The Green Zone's a horrible place. None of us should be here."

"Tell me about Ben."

"He's a bugger, and I couldn't care less what happens to him. He name-drops his senator uncle all the time. After the first hundred times, it gets old." She sniffled.

Payton went back into the kitchen and returned with a box of tissues and handed them to her.

"Before I saw what he was up to with his drug use and sales, I liked him. The Green Zone's one big party to him. I told Leah to keep her distance but she wouldn't listen. Everyone knows how sweet she is. She'll do whatever she can for anyone. When Ben first joined our audit group, I thought he might be here for the right reasons, to help Iraqis get their country back. But he wasn't any better than the rest of us. We all came for the excitement, to pad our résumés, and to take a year's worth of tax-free salary for six months' work before we go back to our boring lives."

"Why's Leah here?"

"The right reasons. While the rest of us pub hop, she tutors English to Iraqi families who live close to our office building. Tonight's only the second time she'd even been to Cliffside."

"What about you? Why'd you come to the Green Zone?"

She avoided his eyes and stared down at her cup. "One too many impaired driving offenses. I skipped my court date."

"They'll find you"

"Already have. My solicitor phoned and said if I didn't get back soon, avoiding ninety days in jail might not be possible."

"When do you leave?"

"Haven't decided. Leah told me to go but I laughed her off. She's the serious one. I'm about, where's the next party?"

She got up and went into the kitchen. He heard her pour more water into her cup and spoon in sugar. Then she opened and closed a drawer. She came back and sat. The bag of weed she put on the table was one of Ben's Kush party bags.

"Ben sold me weed. That's how I got to know him."

"What did Leah say about his drug use?"

"He assured her he'd stop. I told her, don't be fooled. He won't listen. I know the type. They use people. Want to know the sad part? He's a meticulous auditor."

"Leah said he found problems in Fallujah."

"He was furious when he came back. A subcontractor triple-counted military personnel and sent the inflated invoices in for payment. Philip was supposed to go but came down with a stomach bug. Dale sent Ben instead."

"She didn't tell you anything else?"

She shook her head. "I saw Ben in our weekly staff meeting the morning after he came back. He was preoccupied. Dale pressed him to have his Fallujah report on his desk by the end of the day. After the meeting, I heard both of them argue in Dale's office with the door closed."

"Do you know if he gave Dale his report?"

"No idea. When Leah heard Ben was going to Fallujah, she was scared for his safety. Fallujah's a horrible place, where several security contractors were killed."

"What's the process after you file an audit report?"

"Dale handles the follow-up with Colonel Mifflin. I've no idea what happens to all the corrupt contractors we find. Something about Fallujah bothered Ben. Leah said he told her he'd go over Dale's head to Colonel Mifflin if he didn't report what he'd found."

"His job is to let the colonel know what his auditors find. Why wouldn't Dale file a report?"

"Half our recommendations don't make it out of his office. I heard he's told several companies we've audited, he might be for hire once his time's up being the top auditor in the Green Zone."

"So much for ethics," he said.

"We're under strict orders to stay away from contractors we audit. Guess who Leah saw Dale with at lunch last week? Titan United executives." She lifted the tea bag up and down in the cup. "You have no idea the cesspool we deal with every day. The American blood money these contractors make is obscene. Take a guess what kind of money our audit group alone has uncovered being paid without any proof of the work being completed."

He watched her.

"Four hundred and eighteen million—almost a half a billion dollars. Our audits send a bulletin to corrupt contractors: if you're caught, the free ride's over. But what happens if your auditor disappears? The gravy train keeps rolling."

"You think Ben's disappearance might be work related?"

"I'm only saying, not all these contractors appreciate when we snoop around their financials."

"Where can I find Dale?"

"You might try the gym near our offices where he sometimes works out at night, though he doesn't have much to show for it."

Payton stood.

She followed him with her eyes.
"Will you be alright?'
 "Once I'm with Leah I will be," she said.
"She needs you."

CHAPTER 20

DALE LOWSLEY

"**WE LOST TOO** many marines in Fallujah," Blacknife said.

"If Ben told anyone other than Leah what he found, it'd be Dale Lowsley. Maggie said he might be at the gym. Let's go," Payton said.

These contractors are in hand-to-hand combat to get ever bigger government checks. If Dale's on the hunt for a job, would it be too far of a reach to consider he might share something with a possible new employer about an audit his group has underway? Or share a piece of information on a competitor so he could score a choice executive gig?

Carl stopped at a blinking red traffic light and turned onto a cul-de-sac two streets over from Ben's office building.

Payton pointed to a monument sign next to the last circular driveway. Below several company names was "GYM" in bold letters.

Carl turned in.

Once a hotel, the building was now being used for offices. They went across the entrance hall, down an expansive staircase, and into the basement lobby. Through open doors Payton saw a banquet room with every piece of exercise equipment imaginable.

In front of floor-to-ceiling windows on the far side of the cavernous space Payton watched several young men and women run to nowhere on treadmills. Beyond the windows stood a statue in the middle of a rock garden.

All these office workers had every comfort of home and none of the hardships that Iraqis had to endure. A vacation with a résumé kicker—all paid for by American taxpayers.

"Why don't they run outside?" Blacknife asked.

"Can't handle the heat," Carl said.

Blacknife looked into a weight room. He shook his head back to Payton. Carl walked along the row of treadmills.

Payton moved through two lines of stationary bikes with sweat-drenched riders participating in a spinning class and being urged on by an instructor. Here was another group headed nowhere.

"Dale Lowsley?" he asked the nearest girl.

She pumped the pedals with her head down and pointed to a flabby guy at the end of the row in front of her.

Payton walked over to him.

"You Dale Lowsley?"

Irritated, the guy glanced up at him through rimless glasses. Sweat covered the top of his head above a narrow half-crown of brown hair, and while he bobbed from side to side, his meatball knees moved like clumsy pistons. "I'm busy here," he said.

"I need to ask you a few questions about Ben Ater," Payton said.

"I'll be finished in ten minutes."

Payton grabbed his elbow in a vise grip. "You're finished now."

"Okay … okay." He slowed and yanked his elbow away.

"LEAH'S BEEN SHOT?" Dale asked. He spoke with a slight Southern accent that Payton placed in Virginia. With a plastic bottle of water in one hand, Dale used a white towel draped around his neck to pat his double chin.

They stood in the oppressive heat next to the rock garden's ten-foot statue of Aletheia. The thought occurred to Payton to ask Lowsley if he knew what Aletheia represented. "Greek goddess of truth" was carved on a plaque at the base.

"Did you know Ben was involved with drugs?"

"I hear things and told him that if I caught him with drugs the military police would be notified."

"Did he listen?"

"He didn't feel rules applied to him. With a powerful senator for an uncle, he thought he could get away with whatever he wanted to."

"Any idea what he was doing by the river?"

Lowsley glanced past Payton and pointed with the near-empty bottle toward the Red Zone. "He had no logical reason to be out there."

"Why'd you send him to Fallujah?"

"Because Phillip was sick, and he was the only one of my auditors who hadn't been out of the Green Zone yet. All my people carry their own weight, uncle or no uncle."

"Anything out of the ordinary with his audit?" Payton asked.

"Only what my auditors find on a regular basis, a subcontractor who padded their numbers."

"Who was the subcontractor?"

"A Yemen-based outfit brought in by a Titan United subsidiary. Bigger companies don't want to send support staff into dangerous situations. They hire subcontractors who have access to employees from Third World countries."

How'd Vicar square with Colonel Mifflin one of his operations retained a corrupt subcontractor? Payton thought.

"What did you do about the padded invoices?" Payton asked.

"Ben knew the drill. After I review his report and agree with his conclusion that fraud may be involved, a memo's sent to Colonel Mifflin, who's in charge of the Iraq contractor program. For some reason he went behind my back to her office."

"Why?"

"No idea."

Payton recalled that Maggie said Leah told her Ben would go over Lowsley's head if he didn't report what he'd found.

"Ben might have concerns with what his audit turned up."

"Not his job. Once he submits his audit results, he's done." With a self-important tap on his sweat-soaked T-shirt, he added, "I'm the only one who communicates with Colonel Mifflin."

If Ben thought Lowsley would bury his report, he might decide to go straight to Mifflin.

"What if he didn't trust you'd send the audit to her office?"

"He was hired to perform a specific task, to verify contracted work's been completed. No more, no less. I can assure you, I give every audit careful consideration." He dabbed more sweat.

"What did Colonel Mifflin do?"

"When she couldn't see him because of her packed schedule, he wouldn't leave her office. She called security to escort him out. Then she called and read me the riot act. Do you have any idea how busy she is? She can't let everyone barge into her office without an appointment."

"I'm sure Iraq would grind to a halt without her," Payton said.

"She oversees a hundred thousand plus contractors. Iraq doesn't get rebuilt without her oversight."

"Was Ben the first time any of your auditors went to her office?"

"Yes, and I told him if he went around me again, he'd be on the next flight back to Ohio."

"What's the process when you find fraud?"

"I send Colonel Mifflin a fraud memo."

"How many have you sent her?"

"What do fraud memos have to do with Ben?"

"Humor me."

He pointed the bottle at Payton to make his point. "We've found eighty-two fraud cases out of three hundred and twenty-nine completed audits."

"Did all eighty-two end up in her office?"

Lowsley hesitated, then quickly glanced back to the gym windows. "Not all of them." He gestured with the towel. "She told me she doesn't have enough staff to review every case. She only wanted ones where large amounts of money are involved."

Maggie was right when she said Lowsley didn't send all audit results over to Mifflin's office. If he held back certain information, what else didn't he let Mifflin know about?

"Define large."

"At least six figures, and if we suspect the same company more than once, we'll send them over to her."

"Is Fallujah the first time for Titan United?"

"We found a few other occasions."

"How many?"

He hesitated again. Lowsley had a hard time with eye contact. Was the sweat on his upper lip from his workout or nerves?

"Eleven, well, twelve if you count Fallujah."

Why'd Mifflin given Vicar a pass with twelve fraud memos? Payton wondered.

"Did she receive all twelve?"

"Of course she did."

"Were Leah and Ben responsible for the memos?"

"Every one of them."

"All twelve were over a hundred grand?"

"I already said the dollar amount had to be at least that for a memo to be issued."

"How much money are we talking about with Titan United?"

Lowsley didn't answer. He looked to the windows again.

"Let's go back to the embassy," Payton said. "We have little rooms with uncomfortable chairs where we park people for several hours if they have a hard time with questions."

"Four point three million."

"How has Titan United kept their government work with twelve fraud memos?"

"You'll have to ask the colonel. She makes those decisions."

Payton planned on it.

"One of your people said they heard you and Ben argue after he came back from Fallujah. What happened?"

"I told him I needed his report for my weekly meeting with Colonel Mifflin the next day. Speed isn't one of Ben's strong suits. He doesn't like to be rushed. He's a perfectionist, sometimes to the point of being ridiculous."

"I'm curious. Do you miss much fraud?"

"I have exceptional people who don't miss anything."

Lowsley finished off the water and tossed the empty bottle into a garbage can behind him.

Payton put his foot on the cement bench next to Lowsley. "Are you aware Ben told Leah he found something else in Fallujah?"

Lowsley's eyes scudded over to Blacknife, then Carl. When they came back to Payton, he still didn't make eye contact. "He never mentioned anything else."

"Does juggling all these fraud memos interrupt your job search?"

He folded his towel, wiped his upper lip then the top of his head, and still didn't hold eye contact.

"I've done my bit to help Iraq. Why shouldn't I be rewarded? The Green Zone's a dangerous work environment. Look what happened to Ben."

"I may need to speak with you again."

He looked at the statue, then to Payton. "I'll be here. My new job doesn't start for three months."

CHAPTER 21

ARABIAN SEA

PAYTON WALKED A few blocks from the embassy over to a restaurant-lined street.

Maggie indicated Ben was furious when he came back from Fallujah. If she knew Lowsley didn't send all of their audit results to Mifflin's office, Ben would also know. Is that why he went to her office? He didn't want to risk that Lowsley wouldn't turn over what he found?

Payton approached the Arabian Sea, a restaurant operated by Titan United, where Rammer said Otto and Vicar were at dinner. Tinny Arabic music played from speakers hidden behind potted palm trees on either side of the entrance.

Inside the entryway, he saw white kitschy track lights twined with the plastic ivy-covered ceiling. Gray-painted wood scimitars hung on either side of the smudged glass door.

He scanned the crowded lobby and packed cocktail lounge. Chandeliers lit the dining room, and tuxedoed waiters and busboys scurried around dozens of tables covered with white tablecloths.

Otto was on the other side of the room at a table with Vicar, Zaki al-Dulaimi, and Wafiyi Khleifat, who chatted away with Colonel Mifflin. The only one not there was Marco al-Dulaimi.

Khleifat, the politician, would be here for a handout. Zaki, his remora, was right next to him. Catherine called the brothers educated hoods. Why didn't he believe their only interest in Khleifat was to help him get elected? If their guy Khleifat won, he'd make sure the brothers would score plum positions in the new government.

Vicar spoke to Otto, who stood and leaned down beside him. Otto responded and then walked through the double kitchen doors located on the other side of their table.

Payton came up to the table and heard Vicar say to Khleifat, "I don't mean to boast, but we have excellent chefs."

Tens of millions worth of government work, you better have a decent cook, Payton mused.

"We need to talk," Payton said.

Vicar looked up, annoyed. "I'm sorry, but we're in an important business meeting. I can make time for you tomorrow. Call my secretary—"

"I'll be quick," Payton said.

"Tomorrow will be—" Vicar said.

Payton saw Mifflin move her hand over to Vicar's, beside his empty martini glass. She gave him an "I'll take over" pat.

"Special Agent, now's not the time," she said.

Payton didn't acknowledge her. He bent close and smelled vodka and green olives on Vicar's breath. "Tell your South

African director of operations to keep his goons away from my investigation. I want both of you in my office tomorrow."

Khleifat spoke to Zaki, who glanced up at Payton.

Vicar made a show of folding his napkin and setting it beside his plate of deviled eggs and caviar. "You're being preposterous," he said. "Otto would never interfere with an official investigation."

The colonel stood and in full military authority mode said, "Agent, you're out of order."

"A few hours ago my team was ambushed." He stabbed his thumb at Vicar, who now straightened his silverware. "I saw one of his security men nearby before it happened, and I don't care for coincidences."

"I won't be threatened," Vicar said.

Colonel Mifflin's eyes narrowed. "Ladd, this conversation's over."

Vicar murmured to Khleifat, who shrugged his shoulders.

"We've only started," Payton said. "Don't make me come looking for you," he said down to Vicar. He'd made his point and would let Catherine know she might get a call from Ambassador Rhodes after Mifflin phoned to complain.

Payton walked back across the dining room to the front door. The thought occurred to him that Vicar, with his bow tie and manicured fingernails, could be clueless when it came to operations. Maybe he plays the part of being a rain-maker, a major-league hitter, a wine-and-dine guy whose job is to please Colonel Mifflin to keep the contract work coming? No operational heavy lifting for him. Otto could handle any day-to-day dirty work.

When he stepped outside, he saw a narrow space between the restaurant and the adjacent building. Otto might still be in the kitchen. If he was, Payton would save Vicar the trouble and tell Otto himself.

He slipped between the buildings. When he moved onto the sidewalk behind the restaurant, he ducked back into the alley.

A white Jaguar, with Marco behind the wheel, idled at the curb across the street. Otto climbed into the front passenger seat and they pulled away.

On the same side of the street, under a Chinese restaurant delivery sign, Payton saw what he needed. He sprinted over and pushed a three-speed bicycle with a wicker delivery basket off its kickstand, hopped on, and pedaled several times before the small motor attached to the rear wheel sputtered to life.

Marco turned at the second traffic light. Payton gunned the bike. When he made the turn, the Jag's brake lights tapped on several cars ahead at another red light. Payton didn't have enough space to weave between the parked cars and vehicles stacked back from the light, so he bounced up onto the sidewalk.

The light turned green and traffic started to move. Payton veered to miss a man sprawled in the middle of the sidewalk, then hopped off the curb and hurtled through the intersection.

In front of a bakery delivery van slowed at the next light, Yafa Street, Marco maneuvered past a construction site Porta-Jon, glided through the intersection, then accelerated toward another green light.

The light turned red, traffic slowed and stopped. Payton swerved into the empty oncoming traffic lane and with the bike wide open, darted through a brief pause in Yafa Street's traffic. Two blocks ahead, Marco drove into a park.

Payton took the first dirt footpath he came to into the park. Through several trees, and beyond a marble memorial, he saw them idle at a red light.

The light changed and the Jag disappeared into a neighborhood.

Payton followed and saw the brake lights turn. He came to a stop and peered around the edge of a shuttered shop. Otto's door opened, he climbed out, and Marco drove off.

He rested the bike against a light pole and crept around the corner in sidewalk shadows close to buildings. Otto walked beside several empty street vendor stalls, then dropped out of sight.

Payton jogged across the street to the stalls and used them for cover to move opposite the alley entrance. At the far end of the alley, the security wall loomed.

He didn't see Otto.

A forlorn boat horn broke the silence. Payton smelled trash being burned.

Opposite destroyed buildings, now piles of rubble with facades, was a decrepit two-story apartment building.

Was Otto in the apartment building?

Payton moved to the building's padlocked front door. The lock hadn't been touched. He stepped to the right and saw how close the security wall stood to the apartment building. Otto couldn't squeeze through the tight space.

In a vacant lot on the other side of the building, he moved over mounds of debris toward the rear. He didn't see any first-floor doors or windows Otto could use to access the building. Around back, several large stones blocked the only door.

Back at the front of the building, he scanned the alley. How had Otto vanished and why did Marco drop him off?

After he checked the destroyed buildings across the street and found no trace of Otto, he decided to have Blacknife bring his marines for a more thorough search in daylight. He wanted to know how Otto'd pulled off his Houdini act.

CHAPTER 22

EMBASSY

CATHERINE CALLED TO say she'd be late and to go ahead without her. Payton had gotten a bite to eat and was halfway through his coffee when she came into the cafeteria. She looked drained when she sat across from him with her own cup of coffee.

"Any improvement with Leah?" Payton asked.

"Her doctors said she may have an infection. They doubled her antibiotics."

"Have you eaten?"

"I had something at the hospital."

"Are guards in place at her room?"

"Blacknife has a marine stationed outside her door."

"CSH is on par with the best trauma centers in the United States. They'll take great care of her," he said.

"I hope they can work miracles. Did you speak with Dale Lowsley?"

"Another short-timer here for a résumé boost. Said he starts a new job in ninety days and has no idea why Ben would leave the Green Zone."

"What did he say about Fallujah?"

"Ben found a Titan United subcontractor who padded their invoices. Here's something we didn't know. Ben and Leah are on the Titan United audit account and have found twelve instances of fraud."

"I'm sure Colonel Mifflin's on top of the situation."

"She's way too cozy with Vicar. After our run-in with Titan United's two Recces in Cliffside, I wanted to give Vicar and Otto a bulletin to keep their people away from our investigation. I paid a visit to a restaurant where they were having dinner and found Vicar, Mifflin, Zaki, and Khleifat all at the same table. Otto left before I got to their table. I told Vicar that I wanted both of them in my office in the morning. He didn't appreciate the interruption. Mifflin stood up for him."

"We can't be certain the Pizza Hut guy had anything to do with the ambush," she said.

"What kind of security contractor disappears once the shooting starts? Here's something else. When I left the restaurant I saw Otto get into a car with Marco. I followed them to a neighborhood near the security wall, where Otto got out and disappeared."

"What do you mean disappeared?"

"I lost him in a dead-end alley. I told Blacknife to take a few MSGs to comb through the alley in the morning." He couldn't help notice how preoccupied Catherine was. "What's up with you?"

She turned her cup. "I've a lot on my mind."

"I'm not surprised—between Ben, the bank runs, and everything else you have to manage, you're the ringmaster of a three-ring circus."

"Not work." She exhaled. "Personal stuff."

"Want to talk?"

"Leah being shot brought home something I've had on my mind for a while. Over the last five years, I've volunteered for a consulate position in Mazar i Sharif, Afghanistan, and embassies in Algiers, Cairo, and Muscat with a total of ninety days off."

"You've never shied away from work."

"When I started my career, I didn't have the connections many State Department employees have. I knew I had to outwork them."

"Which brought you to the top of the mountain, RSO Baghdad."

"Ambassador Rhodes needed an RSO with no distractions. He asked Director Santiago if I was available. With no husband or children … well, he knew I could give a hundred percent of my attention to assist him with his turnaround plan. You know me, hand raised, always ready to go."

"He wanted the best."

"What I have is another failed relationship behind me." She paused and, with a quick shake of her head, pushed back in the chair. "I don't want to be alone anymore."

"I never thought I'd hear you say that." Her buried emotions were one of the reasons he never gave much hope their relationship would work long term. "Let me top off your coffee." He went over to the coffee machines, refilled both cups, and came back.

She ripped open two sugar packets, emptied them into her cup, then balled and tossed the empty packets in front of her. "Being RSO of a major embassy was what I always wanted. You can count the number of women in those positions on half of one hand. When we were together in Mexico, for the first time in my life I had a relationship choice to make, my career or you, which frightened me."

"I frightened you?"

"You never frightened me. The depth of my feelings for you terrified me."

"Those feelings could've been a reason to stay together, not blow up what we had."

"I didn't know how to handle both you and my job responsibilities. You knew I wanted a serious career."

"Which you accomplished."

"People evolve," she said.

"You said you were close to someone."

"I realized halfway through our time together his sense of humor reminded me too much of you."

"I hope it was only his sense of humor," he said.

"The incident with Leah dredged up feelings I've never really dealt with. I know time speeds forward, but she reminded me I have no one waiting for me. Someone who cares about me, who wants to spend time with me, who wants to hold me. I don't want home to be an empty apartment in Washington, DC, or high-threat embassies. I want a professional *and* a private life."

"It's not easy for an RSO to pull off a family life."

"I'm used to nothing in my personal life being easy, but I want to try. I know second chances make great movie plotlines, and in real life they're rare." She motioned to wait a second and pulled out her cell phone. When she looked at the screen, she moved her head and shoulder in a sorry motion and answered it.

He got up and went to the restroom. When he came back, she was off the phone. She stood, stepped toward him, and looked up into his eyes.

"After we find Ben, I want us to try again. And I promise I won't let you go this time."

After she'd cut him off in Mexico, he never expected she'd ever say she wanted to take another swing at a relationship.

"I'm not sure a reset's possible."

"My feelings for you have never gone away," she said.

Dangerous work environments like the Green Zone can put people into stressful situations and make them reconsider their lives. Even if she had changed, he had no idea if he wanted to let her back into his life.

"All I ask … consider what I'm saying. No strings." She gave him a tiny smile.

"What you need is a good night's sleep."

"Can you at least give me a hug?

"Hugs are easy," he said.

CHAPTER 23

ROUTE IRISH

PAYTON PRESSED the elevator call button to go to his fifth-floor room. For the first time in a long while he thought of their good times in Mexico.

When the doors opened, he pressed five and pulled out his cell phone. Three missed calls from Rammer. He jerked his hand into the space before the elevator doors closed and came back out. Somehow the ringtone had been changed to mute. He hated these phones.

"I've tried to get you for the last forty-five minutes. Wade Loft was killed by an IED on his way back from BGW. Cleveland didn't want to wait for you any longer and went to the bomb site," Rammer said.

GUARDS WAVED THEIR Humvee through the security checkpoint, and Carl sped toward Route Irish.

"Was anyone else with him?" Payton asked Rammer, who was in the back seat next to Blacknife.

"Cleveland said he was alone. The bomb was large enough to blow his vehicle off Irish."

"Have you ID'd the Pizza Hut Titan United security guy?"

"Not yet."

"What's the holdup?"

"He's not in the company's database. Their HR department's several weeks behind on photographs of all the new hires."

"Park in their offices if you have to. I want the guy's name."

Ten minutes later, Payton saw the gridlock. Carl eased onto the shoulder and drove past the stalled traffic toward military vehicles, where temporary road construction lights were in place.

A few minutes farther on, Carl pulled up next to a Bradley Fighting Vehicle with a marine in the gun turret behind a mounted machine gun. More marines formed a perimeter around the area to keep onlookers and vehicles back from the blast site.

Payton saw Cleveland in the middle of the road with someone, next to one of the light rigs. Chunks of concrete and asphalt littered the road. Part of the crater was peeled up like corrugated metal. The smell of burned rubber mixed with gas hung over the entire area.

Cleveland came over to the Humvee with a guy in uniform. "Rammer Fulkins, Payton Ladd," Cleveland said and pointed to the air force lieutenant with him. "Daryl Wright."

"Gentlemen," Daryl said and stuck his hand out.

"Those are his men," Cleveland said.

At the crater were two Explosive Ordnance Disposal Unit personnel in blast suits. One inspected the inside of the crater, while the other waved a metal detector wand over the road.

Payton saw a destroyed SUV under another set of intense lights in the desert behind them. "When did it happen?"

"Ninety minutes ago," Daryl said.

"They found Wade with a broken neck in a swale by his SUV. He's been taken to Ibn Sina Hospital's morgue," Cleveland said.

"We believe the bomb was in the minivan," Daryl said.

On the other side of the crater, several yards out into the desert, a generator hummed next to a pole-mounted sodium vapor light. The light shone on a minivan that rested on its roof with the driver's side blown out. A fire smoldered from the engine.

"If my men find any bomb component parts, we may be able to ID who the bomb maker is. We keep profiles of every IED we investigate," Daryl said.

"How often do IEDs hit Route Irish?" Payton asked. He knew for a random IED to hit Wade was beyond a million-to-one shot.

"Activity's dropped way off since we've started around-the-clock air surveillance. Witnesses said the minivan was pulled over in the median."

"People with shovels attract attention, a vehicle, not so much," Cleveland said.

The guy in the crater waved Daryl over.

"You're sure Wade was alone?" Payton asked.

"I called airport security, and they said he was by himself when he passed through the security gate," Cleveland said.

"Any chance he was the target?" Rammer asked.

"Hundreds of vehicles a day on Irish and Wade's taken out? Whoever planted the IED knew who they wanted," Payton said.

"Daryl said those buildings have been used before to trigger IEDs. They use cell phones for detonators," Cleveland said.

A cluster of buildings stood along a ridgeline a few hundred yards behind Wade's vehicle.

Payton noticed Daryl examine something that his person in the crater handed up to him.

"Whoever had access to Ben's notebook hard drive also got to the company's backup tapes. ESM's IT guy turned up Ben's e-mails deleted from the backup. He found no reference to Fallujah in any of his other e-mails," Cleveland said.

"What about Leah's?"

Daryl started back toward them.

"I told Kailash to check her office. He found her external hard drive, but she only backed up audit Excel files. He's going to look through her server e-mails," Cleveland said.

"Dale Lowsley said Ben found a Titan United subcontractor in Fallujah who sent bogus invoices to the military for payment."

"Didn't Vicar know Ben audited one of his operations?" Cleveland asked.

"If he did, he forgot to mention it. Ben and Leah are responsible for the Titan United audit account, and they've found eleven other instances of fraud."

"How does Titan United hold on to all their military work?" Rammer asked.

"Vicar and Mifflin are tight," Cleveland said.

"Too tight. Where are we with the Kurd attorney?" Payton asked.

"Her office said she would be back in the Green Zone tomorrow," Rammer said.

"Back from where?"

"A Kurdish refugee camp in Irbil."

Daryl walked back with the remains of a metal box the size of a computer battery, wrapped in green electrical tape, with two white wires hanging from one end.

"Forget the IED—they used an explosively formed penetrator bomb, an EFP. We call the bomb maker "Van Gogh" because of the skill he puts into his work. We've been after him for eighteen months. He uses green tape and white wires."

Cleveland motioned for the box, and Daryl handed it to him. He examined the wires.

"We haven't seen his signature on an EFP before," Daryl said.

"EFPs are IEDs on steroids," Cleveland said.

"Iranian bomb makers figured out how to focus the explosion for a more powerful blast. For smaller EFPs, we'll see mortar rounds being used. Bigger ones, they use tank and cannon 155s," Daryl said.

"I saw one obliterate a Bradley Fighting Vehicle," Cleveland said.

"EFPs made their debut two years ago. If anyone doubts Iran doesn't have military advisers in Iraq to assist these insurgents, they're clueless," Daryl said.

"Van Gogh have a name?" Payton said.

"All we know is that he's based in Ishbiliya," Daryl said. "Military raids have found a few of his bomb-making operations. He's a freelancer. Offers his services to the highest bidder."

"Someone paid him to blow Wade away," Payton said.

"My guess, we'll find a mortar round was rigged inside the minivan. If a 155 was used, both vehicles would've been obliterated," Daryl said.

Payton felt his cell phone vibrate. He looked at the screen. *Call me.* From Catherine.

He stepped away and dialed her number.

"Where are you?" she asked.

"Wade Loft was killed on his way back to the Green Zone from BGW. I'm at the blast site on Route Irish now."

"Was it random?"

"What do you think?"

"Quinn Wiley called. They have Evette Azard," she said.

CHAPTER 24

THE ATTORNEY

QUINN STOOD SEVERAL doors down from his office. "In here," he said when Payton joined him. A white sign with black "In Use" letters rotated out from the wall next to the door. "We've lost count how many times she's threatened to sue us."

"Rammer said she wasn't due back until tomorrow," Payton said.

"Her plans changed. She decided to attend a Kurdish Nationalist formal dinner with several prominent Kurds and their donors over by the Golden Dome. Too bad for her that's where my people found her."

"What about the weed?" Payton asked.

"It'll be here any minute," Quinn said.

Payton followed him into a small office.

Evette Azard turned from the narrow room's only window. Payton hadn't expected an Arabian beauty. Her silky black hair flowed over her exposed back. The evening dress she wore clung to her tall lean body. When she moved toward the conference table, a slit exposed one leg up to the middle of her thigh. With her black heels, she was at least five eleven. Her fierce dark eyes moved from Quinn to Payton.

"Be assured, I will not tolerate such disrespectful treatment. Being pulled out of such an important dinner was a huge embarrassment," she said in smoky French-accented English.

"You're hard to track down," Payton said.

"And you are?"

"Payton Ladd, Diplomatic Security investigator."

"You cannot detain me if I'm not under arrest."

"We're here to talk."

"I have nothing to say to you."

"The subject is Ben Ater."

"I do not know him."

"He's one of your customers."

"The NGO I work for offers free legal representation to refugees. Our clients are not customers."

"Have a seat," Payton said. "I want to hear about your other line of work."

Quinn stayed at the door, while Payton pulled out a chair and sat. She stared down at him for a few long seconds, then with reluctance sat across from him and folded her arms.

"How long've you been a dope dealer? " asked.

"I don't do drugs."

"Not *do* ... deal."

"Slander will be added to my lawsuit."

She looked at the picture of Ben he slid across the table.

"Ever see him before?"

"No," she said and slid it back next to a pad and pen.

Payton thought she was too fast with the no. She wasn't an adroit liar.

"A confidential source told us a Kurdish woman attorney employed with an NGO," Payton indicated Ben's picture, "supplies him with drugs. Name another female NGO Kurdish attorney."

She scraped her chair back to stand.

"I don't have time to sit here and listen to you accuse me."

"You partial to double digits, Ms. Azard?" Quinn said.

Her eyes bore into Quinn and her hands went out in a What? gesture.

"A US federal prosecutor has an office at the end of the hall. She considers it an honor to put away drug dealers for double-digit terms. She hasn't gotten a sentence of fewer than ten years in the fifteen years she's been a prosecutor. Here's the good part. She took a leave of absence from a federal drug enforcement task force to come to Iraq to help set up a functioning legal system. She owes me a favor. When I tell her about a dope dealer inside the Green Zone whom I need taken care of, she'll make your extradition to the United States a personal mission."

"You have a choice," Payton said with one palm up. "You can keep showing off your goods in sexy dresses to rich Kurds or," he held up his other palm, "you can trade the dress for an orange jumpsuit."

"You'll be able to borrow a shank to slit the jumpsuit pant leg," Quinn said.

Her breathing quickened.

"We need to know why Ben Ater left the Green Zone."

"I told you I never met him."

There was a tap on the door. Quinn opened it and took something from someone in the hall. He shut the door, came over, and tossed the open bundle of baggies they'd found in Ben's freezer next to Evette's clasped hands. Several spilled out of the newspaper wrapping, and one landed on her lap. She chucked it back onto the table.

"We found one of those in the tunnel he used," Payton said.

"He's a fool if he left to smoke," she said.

"We thought the same thing," Payton said, then waved to the newspaper-wrapped baggies. "Until we found these in his trailer. His roommate said he knew whenever Ben met with his supplier, a bundle like this turned up in their freezer. Ever hear of the Italian restaurant Grande Cibo?'

"I've eaten there, why?"

"I hear they have the best Gnocchi Nicoise in the Green Zone," Payton said.

"They don't serve gnocchi in federal prison," Quinn said.

"Let's not jump to conclusions, Quinn. She still has a choice about how she wants to spend her future. Ben and his roommate were at Grande Cibo when Ben said his supplier was in the large party room. Do you want to guess who we found reserved the room for a free Kurdish legal defense fund Q and A?"

"You believe everything a dopehead has to say?" She nudged several of the baggies away.

"Our offer has a thirty-second deadline. Tell us what you know or you'll spend the foreseeable future in a legal battle with a federal prosecutor who hates to lose," Payton said.

"I'm a French citizen who assists Kurdish refugees with legal problems. You've been given false information."

"Twenty seconds," Quinn said.

Payton saw a brief flash of fear in those big dark eyes.

"Twelve, eleven …" Quinn said.

Payton stood and stepped over to Quinn, who was already halfway out the door.

"If I tell you what I know, I stay in the Green Zone," she said.

Payton stood in the doorway, while Quinn held the door open.

After a pause Payton said, "What do you think?"

"She's over by three seconds," Quinn said.

"I'm a second-chance guy. Make it quick," Payton said.

They came back in and closed the door.

She picked up one of the baggies. "He wouldn't leave to buy these," she let it drop, "because I sold them to him."

"How do you know it's your weed?"

"The size of the buds and the purple tinge. No other weed in the Green Zone has the same color."

"You might have competition," Quinn said.

She shook her head. "I'm the only one who brings Kush inside. He liked the attention of being able to sell the best weed inside the wall," she said.

"How did he make his way to you?" Payton asked.

"We were at a party in the residential trailer park. I overheard him say he couldn't find any quality weed. Before I left, I told him I knew where he could get what he wanted. We met a few days later and worked out an arrangement, one package a month."

If she's right—he didn't use the tunnel for drugs—then why'd Ben leave the Green Zone? Something started to gnaw at Payton. Had Wade lied about what happened with Ben at the river?

"Who supplies you?" Quinn asked.

She hesitated. "I answered your question. Why do you need to know who my source is?"

"The whole picture's always helpful," Quinn said.

"But I've cooperated with you."

"We'll make that decision. Where does the weed come from?" Payton asked. He saw her hesitation and he handed his cell phone back to Quinn. "Call your prosecutor, see if she can come down here."

"An Iraqi attorney in the Ministry of Justice," she said.

Payton pushed over the pad and pen. "We need a name."

She scribbled on the pad and tossed the pen down. Payton and Quinn left her in the room.

Quinn glanced at the name on the pad. "I'm on him," he said.

"What if she called your bluff with the federal task force prosecutor?" Payton asked.

"A woman who runs the basement coffee bar would make an ideal prosecutor if I needed her help."

CHAPTER 25

THE WALK-IN

IT WAS AFTER midnight by the time Payton stepped into his room.

Evette confirmed she could supply Ben with any drugs he wanted. That made Wade's river and tea shop story a problem. Payton considered something else: Wade and Leah were hit because of their connection to his investigation. With those two out of the way, he wasn't only back to square one but he'd lost all the squares.

He'd get over to Fallujah early in the morning to check out what Ben had found with his audit and be back before noon. If Vicar and Otto showed up like he told them to while he was away, they could wait until he got back. For starters he wanted to know why neither of them mentioned Ben was their auditor and had found problems in one of the company's operations. While he was in Fallujah, he'd have Rammer and Cleveland start to interview all of Ben's coworkers. Lowsley would be the first one up. Something about him didn't feel right.

After he showered, he climbed into bed. His last thought was about Catherine and whether they should try to revive their relationship. He didn't know if he wanted to risk another crash-and-burn exercise.

His cell phone chirped. When he lifted it off the bedside table, he saw the time was 4:33 a.m. He'd slept for almost four hours.

"Ladd," he said.

"We had a walk-in forty-five minutes ago who says he may know where Ben is. Cleveland's with him now," Rammer said.

Payton splashed cold water on his face, dressed, and went down to their basement offices.

Rammer hurried along the hallway toward him. "The gate guards called and said they had someone who wanted to speak with the people looking for the kidnapped American. In there." He pointed to a door on Payton's left.

Cleveland leaned on his crutches and peered through an interior door's round window. Payton saw a nervous Iraqi youth on a metal folding chair.

"His sister told him an American's been kidnapped. She's a translator for a Latvian employment agency. He says he saw a man being dragged into a building last night who resembled him." Cleveland handed over a wrinkled piece of paper with a picture of Ben and a caption that stated, "Kidnapped $10,000 Reward." "ESM's plastered the Green Zone with these. His sister brought one home."

Payton opened the door and stepped inside.

The boy sat next to a file cabinet and appeared to be a teenager. His collar-length black hair was pulled behind his ears. Acne blotched his scruffy chin and cheeks.

"My name's Payton. Do you need anything?" He slid a chair over and sat. Payton could see the boy's surprise when he spoke Arabic.

"May I have water?" he asked. His dark nervous eyes moved from Payton to the door and back.

Payton signaled to Cleveland, and when he opened the door, told him to bring in a bottle of water.

"What's your name?"

"Mostafa Alam," he said.

Payton held up the flier. "Tell me about him."

"My sister, Farrah, works in the Green Zone." He pointed to the flier. "She said the man who's been kidnapped comes from a powerful family in America. They will pay for his return."

"Your sister's a translator?"

Cleveland brought in a plastic bottle of water and left.

Mostafa drank half the bottle. "Her company supply workers for construction projects. My father say for her to quit. Militias watch Green Zone gates for Iraqis who help Americans." He took another drink and set the almost empty bottle between his feet. "My father a lawyer. Since war he have no work. When I see man from picture I decide to come to embassy. If reward money real, I risk being seen by militias for my family."

Walk-ins come into embassies all over the world. Payton knew most of their information was worthless but, on occasion, priceless. He stood. "Come with me."

They crossed the hall to Rammer's office and went to a Baghdad street map next to a whiteboard. Rammer and Cleveland stood behind them.

"Show me where you saw him," Payton said.

Mostafa stepped closer and studied the map, then put his finger on a street in the middle of Ishbiliya and slid down several buildings to a midblock house. "They drag him into house here."

Right neighborhood, Payton thought. "Where were you?" he asked.

Mostafa moved his finger to a spot near a ditch farther down the street. "I see him struggle with two men under streetlamp before they pull him into house."

"Did you see where they came from? Was it a vehicle or another house on the street?"

"There no vehicle. I have no idea."

"What time did you see him?"

Mostafa glanced at the wall clock. "Between nine and nine thirty."

Seven hours ago. If he was right, they could move on the house now and might find Ben still with the men who'd taken him.

Payton saw Cleveland nod. "What do you remember about the men?" Cleveland said.

"One wore a militia uniform. He's the one who aimed his machine gun at me before I ran."

"What kind of uniform?" Cleveland asked.

"The men who fight for Nassar al-Dori's brigade wear them."

"Your family, how many are there?" Payton asked.

"Five. My father and mother, Farrah, and my little brother."

"Do they know you're here?"

He shook his head.

"Rammer take him to the cafeteria and get him something to eat."

Rammer and Mostafa left.

"Might make sense. He lives in the neighborhood and happens to see Ben being moved," Cleveland said.

"Or the people who tried to kill Leah and succeeded with Wade sent him to draw us into the Red Zone for another ambush. Did his sister check out?" Payton asked

"Rammer confirmed she's on the Iraqi national translator list. His father was an in-house solicitor for one of Saddam's distant cousins, who owned an import-export aftermarket automobile parts business. He hasn't worked since the cousin disappeared after we invaded."

"Quinn and I questioned Ben's supplier, the Kurd woman. She says Ben would never leave for drugs. She's the only one who moves Kush into the Green Zone. Any drug Ben needed, she could supply him with. Quinn's looking into the guy she gave us who supplies her," Payton said.

Cleveland pointed on the map four blocks from the house. "Here's the tea shop. If he was there they didn't move him far. If I had Ben, I might keep him in the same neighborhood to avoid the random military checkpoints being set up since these bank runs started."

Payton studied the map. "Keep him close, don't move him around."

"The walk-in saw militia uniforms. If al-Dori's involved, Ishbiliya will be the securest place to keep Ben. Nothing happens in that part of the city that al-Dori doesn't know about."

"If we hit the house now, maybe Ben's still there," Payton said.

"Rammer might be able to get us close to the building," Cleveland said.

"How?" Payton asked.

"He has an airplane with a high-resolution camera. Ishbiliya's within her range."

"How many passengers?"

Cleveland smiled. "No passengers. You'll see."

CHAPTER 26

ANGEL

PAYTON AND CLEVELAND climbed the last few metal stairs.

"Daryl said Van Gogh's upped his game. The bomb that took Wade out was the most advanced EFP he's come across," Cleveland said, winded from the stair climb.

"Who paid Van Gogh if he's a contract killer?" Payton asked. More questions added to his list … and the reason why he didn't have time to waste up here on the roof.

They came out of the emergency exit door and stepped onto a crushed gravel roof. An HVAC fan chirped somewhere behind them.

The Green Zone was ablaze with light, but across the river Payton saw neighborhood-sized swaths of darkness where electricity was rationed to only a few hours each day.

They went to Rammer, who stood in the doorway of a brick utility room.

"Why are we up here?" Payton asked.

"Let me show you," Rammer said.

Inside the room were thick greased cables threaded over grooved elevator control wheels. Beside the door was a worktable with a notebook computer on it.

Rammer powered up the computer, then lifted the lid off a crate next to the table. He eased out a three-foot-long, navy blue-bodied airplane with folded yellow wings and handed it over to Payton.

One of the elevator wheels spun with a hydraulic whirl. The cable moved, stopped, and moved again.

The lightweight plane had "Angel" written in yellow script on either side of the fuselage.

Were they up here to play with a toy? If Rammer didn't grasp how short they were for time, maybe he belonged back in San Francisco.

While he typed on the computer, Rammer said, "I tweak radio-control airplanes to improve their performance. A mechanical engineer friend helped build Angel." He held up a small battery. "She can fly on this battery for hours without being recharged and has a range of twenty-five miles." He took the plane back, slid the battery into a slot in her undercarriage, and pointed to a glass bubble next to the slot. "Here's a miniature night optics camera I found from a Japanese satellite manufacturer."

"What's the hole for?" Cleveland asked. A dime-sized hole was under the motor.

"A gun barrel. I can chamber four two-point-seven millimeter rounds. I don't expect her to be a weapons system, but I had the extra space and decided to add a small barrel with a trigger device."

He handed her back to Payton, typed on the computer keys for several seconds, then took her out on the roof.

From the door, Payton watched Rammer unfold and snap the wings into place. They'd all seen high-tech drones and knew what they were capable of. It would be hard enough for one of them to fly deep over the Red Zone, locate the house, and find any trace of Ben, but if Rammer thought his do-it-yourself toy had the same capability of those drones, then he'd overestimated Cleveland about his judgment when he picked Rammer out of the three job applicants. He'd give Rammer five more minutes.

Rammer stepped to the roof's edge, fiddled under the fuselage, and the propeller jumped to life. When he raised the plane over his head, it flew out of his hands.

She disappeared over the roof edge.

Payton's first thought was that he'd lost the plane and they could get back to work. Then Angel shot up and faded into the night sky.

Rammer jogged back past him to the computer and pecked away on the keyboard.

Over Rammer's shoulder, Payton saw on the monitor screen a clear view of the roof and utility room from high above.

"Why can't we hear it?" Payton asked.

"I muffled her engine. You'll only hear her if she's on top of you."

Rammer typed several more keys. "She's at fifteen hundred feet," he said. A detailed street map appeared. "A GPS computer chip is embedded in her nose. I programmed the house coordinates where Mostafa said he saw Ben."

She sailed over the Green Zone. Tiny white letters identified the Council of Ministers building with the enormous reflection pool and Shawaf Square. This is where she turned and soared over the river. Between the Al Jumhuriya and Sinak Bridges she curved over the Rusafa neighborhood into the Red Zone.

Payton saw Baghdad's railway station and where the Khalid Bin Al Walid Expressway sliced through the eastern part of the city. She flew along the wide Army Canal, then veered over Ishbiliya's dense neighborhoods.

A house marked by a blue dot popped up in the top right corner.

"Here's the house," Rammer said.

Maybe this wasn't a waste of time.

Rammer pressed the space bar and a midblock two-story house with single-story structures on either side appeared. One end of the short street stopped at a drainage ditch, and the other intersected another street with more low buildings.

"Here's the ditch Mostafa said he saw Ben from," Rammer said.

She flew in wide circles over the house.

"Take her in closer?" Cleveland asked.

Rammer hit a few keys, and Angel descended in tight circles. Payton saw 5:53 a.m. in the screen's bottom left corner.

Constructed with cinder blocks similar to millions of other buildings in Baghdad, the house had a second-floor picture window and a single window next to the front door. There were no windows in the rear, only a door and a walled courtyard.

"How close can we get to the second-floor window?" Cleveland asked.

Rammer held down a key and Angel's circles widened. She skimmed over rooftops. With each pass the camera's focus brought the window into closer view. A dim light shone in the room.

With the next rotation they saw two figures standing over a third slumped in a chair.

"I'll switch to thermal."

"See if you can tell who's in the chair first," Cleveland said.

Angel made another rotation, rounded the drainage ditch, banked hard, and flew toward the house. Rammer held his Control key down and brushed the touch pad. The view magnified and he pressed Ctrl V twice. A video window popped open and started to record. When Angel passed the house, he hit PgDn, and frame by frame the video reversed. Then he paused.

The man in the chair had his head turned up toward another man, who backhanded him. The guy who hit him had a shaved head. The blurred face of the one seated was turned three-quarters of the way toward the window.

Rammer saved the image and opened another file with Ben's passport picture. He went back to the blurred image, manipulated it to bring the picture into better focus, then slid the image beside the passport picture.

"Ben's in the chair," Rammer said.

"What about the guy who hit him?" Payton asked.

The guy stood with his back to the window.

"Sorry, can't get him."

He hit F1, and bright green thermal images appeared. There were three figures on the second floor. Three more came out the rear door into a courtyard.

"Including Ben that makes six," Cleveland said.

On the next pass they watched the three in the courtyard file around to the street.

Rammer had Angel fly in tight circles high over the block.

The three walked up to the intersection. The tallest one in the rear held something with both hands.

Near the intersection, two of them moved to the left corner and started to dig with short shovels at a house's foundation.

"What're they up to?" Payton asked.

They enlarged the hole where the tall guy pointed with his foot. The other one stopped and then walked with slow precise steps into the middle of the intersection, where he turned and retraced his steps back to the hole.

"He counted paces," Cleveland said.

Angel swooped down.

The tall one knelt, and with care he turned what he held upside down and started to work on it.

"Turn off the thermal," Cleveland said and leaned forward to concentrate on the screen. Angel flew down the cross street, with a side view of the three. "Bring her back around."

She arched over the ditch and up the street with her real-time camera on. When she approached again, Rammer adjusted her speed. She slowed.

"Zoom in on the guy in the middle," Cleveland said.

When she was over the intersection, Rammer hit a key and the men filled the screen. A street lamp set back from the corner threw off enough light for the powerful camera.

"See those wires?" Cleveland pointed with his pinkie to the screen. Wires dangled from a shell. "He's holding an IED or EFP."

"I'm impressed with your toy," Payton said.

CHAPTER 27

RED ZONE

"ALL CLEAR," Cleveland's voice came through Payton's earpiece.

Payton lay prone on the sewer ditch embankment where Mostafa had observed Ben from. Over a half-buried, rusted refrigerator he peered into the dawn gloom up the deserted street. The two-story house was midblock to his left. Rammer was beside him.

Effluent trickled down a narrow trench that separated Payton from Blacknife, Carl, and several MSGs where they waited below the ditch's edge.

Nothing stirred.

Ninety minutes ago they'd seen Ben with Rammer's plane. They'd lost half an hour when a battery warning light flashed on Rammer's computer that indicated only seven minutes of power remained. Rammer didn't believe anything was wrong because the battery was new, but not wanting a potential problem deep over the Red Zone, he flew her back. After a quick examination, he found one of the sensors had malfunctioned. Ten minutes later, with a new sensor, she was back across the river.

Payton couldn't hear Angel's muffled engine where she circled above them. Cleveland was in the rooftop mechanical room at her computer controls. A helicopter gunship hovered several streets away over the river and could be on their position in under thirty seconds.

"House on the right," Rammer said.

Payton saw a man's head poke out of a metal gate several structures up from their position. The guy glanced both ways, stepped out, pulled the gate closed, then sprinted across the street and disappeared into an alley.

"Where's he off to?" Payton asked in a low voice. He fingered the Mini Uzi. Something about the way the guy scanned the street bothered him. Then the second-floor window exploded when a machine gun in the room opened fire. Bullets marched beside Payton in the soft dirt. The gun paused for a second before another burst thumped above Blacknife's head.

Had they been set up?

Payton slid down the embankment, followed by Rammer.

"Spartan One, we are on our way," the helicopter pilot said.

"Do not fire on the house. Repeat. Hold your fire," Payton said into his radio.

If Ben was still in the house, he wouldn't stand a chance once the gunship put a rocket through the window.

The marines' young determined faces turned toward him. Payton motioned to the short wall along the embankment's far side.

"Use the wall and those trees in the side yard for cover. Do not fire until I give you the order. You four, let's go."

Followed by Rammer, Carl, and a brawler, Private First Class Hugo Gomez, Payton moved back the way they'd come ten minutes earlier along the bottom of the ditch. He heard Blacknife give the other marines their orders.

"Latif, Alcorta, McCaskey, take the wall. Lujano, Baros, Exline, in the side yard with the trees. Remember, wait until you hear from Special Agent Ladd."

Payton and his men splashed along a shallow stream back to where a tributary veered into the slum's packed houses. A few blocks from the house, he climbed out and moved between a garage and chain-link fence. The helicopter hovered overhead.

They ran deeper into the rabbit warren of alleys and narrow streets.

Payton stopped several houses down a garbage-strewn pathway at the back of a half-painted two-story house and scanned the courtyard bordered with a hip-high eroded cement wall.

A child's bike balanced against a dented paint can next to the only door. In the middle of the footpath, feet from the door, was a bloated, mangy black and white Border Collie. The dog was dead.

Payton heard another burst from the window machine gun.

The helicopter stayed one street behind them. Payton knew the Gatling gun would be aimed at the house, ready on his command to turn it into a colander.

"With Angel's thermal I count three in the window room inside some kind of structure," Cleveland said.

"And the others who carried the bomb out?" Payton asked.

"I've only got three in the room," Cleveland said.

"Ben one of them?" Payton asked into his radio. He had to be one of the three up there.

"Wait, let me switch off the thermal." A few seconds later. "Negative on Ben."

Had they lost him?

They clustered around Payton. The marines held M4 carbines, and Rammer gripped his Remington 870 shotgun with both hands across his chest. Stench from the dead dog filled the courtyard.

"Watch for booby traps. We go two at a time. Rammer, you take the rear," Payton said.

He motioned Hugo and Carl toward the door and saw the fear in Rammer's eyes. The young agent licked his parched lips. Payton hoped, this being Rammer's first close-quarter action, he could push through his fear and not be controlled by it. He'd seen too many young agents who couldn't.

The bottom of the wooden door was covered with scrape marks. Carl reached over from the side and eased it open. Hugo put his flashlight beam around the door jamb into the dark space. Seconds later, he said, "Clear" and went in.

"Remember your training," Payton said to Rammer.

Rammer gave him two quick nods. Payton patted him on the shoulder and went through the door.

They climbed the flight of stairs.

An open door was to their left.

Weak light filtered through a broken window at the far end of the dingy second-floor hallway. Near the window was another closed door where the men would be with, he hoped, Ben.

Hugo and Carl advanced a few feet, then froze. Carl signaled for Payton.

Payton came forward, and Hugo pointed to a clear wire strung an inch above the floor that came out of the open door.

Payton stepped over the wire and aimed his flashlight and Mini Uzi into the room. The room was empty, but behind the door, molded to a hinge, was a banana-shaped plastic explosive charge.

Back in the hallway, he motioned to Hugo to step over the wire and follow him toward the closed door. Carl made sure Blacknife and Rammer saw the wire, then he followed Hugo.

Payton stepped to the far side of the door. He waved Hugo behind him, then to Carl and Blacknife to stay where they were, and circled to Rammer, who turned and covered the hallway.

"We're at the door," Payton said in a low voice into his radio.

"Our boy might not be in the room," Cleveland said.

Could they've moved Ben during the short period Rammer brought Angel back to fix the sensor? They needed whoever was inside, alive.

Muffled metal against metal came from the room. The machine gun was being reloaded.

Payton reached over, turned the doorknob, and cracked the door open.

An explosion blew several tent-stake-sized pieces of wood into the cinder-block wall across the hallway. Automatic gunfire poured out of the room, followed by acrid gun smoke.

When the gunfire paused, Payton scanned the room. A frantic boy behind a sandbag wall hit an AK-47 with the heel of his hand. Behind him, two men stood at a .50 caliber machine gun aimed out the window.

Payton pulled back.

Another burst of bullets from the boy's AK slammed into the opposite hallway wall. The .50 let loose a burst toward the ditch.

Payton spit grit and dust out of his mouth. He heard the helicopter over the backyard.

"Grenade in the room," Cleveland said.

"Down!" Payton yelled. He fell back on top of Hugo. An explosion from inside the room blew several cinder blocks loose. One missed Payton's head by inches when it cracked and fell.

"What's your situation?" Cleveland asked.

"Our lucky day," Payton said.

They rushed the room.

"Behind you, two targets on the stairs," Cleveland said.

Rammer's shotgun erupted. He fired again, again, and again, followed by an explosion.

By the time Payton made the hallway, Rammer was on one knee. Smoke floated out of his raised shotgun barrel.

A body lay sprawled on the floor several feet in front of Rammer. Through the smoke Payton saw another man covered with wood chips, chunks of cinder block, and dust. He lay on the floor opposite a wide hole where the shaped charge blew. Dead, his head was turned and he stared at Rammer. The fingers of his blown-off hand still gripped a handgun that now rested on Rammer's left foot. Rammer stood and kicked it away.

"Good?" Payton asked.

Rammer nodded and with a shaky hand wiped dust from his eyes.

Back in the room, Payton said to Blacknife, "Secure the house and have your marines set up a security perimeter around the block. Keep clear of the bomb buried at the end of the street."

Blacknife radioed his marines and ran with Carl down the hallway past the bodies. The helicopter flew sideways along the street, nose pointed toward the house.

Behind the sandbags, Payton saw a mangled leg half exposed under a pile of rubble where the fumbled grenade exploded. Rammer and Gomez joined him, and they started to pull off sandbags and debris.

The leg was the teenage boy's.

"Put him over there," Payton said.

Hugo took the AK the boy still cradled in his arms. They carried him to the other side of the room and set him on the floor.

Payton tossed basketball-sized chunks of concrete from the ceiling over the remaining sandbag wall.

A middle-aged man with dark stubble for a beard was draped over a Browning .50 caliber machine gun mounted on a short tripod. Both his arms were gone. Rammer and Hugo moved him next to the boy.

Payton pushed over several more sandbags. When he toppled a slab of cement with twisted rebar, he saw a dead elderly man in a fetal position. Below his trimmed gray beard, a horrible neck wound stretched from his right ear to his Adam's apple.

Payton had the marines take him over to the other bodies.

He was no closer to Ben than when he'd arrived a day and a half ago. Frustrated, he heaved several more pieces of concrete.

With his foot he upended a length of ceiling timber with tiles still attached to it. Something caught his eye in the space where the guy with the neck wound had been. He pushed away fist-sized hunks of plaster and grabbed the cloth handles of a black duffle bag covered with dust and blood. A piece of rebar snagged the bag when he lifted it.

Bundles of hundred-dollar bills tumbled out. Some landed in the bloody pool of sludge. He held the ripped end and set the bag on what was left of the sandbag wall. More bundles fell out.

Hugo picked one up and fanned pristine C-notes. "I guess it's true you can't take it with you. How much is in the bag?" he asked.

Payton pulled the bent zipper and moved rows of bundles. "Rough guess? … a million plus."

"Wonder why the old guy had so much money?" Rammer asked.

Payton pointed to the bodies, "I want pictures of those three and the two in the hallway. Run them through our terrorist and criminal databases. Maybe we'll get a match." He stepped out of the rubble, picked up a flimsy curtain piled below the window, and flung it open. After he rolled up the money, he handed the bundle to Hugo. "Get these to Cleveland."

Blacknife came back into the room. "We found something downstairs," he said.

Carl stood in the first-floor hallway outside an open door with his flashlight aimed into a room.

"Over there," Carl said.

On a worktable pushed against the rear wall lay a disassembled artillery shell with a white wire attached to one end. Tools used to work on electronics were strewn over the table along with bits and pieces of component parts. Plastic storage drawers for more parts lined the back side of the table. Green electrical tape hung from a wall nail.

Rammer joined him.

"Aren't EFPs made with artillery shells?" Carl asked.

"And mortar rounds," Payton said.

"White wires were on the EFP Wade was killed by," Rammer said.

"Along with green tape. The bomb disposal people said they were signature colors of a bomber they call Van Gogh. I want the same Explosive Disposal Unit at Wade's blast site brought over here," Payton said.

They'd found a mounted .50 caliber machine gun, an EFP bomb assembly room, a bag full of money, and five dead bodies, but no Ben Ater.

He was way overdue for a break.

CHAPTER 28

EMBASSY

PAYTON ENTERED HIS ROOM, stripped, and went to the shower. He smelled like a sewer.

He didn't believe Mostafa was sent to draw them into the Red Zone, but he'd still have Rammer talk to him again to see if his story changed.

The hot water didn't wash away his disappointment that they'd come back empty-handed.

From Angel's flyby, they saw Ben being interrogated. Why was he still alive? If they were terrorists, why hadn't they promoted his capture and execution on the Internet? His ransom and terrorist recruitment potential were huge.

He stepped out, toweled off, and dressed.

His cell phone vibrated.

"Rammer told me about the walk-in. Are you alright?" Catherine asked.

"Still in one piece."

"You came close to getting him back."

"Close only counts in horseshoes and hand grenades. Next time, I'll take the horseshoes," he said.

"We have a meeting at eleven with Ambassador Rhodes and a four-star general who arrived last night, whom the president put in place to handle these bank runs. I need you to be at the meeting."

"I don't have time for meetings."

"Don't put me in a position where I have to make excuses for your absence." She paused. He heard her take a deep breath. "Sorry. We've had three more bank runs since Al Kut, and alarm bells have gone off inside the Pentagon. They fear the militia truce Ambassador Rhodes and his team of military commanders worked on for months might spiral out of control. There's a real possibility we could slip back into another sectarian warfare nightmare."

"If the military had invaded with enough personnel, Iraq would be a different story today," he said.

"The manpower-shortage train left the station months ago. Now we have a potential counterfeit money scare to deal with. The core reason the situation has started to improve is the planeloads of cash we fly in and feed into the banking system to prop up the economy. Ambassador Rhodes and the general have a conference call later today with President Timmons and the Joint Chiefs to update them on the bank-run situation. They'll want to know where we are with Ben."

"Tell them, where we started, nowhere."

She didn't answer.

"I'll give them forty-five minutes, then I'm gone. I need you to arrange a meeting with Colonel Mifflin before I leave for Fallujah. Can you make it happen?"

"Let me see what I can do. Eleven in Ambassador Rhodes's office," she said.

Wasted time in meetings was time Ben didn't have. He called Cleveland and told him he needed to see him.

Payton sat in the first-floor embassy grill when Cleveland crutched his way over to his table. "How'd Rammer do?" Cleveland asked.

"Better than I expected."

"The bomb technicians confirmed the bomb room is Van Gogh's. The shell with the white wire is a Russian 152 mm artillery round he was in the process of turning into an EFP. Daryl said his unit has seen EFPs triple since Ambassador Rhodes started the militia truce talks."

"The EFPs could be an Iranian escalation to crater the talks," Payton said.

"A peaceful Iraq is not what the mullahs want." Cleveland opened his leather folder and tossed over a manila envelope.

Payton withdrew four burned one-hundred-dollar bills.

"Catherine asked me to take a look at these from the Al Kut bank run. Several detained Iraqis said they're counterfeit. I put each one under a microscope and was surprised by what I found. They're supernotes."

"You mean North Korean counterfeit one-hundred-dollar bills?"

Cleveland nodded.

"Those are the highest-quality supernotes I've come across. Unless you know what to look for, they're almost exact replicas of genuine C-notes," he said.

"If you needed a microscope to figure out what they are, how did the BUI rioters know they were supernotes?" Payton asked as he examined each of the burned bills.

"Before the shooting started, the marines heard a guy with a megaphone working up the crowd in the square outside the bank. He said BUI gave them fake money and was a pawn of the United States."

"Did they detain him?"

"Disappeared in the chaos."

"We both know what happens if BUI, the only solid bank in the country—our bank—is hit with a counterfeit money scare," Payton said.

"We have another war to deal with," Cleveland said.

"You said Baghdad's where all the action is," Payton said. He replaced the notes in the envelope and slid them over.

Cleveland had one of his I-told-you-so smiles. "Now the fun really starts. One point seven million worth of supernotes were in the bag you brought back from the Red Zone house. They matched these." He tapped the envelope. "The supernotes are connected to the house by Al Kut's BUI bank run."

"Has Rammer made any headway with the five men killed in the house or the Pizza Hut Titan United security guy?" Payton asked.

"He's still going through the databases. Titan United being way behind with their personnel picture files doesn't help. I asked Quinn if he'd join me for a quick trip over to the tea shop. Rammer's right, the load-bearing wall took a bazooka or RPG round. It came from a roof across the street where I found a half-smoked cigar. The shooter or someone with him smokes premium thin gauge, Double Claro Cuban Romeos. Twelve-dollar cigars manufactured in Santiago de Cuba and distributed in South Africa for a limited run last year."

"All we have to do is find a Cuban cigar smoker in a city of several million. Another needle-in-a-haystack exercise," Payton said.

PAYTON AND CLEVELAND walked into Catherine's office. She sat at her desk with the telephone hunched up to her ear as she leafed through a thick document held together with a large black metal binder clip. She motioned them over to a round table and chairs, listened to the person on the phone for another few minutes, then signed off.

"Did you really find a machine gun nest?" She came over and sat with them.

"Inside a sandbag enclosure on the second floor," Payton said.

"The militia uniforms our walk-in saw, fit with what we know about al-Dori, who instructs his people to barricade themselves inside residential houses, some even still occupied with families. He knows we won't destroy the houses and risk innocent lives," Cleveland said.

"Were any of you injured when the grenade went off?" she asked.

"The hallway wall shielded us," Payton said. "The three guys inside the room weren't so lucky. Show her."

Cleveland pushed over a charred C-note. "Here's a note from the Al Kut bank run you wanted me to check out." He followed with a second pristine C-note. "And one brought back from the house raid. They're both supernotes."

"The men who have Ben had them?" She examined both bills.

"Almost two million worth," Payton said.

Cleveland handed her another bill. "Here's a genuine C-note."

She compared it to one of the supernotes.

"Those supernotes being in the same house where we saw Ben are game changers," Payton said.

"Where does that leave us with the drug lead?" she asked.

"I don't think drugs have anything to do with his disappearance," Payton said.

"Are you sure Ben was even in the house? We've all had too many experiences with truth-challenged walk-ins."

Cleveland gave her a printout picture of Ben in the chair from Angel's video. "Rammer has a mini-drone he flew by the house. Ben's in the chair."

Payton pointed to the picture. "We saw him right before an EFP was carried out."

"I didn't hear about an EFP," she said.

"They had a bomb assembly room on the first floor," Cleveland said.

"Thanks to the drone, we saw where they buried it and none of our people were killed," Payton said.

Catherine checked her watch. "We have three minutes before the meeting starts." She stood and went to the door.

CHAPTER 29

THE AMBASSADOR

IT'D BEEN SEVERAL years since Payton last saw Ambassador Elliott Rhodes. He was still a bear of a man, with stooped shoulders. His thick dark hair was streaked with gray now. Baghdad will do that to an ambassador.

"Good to see you again, Special Agent," Rhodes said.

"Ambassador," Payton said.

They shook hands.

"Cleveland, give us a few minutes," Rhodes said.

Cleveland walked over to the conference room. Payton and Catherine followed Rhodes into his office.

"Catherine told me about what happened in the Red Zone this morning and behind the Pizza Hut. You've been busy."

"My quota's two ambushes a day," Payton said.

"Here's another ambush you need to be aware of. Colonel Dara Mifflin complained to her superiors in Washington about your treatment of Titan United's managing director, Graham Vicar, which prompted a call from Defense Secretary Ordway to DSS Director Santiago. You've touched a nerve. Vicar's company does important work for our military."

Payton wondered why Vicar needed Mifflin to run interference. "I told him to keep his security people away from our investigation," Payton said.

"His company's a key player in our work here, and Secretary Ordway doesn't want to jeopardize their relationship with the military."

"Titan United's a sinkhole Mifflin's poured a lot of money into," Payton said.

"She's in charge of the contractor program. Let's make an effort to get along. I've shared my concerns with the president about how undermanned we are and DOD's boneheaded decision to pay their way out of the mess they created by using all these contractors. By the way, Director Santiago called thirty minutes ago and said, 'Don't back Ladd down.'"

Payton knew Emilio Santiago wouldn't be swayed by a call from Ordway. Emilio always covered for him.

"One of Vicar's employees, a security contractor named Wade Loft, said he was taken with Ben into the Red Zone. We won't be able to verify his story because an EFP blew him off Route Irish last night," Payton said.

"A bomb-making room with a half-assembled EFP was in the house Payton and the marines raided earlier," she said.

"We know they carried another EFP out of the same house last night," Payton said.

"Fortunately no one was killed," Catherine said.

"Any connection to the EFP Graham Vicar's employee was killed with?" Rhodes said.

"We're working on it," Payton said.

"Senator Ater's office calls every day for an update. He'll bring a political firestorm down on the White House if his nephew turns up dead," Rhodes said.

"Wasn't he the one who asked President Timmons to find Ben Green Zone work?" Payton asked.

"I agreed over the objections of my RSO." Rhodes looked at Catherine. "Whom I should never second-guess."

"We ran into Gabe Kuttic, who doesn't believe Ben was even in the Red Zone," Catherine said.

Rhodes nodded to the conference room. "Gabe's here." He looked at Payton. "I know you two have a history together. Try to keep it cordial. I'm already in the middle of a militia civil war and don't need another one between the DSS and CIA."

"He knows more than he's told us," Payton said.

"Keep the collateral damage to a minimum." Rhodes picked up a legal pad and pen. "Do we have an update from CSH about the girl?"

"She's still sedated. On top of her blood loss, she has an infection," Catherine said.

"Let me know if her situation changes," Rhodes said. He opened the door and led them into the conference room.

CHAPTER 30

PAYTON SAW KUTTIC glance his way, then ignore him as he came into the cramped conference room.

Ambassador Rhodes made the introductions.

"Meet USCENTCOM Chief of Staff General Fritz Qwen, who arrived last night from MacDill Air Force Base. General, Catherine McCabe is my RSO, and Diplomatic Security Special Agent Payton Ladd is the lead investigator on Ben Ater's disappearance. Cleveland Pinnix, whom you've already met, is our security engineering officer. I believe all of you know Gabe Kuttic with the Central Intelligence Agency."

Qwen was almost Payton's height, a few inches over six feet with short dark hair, light blue eyes, and a granite jaw.

Everyone sat down. Qwen popped open his metal briefcase and withdrew a green folder.

"Over the last seventy-two hours bank-run riots have occurred in Basra, Najif, Al Kut, and Mosul. Each run targeted a Bank of United Iraq branch. Two bank managers barricaded inside the Najif branch were hauled out and hanged from a streetlight. The body count now stands at twenty-nine dead civilians."

He passed out 8½" by 11" maps of Iraq with circles around the bank-run cities.

"Fifteen thousand additional troops have been diverted to BUI locations. Rumors circulated counterfeit money was being disbursed from those branches. We shuttered them until more money can be flown in from the New Jersey Federal Reserve Bank. Joint Chiefs Chairman Major General Riebow, Defense Secretary Ordway, and President Timmons are concerned these runs might be a new tactic by Al Qaeda to destabilize the country."

"General, Cleveland has something you'll want to hear," Payton said.

Cleveland passed several C-notes around. "These came from Al Kut's BUI branch. They're Series PS-201145 North Korean supernotes. The highest-quality counterfeit currencies I've come across."

"You've confirmed they're supernotes?" Qwen asked as he examined one of the C-notes.

"North Korean counterfeiters never perfected the cotton mix we use in our currencies. You can see the fiber discrepancy when you examine them through a microscope. A sizable chunk of North Korea's GDP comes from the sale of counterfeit goods. Currencies are one of their specialties," Cleveland said.

"Evidence of counterfeit money has become a grave concern for the Joint Chiefs. If the problem escalates, the country could be at risk," Qwen said.

"We found over a million and a half dollars worth of the same series in a house where Ben Ater was being held," Payton said.

"Which puts the Al Kut BUI supernotes in the house with Ben," Cleveland said.

"Senator Ater chairs the Appropriations Committee and told President Timmons he'll make the president's war funds requests painful if he doesn't get his nephew back—alive," Qwen said.

"We have every intention of finding him," Ambassador Rhodes said.

"Being stuck in meetings doesn't help," Payton said.

"General," Catherine's eyes cut to him before she turned her attention back to Qwen, "the house is located in Ish-biliya. A neighborhood across the river inside the Red Zone."

"Why would he be over there? We don't have the Red Zone secured," Qwen said.

Catherine gestured to Payton to go on.

"We thought drugs might be the reason, but with these supernotes turning up, we aren't so sure," Payton said.

"Why drugs?" Qwen asked.

"He sold small bags of Afghan Kush."

"He made his own bed if he went into the Red Zone for drugs," Qwen said.

"We came close, but he was moved before we hit the house," Payton said.

"I heard he disappeared from a tea shop," Qwen said.

"We haven't confirmed he was in the shop, but he was in the house," Payton said and peered Kuttic's way. Let's see if he'll show his cards. "The CIA might have an idea about what happened."

All eyes turned to Kuttic.

With a flash of irritation, Kuttic said, "General, Ambassador, what I have to say can't leave the room."

"Let's have it," Qwen said.

"*If* Ben was taken to the tea shop, he might've gone to meet with Yusuf al Dawud."

"What do you mean, if?" Qwen asked.

"We found no physical evidence he was in the building," Kuttic said.

"We've confirmed a bazooka or RPG round was put through the shop's front window," Cleveland said.

"Our only witness, a security contractor who said he was with Ben, was killed last night on Route Irish," Payton said.

"By an EFP," Catherine said.

Payton watched Kuttic's eyes shift around. He probably hoped they'd move on and forget he was in the room.

"What about Yusuf?" Payton asked Kuttic.

For a brief second Kuttic's eyes drilled into Payton. "Yusuf's an associate of Nassar al-Dori. He smuggled weapons for the agency to the Israelis during the Yom Kippur War," Kuttic said.

Rhodes threw his arms out in frustration and stood. He walked back and forth behind the chairs on his side of the table.

"General, were you aware the CIA had someone close to al-Dori?" Rhodes asked.

"No, I wasn't," Qwen said, his eyes locked on Kuttic.

"Our analysts are still not convinced Ater was in the shop. I'd be surprised if he went to meet Yusuf about drugs," Kuttic said.

"Yusuf might be off the reservation and doesn't need the CIA's money anymore," Payton said.

"You don't know him. He hasn't gone anywhere," Kuttic said.

"It won't be the first time the CIA's lost control of a situation," Payton said.

"We don't have a situation."

"Then where's your man Yusuf?" Rhodes asked.

Kuttic hesitated, "We haven't found him … yet."

"What is the connection between Ben, Yusuf, and these?" Qwen pointed to the supernotes.

"I don't think there is one," Kuttic said.

"If you can't put Ben in the tea shop, then how did you connect him to the house?" Qwen asked Payton.

"A walk-in recognized him from a flier Ben's employer plastered all over the Green Zone. Cleveland's assistant flew a mini-drone by the house and confirmed he was inside," Payton said.

"One of your people has a drone?" Qwen said to Rhodes.

Rhodes looked at a loss for words.

"Never underestimate my SEO's office," Catherine said.

Payton motioned to Cleveland, who slid the picture over.

"The drone's camera snapped him being interrogated," Payton said.

Qwen studied the photo. "Why keep him in the city?"

"They might want to avoid military checkpoints put in place since these bank runs started," Payton said.

"You have no idea where he is now?" Qwen asked.

"Best guess, he's still in the same Red Zone neighborhood," Payton said.

"You're down to guesswork?" Qwen asked.

"General, my people are good at what they do. They'll find him," Rhodes said.

"We don't need anymore pressure from Senator Ater. We already have enough on our plate," Qwen said.

"Have you considered that whoever took him dressed in uniforms to make it appear al-Dori's involved? Kuttic asked.

"We don't know who the guys in militia uniforms are, but the drone picture puts him in al-Dori's part of the city," Payton said.

"Do al-Dori's Shiite killers have him?" Qwen asked and tossed the picture to the middle of the table.

"Five guys were killed in the house raid. We're checking them against our criminal and terrorist databases. If we find a match, we'll know more about who might have him," Payton said.

"Tell him about the EFP," Rhodes said.

"We found an Explosively Formed Penetrator bomb in the process of being assembled on the first floor of the house," Payton said.

"We've lost almost three dozen military personnel since insurgents started with those bombs," Qwen said.

"A man killed in the house had a map of several routes our military uses when they go into Ishbiliya. They had a clear line of fire from the second floor to one of the routes half a block away. We watched three men carry an EFP out of the house and bury it up the street where our patrols would've been. The buried EFP and the one being put together in the house had Iranian detonator component parts," Payton said.

"I have a theory, General," Cleveland said.

All heads turned toward Cleveland

"In the right hands, counterfeit currencies can be an effective war weapon. Someone might have other ideas about Iraq's future. Derail any Shiite-Sunni peace talks, flood the financial system with enough supernotes to crash the economy, and put EFPs in the mix to keep our military on edge. Anarchy helps their long-term plans."

"Is your someone Iran?" Rhodes said.

"The Quds Force is an Iranian Revolutionary Guards unit that handles operations outside Iran. They support terrorist organizations around the globe and generate millions in revenue a year from illegal activities. Drug smuggling is one of their specialties. Supernotes and EFP technology are the type of operations they'd be involved with," Cleveland said.

"Iranians are responsible for these?" Qwen pointed to the supernotes.

"With their North Korean contacts, they'd have easy access to them," Cleveland said.

"Iran considers Iraq another front in their war with the West," Payton said.

"Bring me something solid I can take to the president," Qwen said.

"What's our total financial commitment to BUI?" Payton asked.

"Almost two billion. We fly money in by the pallet load on C130s from the Federal Reserve Bank of New Jersey.

A military convoy transports the pallets from BGW to BUI's main branch in central Baghdad, where bank officials handle distribution to the branches. The president ordered another one point three billion flown in because of these bank runs."

"Have the convoys had any trouble?" Payton asked.

"None. Their routes are top secret, known to only a few people. If you plan to attack one, you'd better bring an army," Qwen said.

"Could BUI's central bank be where the supernotes are being put into the bank?" Rhodes asked.

"Green Berets guard the building around the clock. It would be impossible for supernotes to enter the money supply there," Qwen said.

"What about the branches?" Catherine asked.

"Iraqi security forces handle branch security," Qwen said.

"How can we access each branch's deposit history?" Payton asked.

"I'll have my chief of staff give you BUI's contact person. Here's my direct number," Qwen said.

Cleveland jotted down the number.

Rhodes surveyed the table. "The general and I have a conference call with the president and his advisers in a few minutes to discuss BUI and Ben's situation. After the call, we have a meeting with Iraq's prime minister and his cabinet to assure them we're on top of the bank-run situation. I don't want to have to backtrack later and say we were wrong and they're not supernotes."

"You won't, Ambassador. They're North Korean supernotes," Cleveland said.

"All of you know how volatile the bank-run situation has become. Let me be clear—we will not lose Iraq because of counterfeit money," Qwen said.

He and Rhodes left.

Kuttic followed, stopped at the door, and turned.

"Don't involve Yusuf in your embassy games. There's a larger picture here."

"I don't play games," Payton said.

Kuttic made a quick sideways hand gesture. "Leave Yusuf out of it." Then he walked out.

"He always so informative?" Cleveland asked.

"My DIA contact said Gabe's one of the CIA's top Hezbollah experts. He was brought to Iraq after a thirty-six-month stretch in Beirut where he aided a special Mossad unit responsible for Hezbollah informer recruitment. Why would the CIA bring him to Iraq? Hezbollah's not involved with the Shiite-Sunni troubles," Catherine said.

"The Red Zone Shiites and Hezbollah are both Iranian proxy armies," Cleveland said.

"If Yusuf's still on the CIA's payroll …," she said.

"… a big if," Payton said.

"Gabe will do whatever he can to protect his asset," she said.

"You can forget about Ben if he gets caught between Kuttic and Yusuf," Cleveland said.

"Kuttic doesn't have any more of an idea what happened in the tea shop than we do. I want Rammer on those bank deposits," Payton said.

CHAPTER 31

EMBASSY

PAYTON SAW MAGGIE stand up from a chair in the hallway outside of his office when he and Cleveland stepped from the elevator.

Her hair was styled, with no hint of the blue streak. She wore a skirt and blouse he'd expect a CPA firm partner to wear.

"Hello, Maggie," he said and gestured to Cleveland. "Meet Cleveland Pinnix. He's with me on Ben's case."

"I remembered something I thought you should know," she said.

"Let's go into my office," Payton said.

"I don't have time. I'm on my way back to the hospital. You said Ben's external hard drive wasn't in his office or trailer. He told me he had a box in the basement of the Republican Guard building where a UPS store is located. Maybe he put his hard drive in one of the store's rented mailboxes. Sorry, I forgot to tell you. I remembered in the hospital last night."

"I'll get my bag," Cleveland said.

"We'll drop you off," Payton said.

THE CRAMPED UPS store had racks of greeting cards, shelves with clear jars half-filled with different brands of miniature candy bars, and a wall of gold-plated mailboxes.

A middle-aged woman in a starched brown uniform counted and faced bills at a cash register. Her name tag said "Betty."

"Hello, Betty," Payton said and showed her his ID.

She glanced at it, then went back to the money.

"One of your mailboxes might be rented to someone involved with an investigation we have underway. Can you provide us with a list of who the boxes are rented to?"

"The boxes are private property," she said while she edged a handful of ones on the counter.

"Can I borrow your phone?" Payton held out his hand.

She replaced the ones in the register drawer and removed a rubber band from a wad of fives. "Why?" she asked.

"To call Atlanta and tell your CEO how uncooperative you're being with a State Department investigation. If I don't get the list, UPS loses the contract."

She scrunched up her face in a frown and pulled a piece of paper from under the counter, then went back to the fives.

Cleveland scanned the list. "Box 35," he said.

"Don't ask me for a key because owners have the only one," she said. She put the fives in the tray and started counting pennies.

Cleveland withdrew a battery-operated drill from a small canvas tool bag he had couriered over from his office.

"Here," he said and handed the bag to Payton.

Minutes later he stepped back. Metal shavings dropped from the drill bit. He pulled out a foot-long metal box and set it on the island counter.

"Let's see if we found where Ben keeps his secrets," he said and popped open the long narrow box lid. "Bingo." He lifted up a portable backup hard drive.

THEY WERE HALFWAY back to the embassy when Cleveland answered his cell phone. "Ladd's right here," he said and listened for a few seconds. Speaking over his shoulder from the front passenger seat of the Humvee, he then said to Payton, "Quinn found the Kurd's supplier." He mashed the speaker button on the phone and held it between the seats. "Go."

From the speaker, Quinn said, "Evette cleaned out her office and flew back to Paris this morning. I alerted French law enforcement about what she's been up to. Her drug connection, the name she gave us, Zamir Gouda, is a guy who works for an investment firm with an office here in the Green Zone. She introduced Kurds with money to Gouda's firm and received a finder's fee for every new investor she brought in."

"Have you picked him up?" Payton asked.

"My people haven't found him yet."

"What's his background?"

"He's some kind of tax expert/attorney. The investment firm pools money from loaded Arabs, then buys commercial property in Europe with complex ownership entities based in tax havens like the Cayman Islands."

"Sounds like a tax dodge," Cleveland said.

"The firm's founding partners are two brothers who turned up on Interpol's radar four years ago when they were implicated in an exotic-car theft ring. The stolen cars were transported by cargo ship from the Middle East to a warehouse the investment firm owned in Gioia Tauro, Italy. An Italian crime syndicate would then transport the cars to a Chinese Macau-based gang. The real money was in the car trunks … weed from Afghanistan."

"Let me guess, Kush?" Cleveland asked.

"The same weed Evette sold to Ben," Quinn said.

"You said brothers," Payton said.

"Zaki and Marco al-Dulaimi, ever hear of them?"

Evette Azard's connected to Zaki and Marco?

"They're part of Wafiyi Khleifat's play for the prime minister's job. Catherine said they're hoods," Payton said.

"How'd Interpol make the connection between the warehouse and the brothers?" Cleveland said.

"The French coast guard on a routine inspection off Corsica found the cars and weed. They alerted Interpol, whose forensic accountants traced ownership of the ship and warehouse, where the cars were to be stored through a maze of front companies, back to Zamir and the brothers' investment firm. Of course, Zamir and the al-Dulaimis denied any involvement."

"A good attorney would shred any case against them if all Interpol had was illegal activity on the ship or in the warehouse," Payton said.

"Don't you love attorneys?" Cleveland asked.

"Catherine said Zaki and Marco are off-limits because they're two of Khleifat's closest advisers. Khleifat's Defense Secretary Ordway's choice to win the PM job," Payton said.

"We'll be in touch when we have Zamir," Quinn signed off.

"The brothers and Zamir would have contacts who can move large amounts of Kush into the Green Zone," Cleveland said.

"That brings me back to the problem I have with Ben being at the river. If Evette could supply him with whatever he needed, why leave the Green Zone?" Payton asked.

"Is it possible he had direct contact with Zaki or Marco?" Cleveland asked.

"He's a small-time dealer and would be several rungs down the totem pole from those two," Payton said. Still, he had trouble with something about the brothers.

Carl parked behind the embassy. When Payton got out, another Humvee pulled behind them. Blacknife with four MSGs climbed out and came over.

"We picked through the alley and didn't find any way Otto could get past you without being seen," Blacknife said.

"Did you go through the apartment building?" Payton asked.

"Every room. No one's been in the building for a while," Blacknife said.

With the wall so close to the alley Payton was sure he would've heard or seen Otto circle back on one of the side streets. Then how did Otto slip past him? What were he and Marco up to?

"You and Carl get ready for Fallujah."

CHAPTER 32

GABE KUTTIC

PAYTON TOOK THE Glock and extra clips from his desk drawer and set them on top of his Kevlar vest next to the Mini Uzi.

"Might I have a moment?" Kuttic stood in the doorway.

"I'm tight for time," Payton said.

"This won't take long." He stepped in and sat down. "I'm impressed with your washed-up SEO. He's right about the Quds Force history of involvement with illegal drugs and supernotes. He even nailed the EFPs."

"Then why didn't you speak up?"

"Langley said they'll handle General Qwen after they inform the president."

"You're here for?"

"Let's say I have an olive branch."

"You wouldn't be here unless you needed something."

"Here's the CliffsNotes version: Iranians have used supernotes before to wreak financial havoc. In the late eighties, Hezbollah started to exert more influence over Southern

Lebanon with strong-arm tactics on legitimate businesses. One of their shakedown victims who refused to go along was a retired Druze Lebanese Armed Forces general who happened to be the chairman of the Commercial Bank of the Mediterranean, headquartered in the port city of Tyre.

"Rumors started to circulate that his bank passed counterfeit currency. Angry mobs firebombed his headquarters. Soon after, a car bomb killed him along with several employees. The general didn't need another partner. He already had one, the Mossad. He was the highest-ranking Lebanese military spy the Israelis ever had.

"A Hezbollah-controlled armored car company made cash deliveries from local businesses to his bank twice a week. Inside one of their armored vans, Israeli agents uncovered supernotes in dozens of locked canvas bank bags. They traced the bags to a Damascus financial institution controlled by the Quds Force. Mullahs in leadership positions stashed money outside Iran in the bank."

"How's Yusuf involved?"

"With his drug connections, he has access to the Quds Force, which smuggles large quantities of Kush into Iraq."

"Which gives him the perfect cover to spy on the Iranians for the CIA."

"Congratulations, you've seen behind the curtain. The information he passes our way is irreplaceable."

"What happened at the tea shop?" Payton asked.

"I can tell you what didn't happen. Ben wasn't there."

"Yusuf confirmed he wasn't?"

"An associate of mine, a leftover from Saddam's security apparatus, has an informant on one of al-Dori's security details who was there the night it was blown. Ben was nowhere near the shop. Yusuf was there to meet with one of his suppliers to discuss a shipment of heroin."

"Your guy Yusuf might've been the target if his cover's blown and al-Dori knows he's being paid by the CIA," Payton said.

"His cover's solid."

"Then who did the tea shop?"

"Al-Dori's in a vicious battle for control of Ishbiliya with a Sunni militia led by an ex-colonel who controls several blocks in Idris and wants to expand into Ishbiliya. In a raid two months ago, al-Dori's men killed three of the colonel's cousins. Since then, the Sunnis have targeted al-Dori's top people. We believe the shop was a Sunni attempt to take Yusuf out."

"Does the Sunni colonel smoke Cuban cigars?"

"No idea."

"My washed-up SEO found a Cuban cigar on the roof across the street where he thinks the shop was blown from."

"You and your people can chase after Cuban cigars and phantom accountants in tea shops. Iran's our main concern. If we don't have Yusuf in place when the United States pulls out, we'll be in the dark about what the Iranians are up to in Iraq. Saddam's removal wasn't the war's only goal. We needed a firewall to hold back the Iranians."

"Do Iraqis have an opinion about being a firewall?"

"Not my problem."

Payton knew the answer to his next question but thought he'd toss it out there. "I want to speak with Yusuf when you bring him in. He might know where I can find my accountant."

"Won't happen. CIA director Impson said Yusuf stays in place. My opinion, someone started the tea shop rumor to draw your attention away from whatever Ben got himself mixed up with."

"Yusuf knew about the supernotes, didn't he?"

"He hasn't told me."

"You know where he is?"

"In one of al-Dori's private clinics, with a broken wrist. He'll survive."

"You lied to Qwen when you said you had no idea where Yusuf is." Kuttic always had a different shade of the truth.

"I said we haven't found him. We're not sure which clinic he's in. Be assured Yusuf has people inside the Green Zone who take care of his drug business for him. He wouldn't meet Ben."

"Who is Yusuf's contact inside the walls?" Payton asked.

"Sorry, classified," Kuttic said.

"Ben's contact was Evette Azard. A French national who received dope from Zamir Goupa, a tax attorney employed by an investment firm owned by Zaki and Marco al-Dulaimi."

"You didn't hear that from me," Kuttic said

"With Ben's life in the balance, I don't care about Yusuf and your spy games."

Kuttic reached over and closed the door. "The brothers control seventy percent of all criminal activity inside the wall, and DS Ordway doesn't want them touched."

Payton wondered if Colonel Mifflin knew that the brothers ruled over the Green Zone.

"If Khleifat wins and puts the al-Dulaimis in powerful positions, we'll regret Saddam's not still in place," Payton said.

"Yusuf confirmed the Iranians have a spy inside the Green Zone who has access to information only someone at the highest levels of our military or government administrators would know. Director Impson will be patched onto Ambassador Rhodes and General Qwen's call to the president. He'll inform them Yusuf was about to tell us how the spy passes information to the Iranians. Once we know how, we can follow the conduit back to the spy." Kuttic stood. "I'll see if Yusuf has any information about Ben. When you figure out who did the shop, I'd like to know."

He stepped to the door.

"You mean if you find Yusuf?" Payton asked.

"He always comes home to roost. A bone thrown my way would be appreciated." He left.

Kuttic's desperate, otherwise he'd never ask for help. Shared information wasn't in his DNA. If he lost Yusuf on his watch, his career could go up in flames. Payton hoped it'd be a five-alarm fire.

CHAPTER 33

COLONEL MIFFLIN

"BE CAREFUL IN FALLUJAH," Catherine said.

Carl drove. She sat next to Payton in the back seat. He gently squeezed her hand that she'd rested on his knee.

"Ambassador Rhodes wants me to join him and General Qwen when they meet with the Iraqi PM today," she said.

"Kuttic paid me a visit and confirmed Yusuf's on the CIA's payroll."

"It would've been helpful if he shared what the CIA was up to with General Qwen," she said.

"When we ID who hit the tea shop, he wants to know."

"Did you tell him to get in line?"

"Kuttic can find his own answers," Payton said.

"You heard Ambassador Rhodes. He doesn't need any trouble between DSS and the CIA," she said.

"His opinion, the tea shop hit might've been about a Sunni-Shiite militia battle over territory. He also said Cleveland's theory about the Iranians being involved with counterfeit money is not off-base. They've used supernotes before."

"General Qwen wants proof."

"We're working on it. Kuttic has a Red Zone informant who confirmed Yusuf was in the tea shop," Payton said.

"With Ben?"

"His guy said Ben wasn't there."

"Do you believe him?" she asked.

"I'm always skeptical about anything Kuttic says, but this time he might be onto something. The drug lead doesn't feel right. With Evette Azard, Ben could get his hands on any drug he wanted and never leave the Green Zone."

"We're back to where we started, with no answers about why he used the tunnel."

"Quinn tracked down Azard's drug connection. Zamir Goupa, an attorney who works for your well-educated hoods Zaki and Marco, who, according to Kuttic, control a majority of the Green Zone's illegal narcotics trade."

"I told you the al-Dulaimi apple didn't fall far from the tree. With their close relationship to Khleifat, a democratic Iraq will be a pipe dream," she said.

"I plan to press Vicar and Otto on Wade's story when I get back from Fallujah, then we'll start over with Ben's coworkers. Blacknife and his marines checked the alley where Marco dropped off Otto. They couldn't find how he disappeared."

"Maybe he circled back," she said.

"I would've heard or seen him."

"Another question you can ask Otto."

"Whoever took Ben, Kuttic said, wants us to focus our efforts on the shop away from something else he's involved with."

"What is there other than his work?" she asked.

"We'll know if it's work related after I tighten the screws on his coworkers."

"If Azard and Gabe are right, then why'd Wade lie to you?" she asked.

"Vicar and Otto have a lot of questions to answer. I can tell you from prior experience, Kuttic won't stop until he has Yusuf back in play."

"Ben gets in the way of a CIA operation … he'll be buried," she said.

"Kuttic peeled back an onion layer: Yusuf told him a high-level Green Zone spy passes top secret intelligence to the Iranians."

"Does he have any idea who?" she asked.

"Doesn't know, or so he says. Since Yusuf disappeared, he's in the dark."

"If he loses Yusuf with his Iranian connections, he can kiss his CIA career goodbye," she said.

"What a shame."

"Have we found Ben's backup drive?" she asked.

"It was in a UPS box he rented in the basement of the Republican Guard building. Cleveland's at work on it now," he said.

They pulled up to the Council of Ministers building occupied by Pentagon administrators—a "mini-Pentagon," Ambassador Rhodes called it. Massive concrete ribs ran up each side of the several-stories-tall structure. All of the damage the building sustained during the initial air war had been repaired.

"Carl, give us a minute," Catherine said.

Carl stepped out.

She held his hand with both hers. "I meant what I said."

"I'm not sure where we go from here," he said.

"My problem was always being concerned about the future. How about we let the future take care of itself?" she asked.

He didn't let go of her hand. "We'll have to take it slow," he said.

"Slow works for me," she said and kissed him on the check.

COLONEL MIFFLIN'S MALE assistant ushered them into her spacious top-floor office. Sunlight streamed through windows with panoramic Tigris River and Red Zone views.

Mifflin stood sideways behind a boat-sized desk with her telephone hunched up to her ear. She didn't look at them as she snapped through pages in an open legal-sized folder. "I don't care what Tarik told you. Your budget's due Monday and I will not tell the admiral you'll be late. Why are you having problems with a one-facility budget?" She listened for several seconds. "You don't need Tarik's input. An Excel spreadsheet shouldn't take longer than half a day."

Payton considered her serious thin lips, beak of a nose, and black hair that was pulled back and held in place with an army green, braided ponytail holder. She was all business, not one wrinkle in her uniform skirt or starched blouse. The perfect bureaucrat.

He touched Catherine's arm and nodded with his chin toward a side table pushed against the wall under a picture of the president. Several neat rows of bundled money were stacked on it.

"What do you mean 'when'? Today. Our review's tomorrow morning." Another pause. "Noon." She placed the folder on top of a squared stack of more folders, set the telephone down, and turned. "Titan United's a valuable contractor whose people are crucial to the work we do here. I'll not stand for our relationship being jeopardized because of your paranoid aggressive tactics," she said.

So much for niceties.

"Is their contribution worth north of seventy million dollars?" he asked.

"My office pays them a fraction of their true value. Titan United's worth every penny."

"We have a few questions about Ben Ater," Catherine said.

Change the subject. Catherine, always the diplomat.

"I'm not sure what I can say to help with your investigation." She glanced at her watch on the inside of her wrist, then waved to the chairs behind them. "I have a meeting in a few minutes."

She sat in her high-back throne of a chair. Payton thought it fit her Queen of the Green Zone reputation.

"Dale told us Ben came to see you," Catherine said.

"He wanted to discuss one of his audits," Mifflin said.

"Did he say which one?" Catherine asked.

Mifflin perched on the edge of her chair, ramrod straight, with clasped hands between her folder stacks. "I have no idea."

"You didn't ask?" Catherine asked.

"I told him to work through the proper channels. I've put people in place who manage these auditors for me."

"Dale Lowsley a proper channel?" Payton asked.

"Dale's his boss, so yes. After Ben barged in here, I explained in no uncertain terms I only deal with audit supervisors. My assistant escorted him out of the building. I don't have time to meet with every auditor."

"We believe he wanted to speak with you about an MRW facility operated by Titan United. His audit uncovered fraudulent invoices being sent to your office for payment by one of Titan United's subcontractors," he said.

"He should've told Dale. Audit supervisors are responsible for fraud notification memos submitted to my office."

"Have twelve Titan United fraud memos affected your valuable contractor relationship? I mean, if Graham Vicar's a thief, how does he keep all the government work?" he said.

Catherine shot him a glance.

Mifflin straightened several sharpened pencils into a perfect line next to one of the folder stacks. "I don't care for your choice of words. Graham has several hundred employees and double the number of subcontracted workers in the field. Every one of those twelve occurrences was subcontractor related. None, and I want to be clear, *none* were direct employees of Titan United. Graham can't vouch for the behavior of every subcontracted worker not under his direct supervision."

"We'll need a copy of those twelve fraud memos," Catherine said.

The colonel put her hands flat on the desk and stood.

He guessed it was time to go.

"When they're released, your office will be contacted," Mifflin said.

Payton stood with Catherine and pointed over to the money. "You keep a lot of cash on hand."

"They're from the Al Kut BUI branch. I want to know if the counterfeit money rumor's true. These'll be flown to Washington for the Treasury Department to analyze."

"Our technical people confirmed the branch dispersed supernotes," he said.

She didn't miss a beat. "I'll defer to the Treasury Department's analysis. Even if they turn out to be counterfeit, more cash is on the way to be disbursed to every BUI branch."

"Can I have one of those? I'd like my people to check them out," Catherine said.

Mifflin stepped over and handed her a bundle.

"I know you're slammed, but I have one more question. What's your involvement with Marco and Zaki al-Dulaimi?" Payton asked.

"They're Iraqi businessmen who've aided our efforts to secure Iraq's future. With their assistance, Wafi Khleifat should be the next prime minister. I wish there were more business people like them who'd step up for their country."

"Their criminal activity doesn't bother you?" he asked.

"The Middle East is full of questionable characters." Her telephone rang. She picked up the receiver. "Colonel Mifflin," she said. With her hand over the mouthpiece, "If I hear anything that may help your investigation, I'll have my assistant contact you to get on my schedule." She opened a folder and continued her phone conversation.

THEY STOOD IN the building's long shadow.

"She might be clueless about what the brothers are involved with," Catherine said.

"Then she shouldn't be in charge of the Pentagon's money," he said.

"One of my sources on the team of lawyers overseeing the Iraqi election told me Khleifat's in panic mode because the elections are almost here, and even with the full support of the United States, he doesn't know if he'll garner enough votes to win. Zaki and Marco are handing out IOUs like candy to Red Zone militia leaders to have their people vote for Khleifat."

"Once he's in office, the IOUs come due," Payton said.

Catherine held up the bundle. "She'll defer to the Treasury Department."

"How about I bring Cleveland to her office to give a supernote tutorial? Of course, I'll have to make an appointment," he said.

"Don't throw gas on the fire. We still might need her help," she said.

"No way with a dozen fraud memos should she keep Titan United flush with so much work," he said.

"Would you want it known your go-to contractor might be corrupt?" she asked.

"Doesn't the Pentagon run background checks on these contractors before they're awarded any work?'

"Mifflin's office vets all of them."

"Do you know anyone in DC you can ask about her?" he asked.

"Is this about the rumor your old acquaintance shared with you?"

"His tiny security company's after some of the crumbs left over from what she pays larger contractor companies like Titan United. He said he never understood how Titan United rates the volume of work they've received. I'd like to know if Ichabod Crane and the Wicked Witch of the West are tight," he said.

"If she's caught, she'd be court-martialed," Catherine said.

"Relationship or no relationship, Titan United shouldn't be on the government's payroll with all those fraud memos," he said.

"Bob Young oversees the Office of RSOs in Washington. I'll give him a call." She motioned toward Carl and Blacknife at the Humvee. "Will they be with you when you go to Fallujah?"

"Wouldn't go anywhere without them."

"See me when you get back. General Qwen leaves tomorrow. If you find something, I want him to have it before he flies out."

CHAPTER 34

FALLUJAH

THE HELICOPTER ROUNDED on Fallujah from the southeast. Payton adjusted his Kevlar vest. Carl sat across from him and watched brown rooftops slip three hundred feet below the open side door in the late afternoon sun.

They banked hard over a dirt soccer field and started to descend.

Payton checked his watch. Less than thirty minutes to fly twenty miles from the Green Zone.

They leveled and flew over industrial buildings, then were out in the desert again. He saw Camp Fallujah's trailers inside razor-sharp Dannert-wire-topped cement blast walls a few kilometers beyond the city. Another siege operation.

Blacknife sat beside him and pointed out the open door to the camp. "Ben's Waterloo?" he asked over the noise of the machine.

"I hope you're wrong," Payton said.

He asked the pilot to wait while they checked on what Ben found here. If they turned up nothing connected to his disappearance, he wanted to be back in the Green Zone by midafternoon.

"I DON'T NEED distractions," Marine Colonel Pete McVay said. He flicked open his metal lighter and lit a cigarette.

Catherine told Payton that McVay, Camp Fallujah's commander, had a reputation for being a competent enemy killer and a tough taskmaster when it came to camp management. The perfect man to be in charge of a brutal place like Fallujah.

"We'll be in and out, Colonel," Payton said.

They walked into McVay's office trailer and he introduced Payton to Myles Funkhouser, the on-site manager for Titan United Foodservice.

Funkhouser had a right eye tic.

McVay gestured with his cigarette hand. "Myles will handle whatever you need. Titan United does an excellent job in a tough environment. They take care of my people, so I'm satisfied."

"We'll conduct our interviews and keep you informed," Payton said.

PAYTON AND THE marines walked with Funkhouser to his office, a modified construction trailer next to a parking lot with dozens of military vehicles in straight rows.

"We'll wait out here," Blacknife said.

Inside his office, Funkhouser took plastic water bottles with Titan United logos from a small refrigerator beside his desk and handed one to Payton.

"Are you the only manager?" Payton asked.

"I have one assistant, Abd al-Halim Qasem. He oversees the subcontracted workers."

If his assistant was responsible for subcontract work, was he the guy Ben found who ripped off the military with inflated invoices?

"How many workers does he oversee?"

"Eighteen from three different companies. Qasem's employer is a Pakistani company contracted to staff our foodservice operations, a Turkish company handles janitorial and maintenance, and a Kuwaiti firm takes care of all vehicles."

Payton took a long drink. "What contact did you have with Ben?"

"I had to leave soon after he arrived for a Green Zone management meeting. I left him with Qasem. From the little time I spent with him, I could tell he was clueless how we work here."

"How so?"

"Field accounting in a war zone can be tricky. We have to make assumptions from time to time to deal with certain circumstances."

His eye squinted a few times. Being near a city with three hundred thousand residents who wanted to butcher you was enough stress to cause a tic.

"He have any problem with your assumptions?"

"Not after Qasem went over our numbers and toured the camp with him. He said Ben told him what a superb job we've done in a hostile environment."

Squint.

The door opened and a medium-height Middle Eastern guy with a smile, who Payton put to be around sixty, walked in with a cardboard file folder box. His ill-fitting thick black toupee was parted on the left side.

"Qasem, meet Special Agent Payton Ladd. He has questions about Ben Ater."

"Hello, hello, hello," Qasem said with a broad smile. He pumped Payton's hand, then sat on the couch and put his box between his feet.

"Was there anything out of the ordinary Ben was concerned with while he was here?" Payton asked.

"He have no problem with our operation," Qasem said.

Either Qasem wasn't being truthful or he didn't know Ben had found his padded head count invoices.

Qasem reached into his box and pulled up a light-green logbook and handed it over. "We record military people who use MRW."

Payton leafed through page after page of tiny handwritten neat numbers in columns. He set the book down.

"My company paid every two weeks after total head counts sent to Titan United Green Zone headquarters," Qasem said.

"Who's your employer?"

"Rightway, Ltd., based in Lahore. We have contract with Titan United Foodservice."

"Is Camp Fallujah your only responsibility?"

"Yes, Camp Fallujah, keep me busy, busy. Another Rightway manager over other camp."

"What other camp?"

"FOB Stanly in Fallujah, very dangerous. Only five Rightway employees there. I tell Ben he should not go. Stanly sees more action than any FOB in country."

"He went to Stanly?" Payton eyed Funkhouser.

Funkhouser's eye twitched twice, then he said, "I didn't know he left until after I came back from my Green Zone meeting." He licked his lips and took a drink.

"Ben's boss come here from Green Zone looking for him," Qasem said.

"Dale Lowsley?"

Qasem nodded. "Yes, Mr. Lowsley. He arrive on Titan United helicopter."

"Did he say why he wanted Ben?"

"No sir," Qasem said. "When helicopter land, he knew Ben was in Stanly."

How would Lowsley know Ben left Camp Fallujah?

Qasem kept up with his nod and smile.

To Funkhouser, Payton asked, "Why didn't you mention Ben left for another camp?" What else hadn't Funkhouser told him?

"I assumed you already knew."

"Don't make any more assumptions," Payton said. Then to Qasem, "Why'd Ben go?"

"He say his job to check all facilities," Qasem said.

Payton pointed to both of them. "What responsibility do you two have over Stanly?"

"None," Funkhouser said. "We only handle this camp."

"Then who's over Stanly?"

"Qasem's company, Rightway, has the FOB Fallujah contract with Titan United Foodservice. Stanly operates under Titan United's Special Situations Group, and Rightway's on-site manger is responsible for their numbers," Funkhouser said.

"What's the difference between the two?"

"Foodservice comes under the supervision of our corporate country manager," Funkhouser said.

"Who is?"

"Graham Vicar."

"And Special Situations?'

"Mr. Vicar put Otto Van Heerden, Titan United's director of operations, in charge of all Special Situation camps," Funkhouser said.

Was Vicar the type of guy who didn't want to get involved with these Special Situations because they were too risky? Hand off responsibility to Otto and he wouldn't scuff his manicured fingernails or pop a button off his double-breasted suit?

"How many of these camps does Otto oversee?"

"Six—Basra, Amarah, Al Kut, Najif, Nasiriyah, and Mosul," Funkhouser said.

Four of those cities Qwen said had BUI bank runs. He'd have Rammer check if Titan United had contracts in the other two.

"How'd Ben get over to Stanly?"

"On a supply truck," Funkhouser said.

PAYTON TOLD THE helicopter pilot to head back to the Green Zone. McVay would provide several men and two Strykers for the short run over to Stanly. Each vehicle had eight wheels with mounted .50 caliber machine guns, a grenade launcher, and panels of heavy-gauge slate armor welded to its sides. McVay assured Payton that Funkhouser and Qasem weren't going anywhere.

Their driver told them Stanly was built on an abandoned pig farm in Fallujah's Jolan District, where some of the most vicious combat took place when marines attacked the city for a second time. Stanly's site was chosen to give the marines the ability to move into the city on short notice.

Stanly was a quarter the size of Camp Fallujah. Payton saw perimeter walls of ten-foot-high sandbags stacked five deep, reinforced with concrete T-walls. Machine-gun-manned pillbox guard stations were placed every few hundred feet. Thick coils of Dannert wire almost obscured the sandbags.

Payton pulled out his cell phone and dialed Rammer. He told him about the two types of Titan United camps. "I want to know the location of all these Special Situations. Ben left Camp Fallujah to check one out called FOB Stanly."

"I didn't know he left Camp Fallujah."

"Neither did I. Get back to me on those locations."

Their Stryker stopped alongside Stanly's camp commander's trailer, where Major Jock Macaslan, a reed-thin African American, who wore a helmet and body armor, stood with four of his officers.

Payton exchanged greetings with him. Macaslan and one of his officers escorted them over to Titan United's facility, an old barn behind several trailers used for barracks.

The dingy place smelled of mildew, wet rubber barmats, and watered down Clorox. The floor and walls were warped, dark gray-painted plywood. A varnished-top wooden bar ran along the back wall. In a side room were several video games, dartboards, and a pool table. Military personnel sat at tables and watched a NASCAR race on a television suspended from the ceiling.

Macaslan pointed to a short, pear-shaped guy with a black chevron mustache who stood in front of the bar.

"Raj Baz is Titan United's man. Baz, meet Special Agent Ladd, a Diplomatic Security Service investigator from the US Embassy in Baghdad. He wants to speak with you about the auditor who came here. Give him whatever he needs."

Macaslan left.

Baz used a handful of white bar napkins to mop sweat off his bloated face and shaved head. An Asian girl polished the far end of the bar.

"What contact did you have with Ben Ater?" When Payton mentioned Ben's name, he saw the girl pause and glance their way.

"I talk to him only once," Baz said.

"What did he do while he was here?" Payton asked.

"Review our numbers. If you came from Camp Fallujah, Myles and Qasem should half told you."

Why was this guy agitated?

"How long did he stay in the camp?" Payton asked.

"Tree, four hours. His boss took him back to the Green Zone by helicopter."

The girl went through a door to the kitchen. Payton motioned to Blacknife and Carl to follow her. She might know something.

Baz watched the marines disappear, then dabbed his forehead again. "Vere are they going?" He tossed the used napkins on the bar and grabbed several more.

"To check the place out. How long've you been manager?"

"Seven months."

"You're a Rightway, Ltd. employee?"

"Along with the girls. The Rightway supervisor before me vas killed in a mortar attack. The Titan United boss wanted a replacement right away."

"Who at Titan United?"

"Mr. Van Heerden." Baz tilted his head and wiped under his chin. "Ve make our numbers every month and half no problems."

Behind Baz, Blacknife motioned to Payton through the round door window from the kitchen. He told Baz he'd be back in a few minutes.

"The girl spent time with Ben," Blacknife said when Payton came through the door.

They crossed the small kitchen and went out the rear door and around the corner to Carl, who stood next to a timber-roofed sandbag-walled hut. Blacknife knocked on the wooden door.

No answer.

He was about to knock again when the door cracked open. "Can we come in?" he asked.

The girl had frightened brown eyes. "No questions," she said. She spoke above a whisper. Payton heard her Asian accent and saw she was about to cry. "Go away," she said.

Carl slid his foot forward before she could close the door. "We only need a few minutes," he said.

She glanced over her shoulder to an angry voice that came from farther back in the hut, then she stepped away and the door opened.

They stood inside a low-ceilinged room. The wooden plank floor was buckled in several places. A card table with silver metal chairs occupied one corner. Cream material bulged through the chairs' cracked black vinyl. A faucet dripped by the door over a rust-stained white porcelain sink.

On the other side of the room, in front of another doorway, three more women stood. Two were young, and the one in the middle was stocky and older. She glared at them.

"What happened to Ben?" the young girl asked. She went to the table and sat.

"He's disappeared from the Green Zone and we want to find him. What's your name?" Payton said.

"Silma."

"Why would we know about him?" the stocky woman asked and came toward them.

"Manee, they might help us," Silma said.

"We have no idea about him." She walked past them, opened the door, and jerked her hand for them to leave.

Payton ignored her. "If you know something, it could save his life," he said to Silma.

"Out!" Manee held the door open.

Payton heard screams after she slammed the door behind them.

PAYTON STOOD ON the other side of a picnic table draped with a white plastic tablecloth. Silma burst into tears when she saw him.

Blacknife and Carl found her while she hosed off bar mats outside the MWR. They convinced her to speak with them away from the other girls and brought her to Macaslan's logistics room.

"No one saw us, boss," Blacknife said. "Baz is in his hut with the mean one."

"You're safe here," Payton said.

"They have our passports." She teared up.

Carl went to the sink, filled a Styrofoam cup with water, ripped a few paper towels off a mounted roll, and handed them to her. He sat next to her across from Payton.

"Who has your passports?" Payton asked.

"Titan United."

"How did you get to Camp Stanly?"

She hesitated.

"He can help you," Carl said.

"Fifteen girls from Chiang Mai, my village in northern Thailand, we get job with Bangkok Titan United caterer. They offer job for more money if we move abroad. On jet they take our passports. We arrive in Yemen and put in hotel with many scared girls from all over world. Three days later seven girls taken to Kuwait City."

She dabbed tears with the paper towel. "They say we make trouble, put in brothels. Four girls brought to Iraq in freight truck container."

"How long have you been at Stanly?"

"Six months. Mr. Baz say he beat us we talk to anyone about how they bring girls to camp."

Payton would add slave labor to Vicar and Otto's skill set.

"Tell us about Ben."

"He came on truck from Camp Fallujah."

Maggie said Ben was a sharp auditor, maybe he heard about Stanly's operation and decided to check it out. If he was doing his job, why'd Lowsley show up on a Titan United helicopter?

"Has anyone else from the Green Zone come to Stanly?"

"Several weeks ago, two men from Camp Fallujah. Mr. Baz say one important manager in Titan United Green Zone office. The other is manager over Camp Fallujah."

"Do you remember anything about the Green Zone man?"

"I never hear his name."

"What did he look like?"

"Has shaved head and mustache."

"One of these?' Payton drew a Fu Manchu on his face with his finger.

She nodded.

Otto.

"How about the Camp Fallujah manager?"

"He wink many times."

Funkhouser, another Titan United employee with short-term memory loss.

"I see them in Mr. Baz's office. Green Zone man not happy with Mr. Baz's account book where he records head counts. Camp Fallujah manager erase in book. When I clean office, I see where he make changes to total number of army men we served."

Otto and Funkhouser not only knew about the inflated head counts but they were behind them. Otto must've found out Ben was here and sent Lowsley to retrieve him before he could discover their scam. Which meant Lowsley was involved, too. So who alerted Otto that Ben was in Camp Stanly?

"How'd Baz act when Ben arrived?"

"He angry no one from Rightway or Titan United tell him Ben come here. He say he punish any girl who talk to Ben without his permission."

"Tough guy," Carl said.

"Does Major Macaslan or his staff know how he treats you?" Payton asked.

"He never yell in front of army men, only in our hut. When Ben start work, Mr. Baz say give him what he needs. I bring Ben sandwich and soda while he work. Ben very kind. I ask what his job. He must confirm numbers. Your government ... reburs—?"

"Reimburses?" Carl said.

"Yes, reimburse for army personnel served. When Ben look over head counts in Mr. Baz book, he ask if they correct. He say too high. I afraid to tell him how Camp Fallujah man change numbers. If Mr. Baz know I tell Ben, I could be sent to brothel. Ben say it okay to tell him."

"Baz will never hurt you again," Payton said.

He saw her relief and tiny smile.

"I tell Ben each shift, girls write number of army men served on napkin to give accurate count to Mr. Baz. Ben ask if I still have napkin. I keep all of them."

"Did you give them to him?"

She nodded.

"He type in his computer how numbers were changed in account book. When he finish he say, can he see kitchen supply room to check inventory. I show him walk-in coolers and freezer and … " She stopped, and with her head down, clenched and unclenched her fists.

Payton reached across and covered her hands with his. "You're going home. When we leave, you and the other girls will come with us."

Tears rolled from her wide eyes.

"All of you," he said.

"I tell Ben about ice money."

"Ice money?"

"Mr. Baz sell ice to man from Fallujah Tuesday nights. Two weeks before Ben arrive I forget to empty garbage after my shift and go back to kitchen. From dumpster I see Mr. Baz carry black bag into ice truck next to dumpster. When he leave truck, he didn't have bag and he forget to lock door. I curious about black bag and sneak inside truck. I see ice maker with frozen money."

"Ben went into the truck?"

She nodded.

"I show him where Mr. Baz keep key, in desk drawer envelope." She started to cry again. "Manee see Ben come out of truck and tell Mr. Baz."

"Was anyone with Ben when he arrived here?"

She nodded and reached into her back pocket and withdrew a folded piece of paper. "Army man take our picture."

Payton unfolded the paper. Ben was between Silma and one of the other Thai girls. He had his arm out to pull into the picture his security man … Wade Loft. Wade had alerted Otto that Ben was in Stanly.

"One of my men will stay with you until we leave."

She came around and hugged him.

PAYTON MOVED ALONG the sandbag wall to the refrigerated truck. He slid the key from Baz's office into a heavy lock looped through the ice truck's metal door handle. Inside, he flipped the light switch. Industrial-sized bags of frozen vegetables were stored on racks next to boxes of frozen hamburgers, hot dogs, and breaded chicken breasts. On the floor was an ice maker. He lifted the lid and saw blocks of ice.

Something was inside each of the four rectangular blocks. He snapped both metal clips and the hinged front panel popped open. He heaved one of the blocks out. Bundles of one-hundred-dollar notes were cubed inside. The other three blocks also had cubes.

Something caught his eye on the floor beside the ice maker. He reached over and lifted up an empty black cloth bag. It was the same type of bag he'd found full of supernotes in the second-floor room of the house where they'd seen Ben.

Blacknife stepped inside.

Payton tossed him the bag. "Look familiar?"

"Supernotes from the house were in one of these," Blacknife said.

"Take a look at what Ben found." He tapped the ice with his foot. "They'll be supernotes. Ben's life changed when he found them." Payton didn't want Baz to know he'd been in here. He slid the block back into the ice maker and closed the hinged door. "I want to see where Baz goes with the ice tonight."

"DO YOU KNOW how many men we've lost?" Major Macaslan asked.

"Too many, Major, but counterfeit money's being smuggled out of your camp. Tuesday nights, Iraqis come to buy ice from Baz, right?"

"They do, with my approval."

"Whose idea was the ice?"

"Baz said he could sell ice to people in the city and barter for information. I told him to go ahead but only under strict security. Those ice exchanges have provided him with valuable intel about where we can find the enemy."

"Who receives the ice?"

"Hawala brokers."

Hawala brokers. Like Zaki and Marco.

"Baz is involved in more than just selling ice," Payton said.

"If you're right and he used my camp to move counterfeit money, then he's mine. I'll guarantee you he'll tell us what he's up to."

"Hold off. I want to watch him tonight with the ice."

"I'll tell him you and your people were called back to the Green Zone."

"How can I observe the ice transfer?"

"A sniper team rolls out in three hours. They'll get you in a position."

PAYTON MET BLACKNIFE and Carl in the logistics room.

"We'll go out with a sniper team to see Baz hand off the ice money. Carl, the girls will be brought here. I want you to stay with them."

"What about the mean one? I don't trust she'll keep her mouth shut and not talk to Baz," Carl said.

"I asked Major Macaslan to separate her from the other three."

"Does he have any idea who Baz passes the supernotes to?" Blacknife asked.

"Hawala brokers who tell Baz where Fallujah's bad guys are," Payton said.

"I've heard most Iraqis consider hawala systems more credible than banks," Carl said.

"Same here, but I've never been clear how they actually work," Blacknife said.

"They're a trusted way to send money halfway around the world," Payton said

"Competition for banks," Blacknife said.

"Hawala systems have been around forever. Their brokers are honorable members of the community," Payton said.

"Which makes them ideal to move supernotes undetected," Carl said.

"Wait. Didn't Catherine tell you the al-Dulaimis operate a hawala system?" Blacknife asked.

"They have hawala brokers all over the country," Payton said.

Which is why he wanted to know if the guy who received the ice money was connected to the brothers' hawala system.

CHAPTER 35

FOB STANLY

"WE GO OUT EVERY few nights," US Navy Petty Officer Ricco Maaske said.

Maaske, a six-foot-three, broad-shouldered Navy SEAL, hadn't shaved in several days and wore his brown hair pulled back in a ponytail. He sat in front of Payton next to an Iraqi driver named Nuri. Blacknife, along with a driver and a second sniper, followed in another Humvee. Carl had stayed with the girls.

"We never worked from vehicles in my day," Payton said.

"Sometimes being mobile is more productive. Tonight, we'll circle back to several bombed-out buildings on a ridge close to the city. Excellent hunting from there, right, Nuri?"

"The best," Nuri said.

"Where'd you see action?" Maaske asked.

"El Salvador, Lebanon, and the Persian Gulf," Payton said.

"I heard Beirut was a nasty place."

"I was in the Bekaa Valley, and yes, Beirut was a nasty place."

"Major Macaslan said you want to take a joy ride to Fallujah."

"I'm interested in Baz and the ice transfer."

"When I first heard the major let Baz go ahead with his ice meetings, I was skeptical. Baz proved me wrong. We've had fewer casualties because of the information he's provided us," Maaske said.

"Whatever he's up to will cost many more lives than he'll ever save," Payton said.

Nuri shifted and rolled forward.

With their lights off, they drove through Stanly's back gate and disappeared west into the blackness.

They went three kilometers, then slowed to a stop in a depression, Fallujah's lights a distant glow behind them.

Forty minutes later, the Humvees came up the backside of a long rise to a one-room warehouse building. They got out and followed Maaske to the side of the building next to several fifty-five gallon drums that reeked of turpentine. A wide stretch of empty desert separated them from Stanly's lights a few kilometers off to their right.

Payton pressed a button on his watch: 12:48 a.m.

Vehicle headlights appeared on a single-lane road between the city and Stanly.

A modified van with an open trailer back drove through a grove of palm trees below their position and headed toward the camp. The driver slowed when he approached the barricaded checkpoint fifty yards in front of Stanly's main entrance.

"When he leaves, I want to follow him into the city to see where he takes the ice money," Payton said.

"With fifty more men and tanks we can," Maaske said.

"Then stop him before he enters the city."

Maaske pointed to the grove of trees. "We'll take him there."

Payton used binoculars to watch a guard approach the van and after a few minutes wave the driver toward Baz, who stood next to a Toyota pickup truck between the checkpoint and the main gate. The van driver pulled past the pickup, reversed, and backed up to Baz's open tailgate.

Baz clambered up onto his truck's bed.

"Nice move for a fat man. He's in a hurry," Maaske said with his binoculars on the two vehicles.

"We've rattled him. He wants to pass off the ice money before we catch him with it," Payton said.

Baz uncovered four blocks of ice and slid them over onto the van's bed. The driver threw a tarp over the ice. Baz reached into his pocket, pulled out a wad of money, counted out several bills, and handed them to the guy. They shook hands and got back into their vehicles. Baz rolled through the main gate into Stanly, and the van came toward Payton and the others.

THE SURPRISED DRIVER stood next to the tailgate. Maaske stepped up onto the trailer bed and snapped on his flashlight. He flung the tarp off the ice.

"Get them off," Payton said.

Maaske shoved one block after the other off with his foot, then hopped down and shone his light on the jumbled heap of ice.

Payton hit one of the blocks with an iron crowbar that Nuri had retrieved from his Humvee. White-edged chips sparkled and splintered away. He brought the crowbar down again and a chunk calved off and exposed five plastic-wrapped cubes of bills. They tumbled out when he slammed the block again.

Payton lined the cubes along the tailgate.

The old Iraqi stared at him. He had one eye and deep wrinkles on his face. A jagged pink scar started above his right eyebrow and sliced down to the center of his cheek.

"What's your name?" Payton asked in Arabic.

He stared at Payton.

"Give me your knife," Payton said.

Nuri, his head wrapped with a multicolored checked keffiyeh to hide his identity, handed Payton his combat knife. He slit the plastic wrap, pulled a bundle out, and ruffled through crisp one-hundred-dollar bills like the pages of a phone book.

"Did Baz win the lottery?" Maaske asked.

"Seventy-five to a hundred grand per cube," Payton said. "All counterfeit." He turned to the Iraqi. "You speak English?"

The guy nodded.

"If you don't answer my questions, you'll be taken back to the Green Zone, interrogated, and may never go home again. You understand?'

He nodded again.

"What's your name?"

"Malik. Malik Wialheed," he said.

"Why'd you meet Baz?" Payton asked.

"I am hawala broker."

"I know of him. He tells the truth," Nuri said.

"Fighting destroy city's electricity. Ice keep food fresh many days. Mr. Baz offer ice and five hundred American dollars for information where enemies your military want to find."

"What happens with the ice money?" Payton asked.

Malik hesitated. His eye darted from Nuri back to Payton.

"Mr. Baz say use ice money with hawala transactions and deposit rest in bank."

"What bank?"

"Bank of United Iraq in Resafa district."

"Resafa's a commercial district near the river with a BUI branch," Nuri said.

If one of the hawala systems was compromised along with BUI, Iraq's economy was in greater peril than any of them realized.

"How much money has Baz given you?" Payton asked.

He shrugged. "Many millions."

"How do you know Baz?"

"He came to me."

"Why?"

He hesitated.

"Why you?" Payton asked.

"I have business associates who bring me items to sell. Statues and pictures stolen from museums."

"Museums all over the country were plundered after the invasion," Nuri said.

"We take them to man in Baghdad," Malik said.

"Who?"

His eye flashed to the knife and back to Payton.

"Do you want to see your family again? Payton asked.

"Marco al-Dulaimi. He pay with gold and arrange for Baz to bring me ice money."

"You said associates?"

"Hawala brokers in Marco and his brother's hawala system."

"These are worthless. If you want to live, take your family and leave Fallujah. Disappear. You'll be killed if you're connected to the counterfeit money you've put into the hawala system."

"Thank you, sir. Thank you." He nodded several times. "Thank you." Again with both hands he shook Payton's hand. He ran to his van and sped away.

"Will he take your advice?" Maaske asked.

"He's a dead man if he doesn't," Payton said.

THEY FOUND BAZ in his trailer sitting cross-legged on a floor cushion with Manee, the mean Thai woman. He was halfway through a smoky exhale from a hookah pipe when Payton and the marines barged in.

Sparks fireworked from the glass pipe when Payton kicked it over. "Up," he said.

Baz rolled over on all fours and hefted himself up. Carl led Manee out. Blacknife yanked Baz's wrists up behind his back and pushed him out the trailer.

Payton walked into the kitchen and stopped beside a block of ice next to an industrial-sized floor mixer. This was the last block of ice from the ice maker. There was no money in it. Blacknife stood behind Baz.

"What happened while Ben was here?" Payton asked.

"I already told you," Baz said. "He reviewed my account book." Sweat beaded on his forehead.

"And the ice?"

"I sell to people in the city."

"He found the ice money, didn't he?" Payton put his foot on the block.

Baz spread his arms with his hands open. "I've already told you vat I know."

Payton pointed to Baz's pants. "Get them off." He shoved the ice block toward Baz, who jumped out of the way.

"OFF," Blacknife yelled behind Baz's ear.

Baz fumbled with his belt and his pants dropped.

"And those," Payton said.

Baz pulled his red and black striped boxer shorts off. "Sit."

He winced when he squatted on the ice.

The dark green mixer was a four-foot-high industrial behemoth with an auger inside a huge bowl used to knead dough for dozens of loaves of bread or mix gallons of sauces. Payton hit a red switch and the auger started to spin.

"The truth or your left hand goes in. We know Ben found your ice money. Where do you get it from?"

"They vill kill me."

"Not where you're going."

"You don't know these people."

"They don't know me," Payton said.

Baz's eyes bounced between the auger and Payton. "Mr. Van Heerden delivered and set up the ice truck. He ordered me to tell anyone who asked that a Green Zone frozen food company keeps inventory inside. He said I vould receive money in bags on Titan United delivery trucks from FOB Fallujah. I should freeze the money and give the ice to the hawala brokers."

"Why those brokers?"

"They work for the al-Dulaimi brothers."

"Are you the only Titan United camp with an ice truck?"

He shook his head. "There are many others."

"They move money in ice too?"

Baz didn't answer.

From behind, Blacknife nudged his arm closer to the spinning auger.

"Yes, yes." Baz jerked away from the machine. "The girl said she saw Ben go into the ice truck. I told the security man vith him and he called Mr. Van Heerden."

"Wade Loft was his security?"

He nodded. "A few hours after I told Vade, Ben's boss arrived here. He took Ben and Vade back to the Green Zone."

Otto sent Lowsley to get Ben out of Stanly. Ben had no idea the money was counterfeit, but he still had to tell someone what he found. He didn't trust Lowsley to inform Colonel Mifflin, so he went to her office. He never got the chance to tell her because he didn't have an appointment. The only other person he knew to tell was Catherine. That's why he left her a voicemail.

Major Macaslan provided Payton with two additional men to take Baz back to Camp Fallujah. When Funkhouser saw they had Baz, he spilled his side of the operation and confirmed Otto arranged for bags of money to be delivered on Titan United Foodservice supply trucks from the company's Green Zone warehouse.

McVay took Baz, Qasem, and Funkhouser. "We'll deal with them," he said.

Payton called Catherine and told her he'd found the supernotes and who was behind them. Catherine asked the same question that nagged at him. If the brothers owned one of the largest hawala systems in the country, why'd they need Titan United to move supernotes when they could pass them straight to their own brokers?

He told her to bring Cleveland up to speed and send him and Rammer over to Titan United's warehouse where the supernotes were being distributed from.

One question he didn't need to waste anymore time on: Ben's disappearance had nothing to do with drugs.

CHAPTER 36

GREEN ZONE

PAYTON GRABBED A few hours' sleep, had something to eat with McVay, and left at dawn from Camp Fallujah with the marines and the girls on a military convoy headed to the Green Zone.

"Ben's drug involvement was a charade?" Carl asked.

"Total fiction," Payton said. "When he went over to Stanly and discovered the ice money, Wade alerted Otto, who sent Lowsley to retrieve Ben before he could tell anyone."

Otto was behind the e-mail threat Ben received to not tell anyone what he'd found. He was taken after whoever hacked into his e-mails saw he told Leah.

"The Route Irish EFP that took out Wade wasn't random," Blacknife said.

"If he's dead he can't talk. They almost succeeded with Leah, who was about to tell us Ben had found the frozen money," Payton said.

"Dale Lowsley's involved, isn't he?" Carl asked.

"I'll deal with him," Payton said.

"Were supernotes the reason Ben went into the Red Zone?" Blacknife asked.

"I think he was abducted somewhere else, possibly inside the Green Zone, and taken to the Red Zone house where the walk-in saw him."

"How would they move him?" Blacknife asked.

"One possibility is the sewer tunnel where the bag of weed was found, or they had another way past the checkpoint guards," Payton said.

"If these supernotes are tied to BUI's bank-run riots, then whoever wants to bring down the economy knows the millions in cash we use to prop up the financial system is our Achilles heel," Carl said.

"Iranians have the motivation and wherewithal to flood Iraq with supernotes to crash the economy. They use proxies all over the Middle East to fight their battles," Payton said.

"By proxies, you mean Zaki and Marco?" Blacknife asked.

"Their hawala system is perfect cover to wage financial war against the United States," Payton said.

"I can see how the brothers and their crooked hawala brokers might be involved, but I don't get Titan United's connection," Blacknife said.

"Say I'm the Iranians," Payton said, "I might want to hedge my bets and have a backup in case the brothers fail to deliver and supernotes don't get salted into the financial system. With Titan United in play, they have a ready-made distribution network and double their prospects for success."

"Two proxies are better than one," Blacknife said.

Payton got the brothers being involved—they were opportunists—but something about Titan United's connection bothered him. Why jeopardize a fortune in military contracts if they were caught?

When traffic slowed to a crawl on Abu Ghraib Expressway, their driver told them military security had been ratcheted up because of several more bank runs in the last twelve hours throughout Baghdad. Two and a half slow hours later, they entered the city limits.

Army security was everywhere. Twice Payton saw rows of destroyed buildings still on fire.

His cell phone vibrated.

"What's your ETA?" Cleveland asked.

"Not long. We're in the city now."

"Vicar's office said he left the Green Zone for a meeting. We haven't located Otto."

"What about his living quarters?"

"Nada."

"Zaki and Marco?"

"Funny, they've disappeared too."

"Did you call Quinn?"

"He's lent us several MPs. We have every available DSS agent out in the Green Zone hunting for the three of them. I even called in a favor with a Brazilian security company. They supplied another dozen people to join with the search. So far, no luck."

"What about Titan United's warehouse?"

"We've secured the building but didn't find any supernotes. The few Titan United employees inside had no idea about counterfeit money."

"Pull the place apart. I want those supernotes."

"The reason I called, Chief Inspector Akrawi phoned a few minutes ago. He said we might be interested in a body found in his district. The guy had no ID but wore a class ring from Emory."

"Who do we know who went to Emory?"

"Dale Lowsley. Rammer discovered he'd been hired at four hundred and twenty-five grand a year with bonuses, to run, get this, one of Titan United's South American divisions."

"I'll meet you at the main gate," Payton said.

WHEN THEY APPROACHED the security gate, Payton saw Cleveland beside an armored personnel carrier, with a soldier behind the M2 Browning machine gun, parked against the Jersey wall next to the pillbox.

Payton with Carl and Blacknife walked over to Cleveland.

"Waiting for more marines. Catherine said sit tight until she gets here," Cleveland said.

"Take the girls," Payton said to Carl.

Carl went to the Humvee with the Thai girls, got behind the wheel, pulled out of the convoy, and drove through the gate.

Cleveland nodded, "There she is."

Two armored-up Humvees with embassy marines rolled out of the Green Zone past the pillbox and stopped behind the personnel carrier. Hugo Gomez was behind the wheel of the first Humvee. Catherine got out of the passenger seat next to him.

"Who are the girls with Carl?" she asked.

"Slave labor Vicar's company smuggled from Thailand," Payton said.

"Did you tell him we still haven't found Graham or Otto?" she asked Cleveland.

"He knows," Cleveland said.

"Or the al-Dulaimi brothers. I'm not sure what kind of deal Vicar has with Zaki and Marco, but Titan United's up to here in the supernote operation." Payton sliced his hand under his chin.

"If their objective is to destroy any gains we've made, they're starting to succeed with these bank riots," she said.

"Thank the Iranians. They have the North Korean contacts who'd supply them with enough supernotes to implode the economy," Cleveland said.

"Wade Loft was Ben's personal security in Fallujah. When Ben found the supernotes frozen in blocks of ice, Wade called someone in his corporate office, who had Dale Lowsley retrieve him," Payton said.

"Who'd Wade call?" she asked.

"Best guess, Otto," Payton said.

"Drugs weren't involved in his disappearance?" she asked.

"He was taken because he found the supernotes. Anyone he may have told was also a target. First they tried to take out Leah, and then they succeeded when they blew Wade off Route Irish."

"We'll know shortly if Lowsley will be added to the list," Cleveland said.

"Why haven't they killed Ben?" she asked.

"He might already be dead," Payton said.

"The BUI in Amarah was firebombed when it opened a few hours ago, five dead. Last night, an Army Ranger patrol saved the Nasiriyah branch from being destroyed by a mob. General Qwen wants these BUI attacks stopped. He called a meeting of all his commanders. Ambassador Rhodes asked for you to be there."

"No more meetings. You handle the ambassador and Qwen. We'll hunt for Vicar and Otto. Once we bring those two in, they'll give up Zaki and Marco and then we'll know where to find Ben."

"Call me when you have them." She went back to the Humvee, got in, and Hugo drove back inside the Green Zone.

THEY SPED WEST along the river.

"Vicar, Otto, or the brothers would never make it past the pillbox guards," Cleveland said.

"If Zaki and Marco smuggle dope inside, they must have another way in," Payton said.

"Which means they'd have a way out," Cleveland said.

"Like a second tunnel," Payton said.

"What was Wade Loft doing in Fallujah?" Cleveland asked.

"Keeping an eye on Ben for Otto. His involvement got him blown off Route Irish. Have you made any headway with the external hard drive?" Payton asked.

"I was right—Ben backed up his e-mails to the drive. He sent one to Leah while he was in Stanly to tell her he found the ice money and inflated head counts. Several hours after he was back in the Green Zone, someone threatened him.

The e-mail said he wouldn't leave Iraq alive if he didn't forget about what he'd found. It was sent from a bogus Gmail account with a Green Zone IP address."

"When Leah received Ben's e-mail she was put on the hit list. Where's Rammer on the dead guys from the house?"

"One database match. Our money man on top of the bag, Ammar Quadir, was al-Dori's brother-in-law. He owned the house. Here's a bonus: he's a prominent hawala broker who works for the al-Dulaimis."

"We were too late to find Ben, but we surprised the guys in the room," Payton said.

"The machine gun and EFP were meant for one of our military patrols that would've been on the cross street later that morning."

"A hawala broker in Fallujah meets with Baz and now Ammar Quadir. Both are connected to Zaki and Marco's network. See if you can find out any more information about the guy in Al Kut with the megaphone. How did he know counterfeit money was being handed out from the bank?" Payton asked.

"I'll have Rammer check his background. Want to bet he's one of the brothers' money brokers?" Cleveland asked.

"I don't want to take your money," Payton said.

TWENTY MINUTES LATER they stopped in front of a several-story car park garage west of the Green Zone in the derelict commercial center of Chief Inspector Akrawi's Mansour district. MSGs emptied out of the personnel carrier and spread out along the street.

"Down there," Cleveland said.

The driver in the lead Humvee turned into the basement entrance. The second Humvee followed, then the personnel carrier.

On the lower level Payton saw rows of mushroom-topped concrete support columns. They pulled to a stop several yards from a group of men. A man in a rumpled police uniform with rolled-up sleeves walked over and shook Cleveland's hand.

"Special Agent Payton Ladd," Cleveland said, "Chief Inspector Raheem Akrawi."

Keg-chested Akrawi had buzz-cut red hair and a trimmed beard peppered with gray. Splotches of perspiration seeped through his rumpled uniform shirt.

Payton shook his sweaty hand.

They walked toward Akrawi's men.

Payton saw blood pooled on the oil-stained pavement under the body: a man on his side faced the concrete wall.

Cleveland stepped around looked at him and motioned to Payton.

Payton saw the bullet chest wounds and recognized Dale Lowsley.

"He won't be collecting his four hundred K a year," Cleveland said.

Akrawi pointed to a Fiat parked in a space opposite them. A man watched them from the front passenger seat. "One of my patrols heard gunshots and caught him when he ran out of the garage. Another one escaped."

They walked over. Akrawi's man by the passenger door hauled the guy out.

Payton recognized the straight hair over his ears. He was the Pizza Hut shooter and one of the guys in the car outside Ben's office building. His right eye was swollen shut and dried blood caked around his left ear.

"If you don't cooperate, you'll join him," Akrawi said and pointed to Lowsley. "Tell these men what you told me."

He tilted his head back and focused with his good eye on Cleveland, then over to Payton. He didn't say anything. His greasy hair flew over his face when Akrawi's man cuffed him hard on the back of the head.

"We were paid to kill him," he said.

"Get the box," Akrawi said. Another of his men took a shoebox out of the back seat. "He had these." Akrawi lifted the lid.

Payton saw several wrapped bundles of one-hundred-dollar bills. Akrawi handed one to Cleveland.

Back to the man. "You and who else?" Akrawi asked.

"My brother."

"Who paid you?" Akrawi asked.

Another hesitation. Akrawi motioned with his head to his man behind the shooter.

"Wait," the shooter said. "A hawala broker from Ishbiliya."

"The name," Akrawi said.

"Ammar Quadir."

"The guy with the money bag killed in the house. One of Zaki and Marco's hawala brokers," Cleveland said.

"How are you associated with the al-Dulaimi brothers?" Payton asked.

"We are security for their brokers. When they travel with money, my brother and I protect them."

"Why kill him?" Payton pointed to Lowsley.

"Questions are not our business."

Akrawi turned to Payton and Cleveland. "You work for those brothers, you do what you're told."

Cleveland moved a flame from his lighter behind one of the bills. "They're supernotes. The same number series from Al Kut and the money you found in the bag under Quadir." He flicked the bill to the shooter. "Fake money."

The shooter moved his head toward Lowsley's body. "Marco al-Dulaimi wanted him dead."

Akrawi gave an order, and the shooter was manhandled back toward the Fiat.

"Who was your target behind the Pizza Hut?" Payton asked.

The shooter looked back at Payton and smiled. "I recognize you. You were with the girl. Marco said kill her, but you surprised us with your guns. We waited at her office building, but you saw us."

Akrawi's man slammed the door with the guy back in the Fiat.

"Wade and Dale knew Ben found supernotes and were killed for it. Leah's hanging on to life because Ben told her. I don't get why he's still alive," Cleveland said.

"They want something from him. The bald guy next to Ben in the second-floor room we saw with Rammer's toy plane was Otto," Payton said.

"Raheem heard something about the tea shop," Cleveland said.

"One of my Sunni counterparts across the river said Zaki and Marco were behind the tea shop hit. They wanted to send a message to Nassar al-Dori: you want to do business in the Green Zone, you deal with us," Akrawi said.

"We know the brothers are involved with criminal activity inside the wall," Cleveland said.

"Nothing happens there they don't get a cut of," Akrawi said.

"The shop was hit to make a point. The brothers wanted their cut of the drug profits Yusuf generated for al-Dori," Cleveland said.

"Did your source know who they targeted inside the shop?" Payton asked.

"He only heard the guy al-Dori put in charge of his drug operation might've been inside," Akrawi said.

"Kuttic's spy Yusuf," Payton said to Cleveland. He pointed to the Fiat. "Marco's contract killer was after anyone who knew Ben found the supernotes."

"You'll never connect Marco or Zaki to your kidnap victim. They separate themselves with too many layers," Akrawi said.

"Ben's Stanly visit should've gotten him killed," Cleveland said and tossed the supernote bundle onto the box.

"Let's hope his kidnappers still have a reason to keep him alive," Payton said.

CHAPTER 37

PAYTON HAD BEEN in his office for less than twenty minutes when Blacknife called his cell. He'd sent Blacknife over to Titan United's offices to check in with the MSGs posted there.

"Graham's assistant said he's still out of the Green Zone for a meeting. She's left messages on his cell phone to let him know we want to speak with him."

"When will he be back?"

"He hasn't responded. No one over here knows where Otto is either."

"If either of them turns up, take them into custody."

There were hurried footsteps in the hallway.

"Ben's still alive," Rammer said from the doorway. "I need your computer."

Payton moved out of the way and let Rammer sit in his chair. He inserted a disk into the desktop's disk drive. "Here's the list of facilities Otto was responsible for." He handed over a folded piece of paper, then started to type.

Cleveland came in from his office across the hall.

"Something bothered me about the guy who sprinted across the street while we were in the ditch before the machine gun opened up from the second-floor window. Why'd he run?" Rammer asked.

Payton had a problem with the same guy when he ran out of the gate.

On the computer screen, city blocks scrolled under Angel before she was over the ditch. Rammer hit pause and magnified the image. "Here's the gate he came out of," Rammer pointed to the screen.

Across the street from the house where they'd seen Ben was a walled compound with metal gates the guy ran from. Behind the wall was a one-story building with a roof-mounted satellite dish, a courtyard, and a narrow drive along the right side of the building that led to a rear yard with playground equipment. A motorcycle and a dark Mercedes sedan with a cracked sunroof were parked in the courtyard.

"The building's being used for a school," Rammer said.

A man stepped out of the school's front door with a machine gun slung over his shoulder. He opened the gates and scanned the street. After a few minutes, he fished keys out of his pocket and popped the Mercedes trunk lid.

Another man came out who wore a motorcycle helmet with the visor down. He climbed on the bike, kick-started it, and drove out the gate, where he turned left toward the ditch.

Two men dragged a hooded man out of the house with his arms secured behind his back. A fourth man followed, walking to the front passenger door.

At the car, when one of the two men with the hooded guy reached down to move something in the trunk, the guy with the hood bent forward, whipped sideways, and rammed his shoulder into the man behind him. The guy in front grabbed his arm, twisted him around, and smacked him on the side of the head. The hood slipped off, and the one behind shoved him into the trunk and slammed the lid shut. The man at the passenger door said something to the two at the trunk and then got into the car.

Rammer reversed, and when the hood slipped off, he stopped and magnified the image.

"Ben's in the trunk. They moved him from the house across the street where we found the supernotes."

"When did you record this?" Payton asked.

"Forty-five minutes ago," Rammer said.

"He still has some fight left in him," Cleveland said.

"It might keep him alive," Payton said. If only they'd moved faster to take the house, they might've gotten him before he was transferred to the school.

Rammer advanced the video. Angel's altitude increased and street blocks became small cubes. The Mercedes wove through a maze of narrow streets and came to a stop at a four-lane street. "They're headed out of Ishbiliya on Quds Street. I wanted to see the guy on the bike one more time before I stayed with the Mercedes."

Angel circled back. Payton watched the motorcyclist weave in and out of roundabouts and squares.

"He's entered Rusafa, an old business district along the river. I didn't want to lose the Mercedes, so I pulled off."

Angel streaked higher. Endless blocks of houses and narrow streets slipped below her. "They're on Abu Ghraib Expressway," Rammer said.

Payton saw the cracked sunroof move fast in light outbound traffic. Inbound traffic was still bumper-to-bumper for miles because of the extra military security put in place once the bank runs started to get out of hand.

"The expressway turns into Highway One, then becomes Highway Ten and runs west through Fallujah toward Ramadi and Anbar Province all the way to Syria. Here's where they moved out of Angel's range, so I went back to try to find the motorcycle."

Angel soared over the river.

"Any ideas where they're headed?" Payton asked.

"If it was me, somewhere in Anbar," Rammer said.

"The bad news, Anbar's fifty thousand plus square miles," Cleveland said.

"Zaki and Marco will know where to hide. Their father and grandfather were smugglers based in Anbar near the Syrian border," Payton said.

"I knew it was the motorcyclist from the school by how he sits with his knees almost to the handle bars," Rammer said.

Payton saw the motorcycle speed over one of the Tigris River bridges.

"He's on the Ahar Bridge close to the Green Zone," Cleveland said.

In seconds, the bike was over the bridge and slowed at the Green Zone wall next to Jamal Abdul Nasser Square. He veered left at the guarded security entrance onto a dirt road. With the wall to his right and houses on his left, he

U-turned at a bluff above the river and drove behind the houses to one closest to the wall, where he slid to a stop, jumped off, and disappeared inside.

"I contacted an Air Force Major Gunstler at Camp Jackson, a base north of Baghdad. Air controllers there coordinate with drone operators in Nevada, of all places. I told him we needed immediate air surveillance to find the Mercedes. He asked on whose authority, and I said the embassy's regional security officer, Catherine McCabe. I hope she doesn't mind. Fifteen minutes later he called and said General Qwen's instructions are, whatever Catherine asked for, do it," Rammer said.

"I want to see when they came out of the school again," Payton said.

Rammer reversed.

"Slow it down," Payton said.

The guy with the helmet strode toward the motorcycle, followed by the two men with Ben. Then the last guy went to the front passenger door. Something about the way this guy walked.

Payton pointed to the screen. "Magnify him."

The image expanded on the one at the open passenger door who watched Ben struggle before he was shoved into the trunk.

"I can't do any better," Rammer said.

Payton didn't need to see anymore.

"Hello, Marco," he said and went to the door. "Catherine needs to know Ben's alive before she meets with Ambassador Rhodes and General Qwen. How many of our agents are still in the Green Zone searching for Vicar, Otto, and the brothers?"

"Not many. Ambassador Rhodes told her the military asked for all available embassy security personnel to be redeployed to BUI branches," Cleveland said.

"Then call Quinn. Have him pull his men off the search. I want them to join us when we take the house with the motorcyclist. I'll meet you in front of the embassy in thirty minutes," he said and left.

CHAPTER 38

EMBASSY

"HE'S ALIVE?" Catherine asked.

She stood in front of a wall map with scattered red BUI bank-run flags.

"Thanks again to Rammer and his drone, we know one of them disappeared into a house close to the river entrance gate," Payton said. He pointed to the houses and dirt road tight against the Green Zone wall. "We leave in fifteen minutes for the house."

"Where's Zaki if Marco's in the Mercedes?" Catherine asked.

"We haven't found him," Payton said. He waved over Anbar's vast expanse. "Rammer told the air force you requested a drone fly over Anbar to find the Mercedes."

"I did?"

"And with any luck, they'll find the car."

"Ambassador Rhodes said General Qwen wants to be informed when you bring the brothers in. He wants to micromanage any political fallout." She held up her finger and thumb with a tiny space between them. "We're this close to free elections. The first time in generations Iraqis will choose their own leader, and these two low-life brothers can ruin all of it. The president and Ordway don't want what Zaki and Marco are involved with to diminish Khleifat's shot at the gold ring," she said.

"I'll leave Political Science 101 up to you. Either way, those two are through, and if Khleifat goes down with them, too bad," Payton said.

"You heard Ambassador Rhodes, no surprises. Do you have any idea where Graham and Otto are?"

"Vicar's at a meeting outside the Green Zone. When we find him, Otto won't be far behind," he said.

Catherine pointed to a flag. "Another BUI branch was firebombed last night in Al Hillah. Four more dead Iraqis," she said.

"How close is the nearest Titan United operation?" he asked.

She slid her finger over. "FOB Idaho, a kilometer and a half away with an ice truck and two million in supernotes."

"Ben discovered Stanly's frozen money and went to see Mifflin because he didn't trust Dale with the information," he said.

"Without an appointment, so she didn't listen to him," she said.

"You helped place him with ESM. That's why he left you a message. What if he did tell Mifflin?"

"About what he found in Stanly? Then she'd have Graham and Otto thrown in jail," she said.

"Maybe not. She'd be sent packing once it got out she handed over a fortune in contracts to a corrupt company. She's either clueless or wants us to believe she is," he said.

"You heard her. Titan United's subcontractors are to blame," she said.

"Consider the bigger picture. Who benefits the most if Iraq craters?"

"The Iranians?"

"They use Zaki and Marco's hawala system and Titan United to put supernotes into the financial system," Payton said.

"You believe Titan United's connected to the Iranians?"

"Iran's raised the use of proxies to an art form. Phony companies might be another proxy they use."

"Do you have any proof Titan United's an Iranian front company?" she asked.

"Not yet."

"I wonder if the Green Zone spy that Yusuf al-Dawud told Gabe about is involved with the supernotes and Titan United," she said.

"Otto and Vicar might have something to add to any Iranian spy discussion," he said.

"Ben could run out of time if we have to chase down another rabbit hole the size of Anbar Province," she said.

"They've kept him alive for a reason. I don't think they plan to kill him."

"*They?* Marco and who else?" she asked.

"We confirmed Otto was in Stanly to oversee the padded head count scheme. I don't believe Vicar's pulling the strings at Titan United. Otto's the main guy. He orchestrated Wade and Dale being taken out because they knew Ben found the supernotes. They almost succeeded with Leah."

"Otto found out Ben discovered the supernotes and arranged for him to disappear?"

"He was the guy in the second-story room we saw interrogate Ben. They need something from Ben he hasn't told them."

"The brothers and Otto are behind the supernotes with the Iranians," she said and opened a side desk drawer. "And here we've doled out millions to Titan United."

"Titan United's people are even on Ambassador Rhodes's security," he said.

"Which I plan to fix. They'd have to know we'll get the bank-run situation under control. What was achieved besides scores of dead Iraqis and a few burned bank buildings?"

"I don't know yet."

"Mifflin's in the dark with Titan United," she said.

"Or she doesn't want to face reality."

"Why?" she asked.

"For starters, a ruined career for not catching a corrupt contractor the size of Titan United."

"She can join the list of everyone else Titan United deceived," she said.

"Ben being at the river and tea shop's a fabrication. He was taken because of the supernotes. They smuggled him out through one of the entrance gates or a tunnel," he said.

"The same tunnel where the weed was found?"

"Or another one."

She pulled up her holstered SIG. "The guy on the motorcy-cle will know where we can find Ben," she said and strapped on the thigh holster.

He didn't want her to take unnecessary risks and join him. Besides, she had her hands full with Ambassador Rhodes and General Qwen. Were his feelings for her not so deeply buried after all?

"I'll take the house. We have no idea—"

She stood. "No idea what?"

"Who knows what we'll run into?"

"I hope Ben. You don't need to tell me my job. Let's go."

CHAPTER 39

THE HOUSE

PAYTON AND CATHERINE hurried past Post One and climbed into Quinn's Humvee.

"Your motorcyclist hasn't left the house," Quinn said from the front passenger seat.

They sped toward the Damascus Square security checkpoint. Cleveland, Blacknife, Carl, and more MPs followed in two Humvees.

Minutes later they drove through the security gate and went right on Qahira Street toward Mat Haf Square. Through the square they veered onto Thawar Street and entered Jamal Abdul Nasser Square's roundabout and sped along the dirt road parallel to the Green Zone wall.

Up ahead Payton saw the river and houses and how close they were to the wall.

"Have you seen anyone in the house?" he asked while Catherine took a call from Ambassador Rhodes's assistant.

"My people say it appears empty," Quinn said.

Their driver slowed and pulled into an abandoned gas station. Inside, several MPs gathered around an enlarged satellite photograph spread over a discarded desk. A sergeant pointed to the houses on the photograph. Payton saw the short dead-end alley the motorcyclist used behind the houses. The Green Zone wall was less than a hundred yards from their front doors.

"These two are occupied and the others are vacant. The guy on the bike went into the circled house."

One of the houses where the wall angled away from the river was circled in black.

"We'll take the front," Payton said.

Quinn nodded.

TWO TEAMS OF MPS RAN over garbage-strewn vacant lots and veered toward the alley. Payton, Catherine, Blacknife, and Carl jogged along the dirt road next to the security wall. Their backup team of three MPs followed. In a Humvee, Cleveland and Quinn rolled to a stop halfway between the house and gas station.

Payton saw the one-story house was constructed of irregular stone with a bad mortar job. A cement wall surrounded the barren dirt front yard. Several yards from the front door, a dog chain snaked beside an iron pipe hammered into the ground.

Curtains were pulled shut across the only window to the left of the door.

Blacknife and Payton took up positions between the window and door. Opposite them, Catherine stood behind Carl, against the wall. She held her SIG straight-armed. "Go," she said in a low voice into her radio to Quinn's men in the alley.

Blacknife reached over and turned the knob. It didn't move. Payton motioned with his head to Carl.

Carl stepped over and kicked the door beside the handle. Wood splintered when it flew in.

With the Mini Uzi up, Payton rushed left, tight behind Blacknife. Carl and Catherine followed and went right.

A flash, then, like being hit by a truck, Payton slammed to the floor.

The explosion blew Carl up against the interior wall. Catherine flew back out the door. Blacknife, a few steps down a hallway, was shielded from most of the blast.

Thick smoke clouded over them. Another explosion from the rear shook the house, followed by screams.

Acrid gunpowder filled Payton's nostrils and he choked on a metallic rush at the back of his throat. Covered in dust and debris, he heaved himself up and found Carl, who sat with his back against the wall. Blacknife joined him.

"You alright?" Payton asked. His ears rang from the explosion.

Carl didn't respond.

He didn't see Catherine. Where was she?

"Out here," an MP yelled.

"Take care of him," he said to Blacknife and ran out.

Catherine lay on her side beside the iron pipe and chain with her left leg at an odd angle under her body. Payton joined two MPs who crouched beside her.

She moaned. "My shoulder …," she said.

"Better your shoulder than your hard head," he said with a forced smile. The ringing in his ears started to dissipate. He glanced down and saw a piece of metal shrapnel the size of a stubby pencil protruding from the Kevlar vest near her heart. Another MP joined them. "I'm a medic," he said.

She grimaced in pain.

Payton balled his right hand into a fist. If he discovered Otto or Vicar were responsible, he'd bring his wrath down on them.

"Boss," Blacknife said from the doorway.

Payton gently brushed a dirt smudge from her cheek. The medic started to work on her.

"I'll be right back," he said.

Inside, Carl still sat against the wall and sipped from a plastic bottle of water. Payton gave him thumbs-up and he nodded. "How is she?" Carl asked in a weak voice.

"She's tough like you," Payton said.

He and Blacknife picked their way toward the kitchen, where a young MP with a nasty chest wound lay on the floor. Quinn knelt beside another MP, who sat on the floor in the corner with a hideous four-inch wood splinter buried above his ear. Payton put his hand on Quinn's shoulder.

"He was only nineteen. Arrived last week for his first tour," Quinn said.

Cleveland hobbled into the kitchen from the front of the house. "Whoever planted the front door bomb must've been in a hurry. Their trigger timer was off. Otherwise, all four of you would be dead," he said as he surveyed the carnage and pointed with his cane to a destroyed broom closet. "The blast back here came from there. Have you checked the basement?"

Payton stepped over and pulled the basement door off the hinge it hung by and leaned it against the wall. An MP handed him a flashlight. He checked for trip wires and started down.

Opposite the flight of wooden stairs, a rock-and-dirt cave-in filled half the undersized empty room. He scanned with the light upward over the debris and saw a wire fed through eye hooks screwed into a support beam. The wire disappeared into a hole drilled in the ceiling.

Cleveland joined them.

Payton heard the muffled ambulance siren in front of the house.

"They're here for Catherine," Cleveland said.

Payton showed Cleveland the eye hooks, handed him the flashlight, and took the stairs two at a time.

Medics had Catherine on a stretcher at the open rear doors of a military ambulance. "Her collarbone's broken and she might have a fractured skull," one of the medics said. "The Kevlar vest saved her life. I gave her something for the pain."

Payton bent over and held her hand. "You'll be okay," he said.

She flinched when they lifted her and fed the stretcher inside.

Payton pushed both doors closed. "Easy," he said under his breath and took a deep inhale to focus his rage.

"Whoever rigged the house didn't plan on any survivors," the medic driver said.

"They'll pay when I find them," Payton said.

The driver climbed in and pulled away.

When Payton came down the steps he saw Cleveland watching Blacknife and an MP move rocks from the cave-in. Cleveland looked at Payton and slid his cane into a golf ball-sized hole. "You were right. They have another tunnel."

Now Payton knew why they'd chosen the house. It was the closest to the security wall. "Ben could've been moved through here undetected. The guy on the motorcycle is inside the Green Zone. Get an explosive disposal unit down here," he said.

FIFTY MINUTES LATER, a bomb disposal unit member dressed in a heavy suit stepped over the rubble out of the tunnel and came back into the basement with a leashed Dutch Shepherd dog. The woman lifted a bulky helmet off her head and rubbed the dog behind the ears. "You're clear of explosives, though Sally here detected trace amounts of drugs all through the tunnel," she said.

"Unless we find another tunnel, this is how Zaki and Marco moved dope inside. No security checkpoint guards or drug-sniffing dogs to deal with," Cleveland said.

"And how they could smuggle Ben out," Payton said. He stooped and went into the low-ceilinged tunnel, followed by Blacknife.

He'd gone about seventy-five yards when he came to a sharp right turn where a rope ladder disappeared up into a shaft. One wobbly rung after another he went up to an iron cover over the top of the shaft where sunlight glimmered around the edges. With a heave, he toppled the cover over and climbed out into a narrow alley. It was the same alley he'd followed Otto into. Blacknife came out behind him.

"Don't know how we missed it," Blacknife said.

"Here's why," Payton said, and kicked the iron manhole cover with crushed brick and rock mortared to one side.

"I'll be right back," Payton said. He went to the crowded food vendor stalls. A legless beggar sat on a wooden-wheeled cart next to a stall mounded with dates. He held a filthy plastic bowl with a few pieces of change up to Payton.

"Did you see a man come out of here today?" Payton asked in Arabic and pointed back to the alley. He bent over and dropped a twenty into his bowl.

The beggar nodded with one large tooth in his smile.

"He can't hear you," a woman said. She placed avocados in neat rows and looked at Payton with suspicious eyes through her slitted hijab.

"Did you see a man?" Payton came over to her.

In silence, she lined each avocado.

"If you did, you might help save Iraqi lives," Payton said.

"Save Iraqi lives." She scoffed. "You invade our country, and every day we hear more rumors of fake money Americans put into our banks. Keep your worthless money."

He laid a fifty on her counter. She paused, and with a quick hand movement, the bill was under her jilbab and she was back to her avocados. "The man was tall with light curly hair and wore gold glasses," she said.

Payton went back to Blacknife. "Graham Vicar was on the motorcycle. Let's go," he said.

Blacknife went down first and Payton followed him.

Vicar came out of the tunnel and knew the house was rigged with explosives. Otto would also know. If Jack Underhill was right, Mifflin and Vicar were in a relationship, then maybe she sat on those twelve fraud memos for some other reason than to protect her reputation.

They followed the tunnel another sixty yards deeper into the Green Zone, went up a slight incline, and came to the end. A square piece of wood was fitted over a hole above them. Payton handed his flashlight to Blacknife and pushed up. They were in the corner of a warehouse.

They climbed out and surveyed rows of empty racks. Payton motioned, and Blacknife with his M4 carbine up went to the right. Payton moved through the racks.

Blacknife joined him when he stepped out into an open area at the end of the racks. They moved left toward a white sheetrock structure with a single window built close to several dock doors.

Payton glanced through the window and saw kitchen equipment. No one inside. He opened the personnel door into a fully equipped institutional kitchen that, like the warehouse, had never been used. They checked the walk-in cooler and freezer. Both empty.

"Over there," Blacknife said and pointed out the window.

Payton saw a blue tarp-covered mound by the dock doors.

They stepped over and Blacknife threw back a corner of the tarp. Dozens of black bags with cloth handles were heaped in a pile. Blacknife lifted one and pulled the zipper. C-notes were jammed inside. "I guess we found where they stored the supernotes," Blacknife said.

Payton counted over five dozen bags.

"Get Cleveland," he said.

CHAPTER 40

GREEN ZONE

RAMMER EXITED THE lead Humvee and came over to Payton, who stood with Blacknife in front of Titan United's headquarters building. Carl followed with several embassy marines.

"The actual warehouse Titan United uses to supply their FOB operations is located on the opposite side of the Green Zone from the one you found. Cleveland questioned a Titan United controller we brought in. He said Otto's Special Situations Group leased the off-the-books warehouse you found from a shell corporation connected to the al-Dulaimis. Rent checks are sent to a Damascus-based financial institution," Rammer said.

Payton remembered something Kuttic mentioned. "Kuttic said the Quds Force controls a Syrian bank located in Damascus where Iran's leadership stashes money outside Iran. See what bank receives the rent checks. We may have found the Iranian connection."

"Could the brothers be connected to the Iranians?" Rammer asked.

"If their rent money turns up in a Quds Force-controlled bank, you tell me."

So the brothers, if they're involved with the Iranians and Otto and Vicar, how much of a leap would it be to consider money the United States pays Titan United finds its way back to the mullahs? Or worse, the Quds Force uses our money to help fund their efforts to bring down Iraq. "How were the supernotes transported to Otto's Special Situation Group locations from that warehouse?"

"Hidden under kitchen supplies in Titan United delivery trucks. Titan United vehicles are waved through army checkpoints without being inspected, thanks to the security clearance Colonel Mifflin gave the company," Rammer said.

Payton wanted to know, with a dozen fraud memos, why she'd given Vicar a get-out-of-jail card and not revoked the company's security clearance.

"Catherine said Titan United will pull down seventy plus million this year," Payton said.

"Closer to eighty. The Special Situations Group alone will rake in north of twelve million. It wasn't until Colonel Mifflin arrived that Titan United started to rack up contracts. Twenty-seven in total, and eight are no-bid solesource contracts," Rammer said.

"A free ride," Payton said.

"Let's say the Iranians are somehow involved. Do you think Otto had any idea where the warehouse rent money ended up?" Rammer asked.

"He and Vicar aren't fools. That's why they're on the run."

"Ben's frozen money discovery threw a wrench in the whole supernote operation," Rammer said.

"Dale and Wade were killed because they knew too much," Payton said.

"Cleveland told me to tell you he hasn't been able to confirm if Mifflin and Graham have more going on than just business," Rammer said.

"There's a reason she favored Vicar with all those contracts. Let's go," Payton said.

On the second floor, Payton stopped at the desk of the surprised young woman sitting outside Vicar's office.

"Where is he?"

She started to get up. "You don't have the right to barge in here," she said with a Scottish accent so thick Payton had a hard time understanding her.

"Where. Is. He?"

"Who are you people?"

"Diplomatic investigators."

"I have to call my—"

Payton swept several files off her desk and leaned toward her. "Where?"

She sat back down. "He left on a company helicopter earlier today to inspect Forward Operating Base kitchens," she said.

"Why didn't you tell my people when they were here earlier?"

"I only found out a short while ago."

"Flew where?"

"Anbar Province."

"Call Cleveland and tell him to track Vicar's helicopter," Payton said to Rammer. To Blacknife and Carl, "Secure the building."

He went into Vicar's office. The BBC News played on a wall-mounted television. A laminated map of Iraq was spread over an oval conference table. White and black dots indicated Titan United operations. "Foodservice" was written next to a black dot in the upper right corner. Below it was a white dot for Special Situations.

Rammer joined him. Payton picked up the remote and muted the television. "General Qwen's office instructed every camp commander where Titan United has staff to put them under guard and confiscate their computers and cell phones," Rammer said.

Payton moved his finger from one Special Situation location to another. "Fallujah, Basra, Amarah, Najif, Al Kut, Nasiriyah, Mosul, and Hillah. All Otto's operations, and every one of them except Fallujah has had a bank run."

"I haven't finished with all the BUI deposit histories, but I've found two with large amounts of cash being deposited by hawala brokers. Al Kut three million, Hillah over four million," Rammer said.

"And no one at BUI had an issue with large cash deposits?"

"Not when the depositors are Hawala brokers."

"If similar amounts are being put in other BUI branches, that means tens of millions of supernotes are already in the banking system," Payton said.

"Ben's hard drive had audits he and Leah completed for the Basra and Nasiriyah branches," Rammer said.

"Any problems?" Payton asked.

He shook his head. "They signed off on them. These supernotes in BUI are financial IEDs."

"The BUI bank riots will be pocket change compared to what'll happen when the rest of the population realizes how much counterfeit money has been fed into their money supply," Payton said.

"Cleveland said you wanted to know about the Al Kut guy with the megaphone. I spoke with the marine captain in charge. One of the Iraqis they detained told him the megaphone guy yelled at the crowd that the bank passed out counterfeit money for the United States. He's a semiprominent sheik with a reputation for anti-American rhetoric. When the marines went to bring him in, they discovered he'd flown to Qatar."

"Convenient time to leave the country," Payton said.

Rammer's cell phone rang. He listened and pressed the speaker button, then held the phone up.

Cleveland said from the phone, "Vicar's helicopter landed in FOB Lynchpin in Ar-Rutbah in western Anbar Province, where a Stryker brigade and several British armor units are based. Lynchpin's commander said Vicar wasn't in Titan United's office when he sent security to take him into custody. He did say one of his Iraqi interpreters can't find his motorcycle."

"What about an ice truck?" Payton asked.

"It was parked behind the kitchen with eight hundred grand in four blocks of ice."

Payton studied the map. "Where's Lynchpin?"

"Fifteen kilometers northwest of Ar-Rutbah," Cleveland said.

Payton saw a white Special Situations Group dot next to Ar-Rutbah.

"By the way, your South African Recces Otto enjoys Cuban cigars. Which puts him on a very short list of suspects who could've been on the roof across from the tea shop," Cleveland said.

"A list of one," Payton said.

Cleveland's desk telephone rang in the background. "Hold on." He said something to whoever was on the other telephone.

"Otto could have blown the shop to make Wade's story more plausible," Rammer said.

Cleveland, back on the cell phone, said, "Gunstler says his drones have flown along the expressway all the way to the Syrian border. No luck with the Mercedes. He has one drone north of Al Qaim near the border and another one hundred and thirty-five miles southwest of Nukhaib."

Rammer pointed to both drone locations.

"Tell Gunstler to forget Marco and the Mercedes. I want to focus on Vicar. He's on a stolen motorcycle near Ar-Rutbah going in the same direction the Mercedes with Ben and Marco is headed. Get one of those drones after him," Payton said.

Cleveland spoke on the other phone, then said back to Payton and Rammer, "You've got one drone for two hours before it needs to be refueled."

"Tell Gunstler to find that motorcycle."

Cleveland signed off.

Payton surveyed the map. "You're Marco, where do you go with Ben?"

Rammer ran his finger along the border. "The topography all through here is South Dakota Badlands. Nothing but cliffs, switchbacks, and canyons. Bedouin tribesmen are the only inhabitants who've lived out there for generations. If I wanted to disappear, I'd go there."

"How long would it take them?" Payton asked.

"A couple of hours at the outside. If they cross into Syria, we'll never find them."

"Not a smart move. Syrian border patrols are trigger happy," Payton said.

He looked at the vastness of Anbar Province, home to the al-Dulaimi family's smuggling business.

"Look," Rammer said. He took the remote and turned up the volume.

"A mob of Iraqis marched on a Bank of United Iraq branch in the northern Iraq city of Tal Afar today," said the BBC newsreader.

A crowd chanted anti-American slogans behind a reporter. One of them picked up a tear gas canister and threw it somewhere off-camera.

The newsreader continued, "After several hours of demonstrations, the bank manager was pulled into the street where he was shot and killed, and the building was firebombed. Shots were fired when marines arrived. Five Iraqis were killed and twenty-one wounded. No marine casualties. Rumors of counterfeit money being disbursed from BUI have spread in many other cities. BUI is the only US-endorsed financial institution in the country. One of my sources told me military commanders are concerned Iraq might slip back into war because of these bank riots."

"Death to America!" a man screamed as he flapped open an American flag. It floated down over a body set on fire, then disintegrated in the flames. A young boy tossed a handful of money at the body. The bills fluttered into ashes.

Rammer's cell phone rang. He pressed speaker again.

"We got lucky, wait a second," Cleveland said and put them on hold, then clicked back on. "Go."

"A Chinook helicopter pilot heard our alert about a motorcyclist in western Anbar. He might've ID'd your guy. Are you near a computer? I'll give you the link to access the drone's optics," Gunstler said from Cleveland's other phone.

Rammer set the cell phone on the desk and pulled out the keyboard. "I'm on," he said toward the cell phone, typing while Gunstler spoke.

On the monitor screen Payton saw an overhead camera view of a motorcycle with a rooster tail of dust on a ruler-straight desert road.

"Got him. Cleveland, you have him?" Rammer asked.

Several seconds later Cleveland said, "I'm there."

"He's twenty kilometers northwest of Wadi Ubaila, headed west," Gunstler said.

"Can you zoom down?" Payton said. He watched the guy on the bike come into clearer focus. Sunlight reflected off gold glasses below a thick mop of curly hair and lanky legs folded up on the bike's footrests. "It's Vicar," Payton said.

"He's eight kilometers from the border," Gunstler said.

"Vehicle from the west. Two minutes to intercept," the drone operator said.

The computer screen split in two. Vicar on one side, a car on the other. White script along the bottom indicated their speed. Vicar sixty kph, car fifty-five kph. Vicar started to slow … fifty … forty-five kph.

"He sees the car now," Rammer said.

Thirty-five kph.

"You looking for a cracked sunroof?" Gunstler asked.

The image zoomed in closer. It was the same car they'd seen with Rammer's plane.

"That's our car," Cleveland said.

Vicar stopped beside the Mercedes. With his feet on the ground, he motioned west. Whoever was inside stayed there.

"Gun, rear window," the drone operator said.

Payton saw the barrel of a gun stick out the rear driver's side window.

Vicar fishtailed and sped away. The driver reversed into a cloud of dust and accelerated after the motorcycle.

Payton saw their speed increase. Sixty-eight … seventy-five … eighty-three kph.

Vicar was bent forward.

The car gained on him. Flash, flash from the front passenger window. More flashes from both back windows.

At ninety kph Vicar started to slow and careen out of control. Seconds later, he swerved over an embankment and flew several yards. The bike went one way and Vicar the other.

The Mercedes slid to a stop. The driver and three men from the rear seat climbed out.

The drone operator magnified by twenty-five percent.

They ran toward Vicar, sprawled next to several jagged rocks.

Payton recognized the shaved head of a man who came out of the front passenger seat. "Otto," he said.

Vicar rolled over and knelt with his hands raised. Payton watched him plead. Otto said something to him, then with his arm extended, shot Vicar in the head. Vicar fell backward. Otto and his men returned to the Mercedes and sped off.

"Marco's not in the car," Payton said.

"He was when they left the city," Rammer said.

Payton watched the Mercedes.

"What direction are they going?" he asked.

"Where they came from, the west, toward the border," Rammer said.

"Is your man still in the trunk?" Gunstler asked.

"Let's hope he is and they didn't dump his body somewhere," Cleveland said.

"He's not dead. They've kept him alive for a reason," Payton said. He leaned toward the cell phone. "Don't lose them."

"How'd they know where to find Graham? He's been on the bike for less than an hour," Rammer said.

"Vicar called Otto or someone else who told Otto where to find him," Cleveland said.

"Why would Otto kill him?" Rammer asked.

"Maybe Vicar got cold feet," Cleveland said.

"Or like Dale and Wade, he can't talk if he's dead," Payton said.

"No loose ends," Cleveland said.

"Where's our nearest base?" Payton asked.

"Al Jid, fifty miles southeast," Gunstler said.

"How long before we can have someone to Vicar's location?" Payton asked.

"Under two hours," Gunstler said. He paused and spoke in a low voice to one of his people.

"Otto has to know we have drones up along the border," Payton said to Rammer, then listened to the drone operators' background chatter.

Gunstler came back on. "If they go into Syria, we can't follow them. The Syrian air force won't tolerate a violation of their airspace. They've shot down two drones in the last eighteen months to prove their point. I won't lose another one."

"Don't pull off the Mercedes," Payton said.

"If they cross the border and that drone goes down, it's on you."

"I'll take the heat."

"Border, two minutes," the drone operator said.

Payton watched them speed through a narrow valley with rock walls and accelerate on a narrow dirt road out into the open. Beyond a river to the west, a village appeared.

"Abu Kamal, they're in Syria," Gunstler said.

For the next few minutes they watched the Mercedes race toward the village.

BEEP … BEEP … BEEP.

"Radar contact. We're being tracked," Gunstler said.

Payton bent closer to the phone. "Stay with them."

"I don't like this," Gunstler said.

The car hurtled toward the village, then the screen went fuzzy. "We lost the drone. Ladd, you'd better have some serious juice up the chain of command," Gunstler said.

"Direct any blowback my way," Payton said.

He had to get to Abu Kamal.

CHAPTER 41

IBN SINA HOSPITAL

PAYTON CAME INTO Catherine's room and saw Ambassador Rhodes conferring with one of two nurses at the foot of her bed.

The second nurse saw Payton.

She adjusted Catherine's IV. Her nametag read "Martyna, Warsaw Poland."

"Both of you will have to leave," Martyna from Warsaw said. "She needs sleep."

"We'll only be a few minutes," Rhodes said.

"Yes, you will," she said and left with the other nurse.

Payton stepped over and held Catherine's hand. An IV needle was taped in place on the back of her other hand.

"She has a serious concussion and her collarbone was broken in two places," Rhodes said.

Payton pushed the thought away that if she'd hit the stake with her head they wouldn't be here right now. She'd be dead.

"How do you feel?" he asked.

"Whatever's in the drip works," she said in a weak voice.

"You need anything?"

"Ben being found would be a good start," she said.

"What's the latest?" Rhodes asked.

"We believe he's in western Anbar Province or a village over the border in Syria. I'm going there when I leave here." Payton told them about Otto, Vicar, and the Mercedes in Syria.

"You get caught in Syria, you're on your own," Rhodes said.

"I think they plan to circle back."

"How have you connected Titan United's director of operations and the tea shop?" Rhodes asked.

"He used a roof across the street to put an RPG or bazooka round into the shop," Payton said.

"His background's with the Recces South African Special Forces. Several men who served with him are on Titan United's payroll," Catherine said.

"They're trained killers," Payton said.

"Otto's behind the supernotes and Ben being kidnapped?" Rhodes asked.

"With help from Zaki and Marco al-Dulaimi, who are involved with the Iranians," Payton said.

"Don't tell me the Iranians are also mixed up in this," Rhodes said.

Rammer had called Payton before he arrived at the hospital to tell him about Zaki and Marco's shell company, the Syrian bank, and the rent checks. Kuttic told Cleveland the bank was a Quds Force front company.

"The leased Titan United warehouse where we found the supernotes is owned by a shell company controlled by the brothers. The off-the-books rent Vicar and Otto paid them ended up in a Damascus financial institution controlled by the Iranian Quds Force," Payton said.

"Are you saying the fortune we pay Titan United finds its way to Iran?" Rhodes asked.

"The CIA confirmed the Syrian bank is a Quds Force operation."

"We know Iranians are involved with their introduction of these EFPs, but an all-out war against Iraq's financial system with supernotes is something else," Rhodes said.

"They have the motivation, means, and North Korean contacts. Cleveland used the analogy we could be in the middle of an Iranian Tet Offensive," Payton said.

"We'll crush them," Rhodes said.

"Tet was a military victory for the United States, but destroyed American public opinion for the war," Payton said.

"Why did they want to kill Ben in the tea shop?"

"He wasn't there. They knew we'd focus on his drug use and sales. Him being in the Red Zone for drugs was a ruse to draw our attention away from his audit work."

"Why kill Graham?" Rhodes asked.

"We're not sure," Payton said.

"What about the security contractor who said he was with Ben? The Route Irish bomb was meant for him?" Rhodes asked.

"Wade caught a bad break when Ben found the supernotes. Otto and whoever he's involved with didn't want to risk their supernote scheme would be discovered. They eliminated anyone who might pose a threat."

"Like Ben's boss, Dale Lowsley," Catherine said.

"Dale's job was to keep his auditors away from the frozen supernotes in Titan United facilities. He dropped the ball when Ben found the ice truck. Otto didn't want to chance Dale would crack once we put pressure on him," Payton said.

"The military has marshaled thousands of troops from all over the country to stop the spread of these bank runs," Rhodes said.

"It may be too late. BUI isn't the only place supernotes have turned up. The al-Dulaimis operate Iraq's largest hawala broker system. Their brokers made the BUI supernote deposits and distributed them throughout their hawala system."

"Why the bank and the hawala system?" Rhodes asked.

"To guarantee their plan to crash the financial system worked. Take down two financial institutions Iraqis have faith in. Between the hawala system and BUI, tens of millions of supernotes have been put into Iraq's economy," Payton said.

"If these riots spread, the military may put the elections on hold," Rhodes said.

"No elections would hand Iran what they want," Payton said.

"More bank riots are being broadcast on the nightly news every day. Sooner or later, the American people will say enough is enough," she said.

"Kuttic told me a high-level Green Zone spy who passes information to the Iranians might also be involved with Ben's disappearance and the supernotes," Payton said.

"I'll alert the FBI's spy hunters," Rhodes said.

"When does the one point three billion arrive?" Payton asked.

"Day after tomorrow. A team from the US Treasury Department along with Iraqi treasury officials and BUI executives will distribute the money from BUI's headquarters. On Qwen's orders, military commanders will be at each branch with local politicians and sheiks to assure Iraqis we have the situation under control," Rhodes said.

"Tell Qwen he needs brokers who aren't involved with Zaki and Marco's hawala system to be at those branches when the money arrives," Payton said.

"Is Colonel Mifflin in charge of cash transfers to BUI?" Catherine asked.

"She and the convoy commander make the decision what route to take," Rhodes said.

"I spoke with Bob Young in Washington, and he said Pentagon administrators are so pleased with how she managed to put the contractor program back in order, she'll be promoted when her tour ends," she said.

"A debacle with Titan United should put an end to any promotion talk," Payton said.

"Leave those with me," Martyna said from the doorway. An embassy courier stood outside with several files for Catherine.

"She works all the time," Payton said and looked at Catherine, who'd closed her eyes.

"Not today, she doesn't," Martyna said.

CHAPTER 42

WESTERN IRAQ

WHEN THEIR HELICOPTER landed in Al Jid, Payton, Carl, and Blacknife were greeted by Major Patrick Huff, a cavalry commander of a squadron of Apache helicopters. Payton and the two marines went to Huff's office next to a firing range.

"We have a group of special operators, Seals, British SAS, and a few Green Berets we call on from time to time, to tidy up along the border when our Syrian friends get chippy. They'll take you over the border. Perfect flying conditions tonight. You'll be in the operators camp in under an hour," Huff said.

THE PILOT FLEW low and fast, and Payton watched the star-lit desert out of the open side door.

He didn't think Ben was still in Baghdad. Marco and Otto would want to keep him close. He had to be in the Mercedes. Besides, what better place to hide him than Syria or western Anbar Province? He saw Baghdad's glow on the far eastern horizon when they arched west toward Syria.

What would be the Iranians' endgame? They had to know we'd flood the financial system with more cash to stabilize BUI and a compromised hawala system. Was their goal to create enough financial carnage to delay the elections? He had the uneasy feeling a piece was missing.

Forty-five minutes west of Al Jid, their helicopter slowed, hovered, and landed. Hundreds of stars gave off enough light for Payton to see a cluster of sizable boulders surrounded by a sea of flat desert. They tossed their gear out, leaped down, and ninety seconds later the helicopter lifted and disappeared.

They were met by a cold breeze.

A bearded man who carried a machine gun emerged from the boulders. "Follow me," he said.

He was of medium height and from his ragged appearance must've been out here for a long time.

They grabbed their gear, and he led them through the boulders down a narrow footpath into a depression where Payton saw several more grizzled men. "Put your gear over there and join us at the maps," the guide said. He pointed to a smokeless fire on the edge of a smooth, flat area with tall boulders on three sides.

A few men cleaned their weapons.

Two men joined them in front of a minivan-sized boulder with maps attached to it. One of the men snapped on a flashlight, and Payton saw an enlarged satellite photograph next to a topography map.

"I'm Plum," their guide said. "Meet Cherry and Apple."

Payton introduced himself and the marines. Cherry was a black guy almost his height, six foot four, with short stubble for a beard. Apple, a stocky Asian who wasn't a pound under 250, had cheerful eyes.

"Ten klicks west of here jihadists have a trail they use to cross into Iraq. We're their Welcome Wagon," Plum said. He pointed to a circled city inside Syria. "They gather on the outskirts of Abu Kamal before they cross the border and disappear into rough terrain on the Iraq side. A no-man's-land, the perfect place to smuggle fighters into Iraq. Major Huff's orders are to take you to Abu Kamal."

"We're after four men in a Mercedes we believe have an American they kidnapped with them. They're involved with these bank runs that have happened all over the country," Payton said.

"Why'd they choose Abu Kamal?" Cherry asked with a Dublin-influenced Irish accent.

"They might know we keep drones up on our side of the border. They go into Syria, lay low, and circle back," Apple said.

"Syria's a police state," Cherry said. "They won't go far. Military's everywhere. They'd have to drive hundreds of miles to make it to Turkey or Jordan. They'll come back our way."

"We have an informer in Abu Kamal who confirmed your Mercedes is there," Plum said. He took a pack of cigarettes and a lighter out of his shirt pocket and lit one. "Omar Deeb, Al Qaeda in Iraq's new leader, arrived yesterday with several men. They're in a mosque on the opposite side of the village from where your kidnappers are holed up inside a house. We've had an operation planned for weeks to take Deeb once he arrived. The men you're after must be important because we received orders to accommodate you three. When we go into Syria, will you boys know how to take care of yourselves?"

Payton smiled. "What do you think, boys?" he asked the marines.

"Another day at the office," Carl said.

CHAPTER 43

AT 3:00 A.M. word spread … time to move.

"Deeb's in the mosque dormitory with his bodyguards," Plum said.

Payton, Blacknife, Carl, and several operators stood in a semicircle. Payton saw grease pencil circles with different team leader names where Plum pointed to Abu Kamal on the satellite map. "Deeb moves at 0600. Cherry and my team will take the house, Apple and Orange the dormitory. Pear, your sniper teams are here and here." Plum indicated a ridgeline with two X's along the border above the river and village. "Our source puts your kidnappers in this house." Plum touched a circle around an X over a house in a group of structures farther east of the dormitory toward the river.

"Could they be part of Omar's group?" another operator asked.

"We don't believe they are," Plum said. "Anyone comes our way, Pear, deal with them. We're out of the village by 05:15."

PAYTON'S WATCH SAID 3:40 a.m. It'd gotten colder and he saw fewer stars now.

If he was Otto, he wouldn't go any deeper into Syria and risk being intercepted by a Syrian military patrol. He agreed with Cherry: they'll come back over the border and disappear somewhere in the rough terrain.

They loaded their gear into modified ATVs with oversized wheels and mounted machine guns.

A shaggy, dark-haired, compact operator who hadn't shaved in days stacked boxes of ammunition into the nearest vehicle.

"Mango," he said and stuck his hand toward Payton.

Payton introduced himself and shook Mango's calloused hand.

"Exceptional morning for killing," Mango said with a toothy smile. He sounded like he was raised in Cajun country.

Payton and Blacknife climbed onto a narrow bench seat behind Plum and his driver. Mango stood in the gun well. They drove in single file with Plum's vehicle out front.

Mango pulled the machine gun's side lever and loaded a belt of finger-sized bullets, then rotated and turned the barrel forward.

They all wore night-vision goggles. Payton noticed how quiet the vehicles were. They sped toward Syria, their way lit by dim bluish headlights. He watched flat terrain give way to several rocky inclines, each taller than the next. They started up one Payton figured was two thousand feet.

Fifteen minutes later Plum turned. "Welcome to Syria," he said.

They drove ten more minutes, then stopped at the edge of a plateau. Payton saw lights clustered in a vast plain below them.

"Abu Kamal," Plum said.

Pear's sniper teams peeled off in opposite directions, and Plum's vehicle started down a rutted trail. At the bottom the trail flattened, and Apple, followed by Orange, veered right and disappeared. Cherry's team followed Plum toward the village, where they pulled to a stop behind a rock cluster a thousand yards from the first group of buildings.

A weak breeze blew from the village. Payton smelled charcoal fire. They rolled forward.

Two hundred yards from the first line of houses, they entered a shallow wadi and snaked back and forth parallel to the houses. Mango pointed the mounted machine gun up to the scrub brush lip several feet above them. Minutes later, they drove a few dozen yards out into the open and stopped behind a thicket of bushes.

They started on foot. Mango stayed behind and covered them.

4:30 A.M. ON Payton's watch.

They stopped when Plum raised his hand. He and Cherry slipped away toward a group of low buildings.

"Move," Plum said through Payton's earpiece.

Yards from the closest house, Payton's group clustered around Cherry and Plum. Plum motioned three of his men forward, and one rapped on a window next to the rear door. Seconds later, the door cracked open and they disappeared inside.

In his earpiece Payton heard confirmation Plum's source was there. Plum rose and one by one they sprinted to the door. Cherry was the last in. Carl stayed outside with another operator.

Through a doorway Payton saw an old man sitting cross-legged on a floor mat. Plum squatted next to him and they spoke in low voices. A few minutes later, Plum unzipped one of his jacket pockets, withdrew a cloth pouch, and shook out several gold coins. Payton watched the man count each coin, then put them inside his robe. He spoke and motioned toward the mosque.

Plum stood. "Seven in the dormitory, eight in the mosque," he said.

"More than we expected," Cherry said.

"Four more joined them before midnight. All Saudis," Plum said.

To Payton, he said, "Your targets are still in the house. They've had no contact with Deeb's men."

They left the house and moved behind several buildings, then stopped beside an eight-foot-high mud wall. An operator went down on all fours, and another stood on his backpack and peered over the wall. He stepped down and nodded to Plum. Two men laced their hands together, and

Plum stepped up and hauled himself over. Payton followed and dropped inside a dirt yard.

Three houses stood close together with a shared courtyard. A rusted fifty-five-gallon drum stood beside the only door of the middle building.

"Go," Plum said into his radio.

Payton heard a muffled explosion on the other side of the village, followed by another, then screams and automatic machine gunfire.

Plum eased the door open, and four of his men disappeared inside. Less than a minute later, one reappeared and said something to Plum, who motioned them inside.

More explosions came from the mosque.

Payton saw four hijab-covered women huddled in a corner of the front room. One whimpered when Plum asked where Otto was. "Where?" Plum asked again with more force.

"No men here," the large one who sounded like a teenager said. She pointed to the house on her left. "They kill man and woman."

"Wrong house. Your targets are next door," Plum said to Payton.

They rushed back into the courtyard. "Apple?" Plum said into his radio.

Payton heard Apple at the mosque say, "One of ours is down, hit in the leg. Five enemy confirmed dead. We're in the mosque's courtyard. I make five more in the dormitory basement."

"Orange?" Plum said.

"Three enemy dead. No more movement," Orange said.

"Apple, can you take the basement?" Plum asked.

Apple said, "Problem, they took women and children with them."

"How many?"

"Can't confirm."

"Is Deeb with them?"

"Affirmative," Apple said.

"Use gas. Do it now," Plum said.

He nodded to Cherry toward the door of the second house. When Cherry reached to open it, Payton heard vehicles speed away from the front of the house.

"Mercedes and jeep moving," one of Pear's sniper team spotters said through Payton's earpiece.

"Don't let them get away," Payton said to Plum.

"Go, Pear," Plum said.

Seconds later, Payton heard one of Pear's sniper rifles from the ridge. The Barretts they used could disable a vehicle from great distances with five-inch brass-tipped bullets.

"Jeep down," Pear said. "Two men got out and are now in the Mercedes."

"Take the Mercedes," Plum said.

"Lost contact. They're in a wadi," Pear said.

"Did they open the Mercedes trunk?" Payton asked into his mic.

"Negative," Pear said. "Contact lost, repeat, contact lost."

"Do they still have Ben?" Blacknife asked Payton.

Payton turned to Plum. "We have to check the house," he said. Plum nodded and sent two operators with Payton and Blacknife.

An operator eased the door open. Tight behind each other, they crouched and rushed inside. Payton saw the dead man and woman in a closet but no Ben.

They rejoined Plum, who said, "I'd run to the mountains and canyons along the border where smugglers have used the topography for decades to hide from Saddam's army."

Marco will know where to hide, Payton thought. His family has made their livelihood from those canyons and hills for years. The time was 4:44 a.m. "We have to go after them now," Payton said.

Plum said into his mic, "Mango, take our visitors after the Mercedes." He turned and spoke to one of his men, then to Payton. "We'll rendezvous back in the wadi."

Plum disappeared toward the mosque with Cherry and the rest of his men. Mango pulled up, and they climbed in and sped away.

A kilometer and a half east, Mango rolled into a ravine. Payton could see in the dim headlights tire tracks disappear around a bend on the dry stream bed. He knew if the Mercedes stayed at the bottom of the ravine, Pear's snipers wouldn't have a shot.

"The ravine cuts straight through toward the border. They'll vanish if they make it back over," Mango said.

"We need to stop them," Payton said.

Mango accelerated through an S curve and approached a crease between two hills where the stream bed disappeared.

Another explosion came from the village, a pause, then an intense firefight erupted. Payton saw an orange glow in the night sky from the mosque.

"Deeb and his men are dead, children and women unharmed," Payton heard Apple say to Plum.

"Eight vehicles approaching from the west," Pear said.

"Mango, break off, repeat, break off," Plum said.

Mango slid to a stop.

"Don't stop. We're too close to them," Payton said.

"They're gone," Mango said.

More gunfire erupted from Abu Kamal. Mango pointed with his thumb to the mounted machine gun. "Do you know how to use one of those?" he asked.

Payton stepped into the well.

Mango made a U-turn.

Payton swung the big gun around to the rear, furious they'd come up empty-handed again. When they regrouped, he'd call Cleveland to tell him he needed another drone.

Mango raced back toward the village.

Payton saw Plum with his men beside a destroyed pickup truck not far from the bushes where they'd left the other vehicle. One of Plum's men lay on his back while another attended to his leg wound.

Mango slid to a stop. Blacknife and Carl moved and sat on the edge of the gun well so the wounded man could be placed on the bench seat. Plum and his men went over to the other vehicle. Both vehicles sped toward the plateau.

Payton heard rapid gunfire from Apple and Orange's direction and saw white tracer bullets arch back toward the village. Two sets of operator vehicle headlights raced toward Mango, who'd started up the incline toward Pear's snipers. Payton heard the Barretts fire again and again.

A quarter of the way up, Mango stopped. Payton swiveled the gun toward the village. Plum's vehicle rolled up past them. Apple and Orange rounded the last wadi bend.

Payton saw several sets of headlights Pear warned them about, speed out of the village.

"Syrian military, five hundred meters," Pear said.

Apple and Orange's teams bounced up past Mango.

Payton figured the Syrians had closed to three hundred meters when he saw flashes from the lead vehicle. Several rounds zipped into the ground next to their rear right tire. He fired, and spent metal bullet casings clanged onto the gun well's floor. His tracers poured into the vehicle out front. The vehicle lurched and stopped.

"Any time now, Pear," Plum said.

The Barretts roared once, twice, three times.

Mango started up.

Payton fired and saw red sparks mushroom out of another vehicle before its lights went out.

Mango came up and over and sped past one of Pear's teams. Payton watched the sniper and his spotter hop up from their prone position, climb into their vehicle, and speed after them.

TWENTY MINUTES LATER they pulled into a shallow wadi inside Iraq. Plum spoke to Cherry, who with another operator drove the wounded man back to their camp.

Plum unfolded a map over the hood of Mango's vehicle.

Payton replaced the radio handset in the other vehicle and came over.

"Your embassy people have any luck with another drone?" Plum asked.

"Too much blowback from the one lost to the Syrian Air Force," Payton said.

"It'll be light in an hour," Plum said. "We'll come back tonight and track them from where they disappeared."

"We can't wait," Payton said. They had to go now.

"We only brought enough fuel to make it to Abu Kamal and back," Plum said.

"Chief, what about the Bedouins?" Mango asked.

Plum considered what Mango said, then clicked on his flashlight and pointed to the map.

"Here's our position. We've had contact with Bedouin tribesmen ten klicks northeast here." He moved his finger north and west into the desert. "They might be persuaded to part with a few camels. If you make their encampment and they're gone, wait for us."

Bedouins or no Bedouins, Payton wouldn't wait. Ben was in those hills, and he wouldn't leave without him.

CHAPTER 44

THE BEDOUINS

SUNLIGHT PIERCED the horizon, and the heat came in a steady slow surge.

Plum had given each of them a black and white checked keffiyeh to wrap around their heads.

They walked in silence for two hours before Mango stopped. "The Bedouins are in those hills," he said.

Through a narrow slit, Payton saw a dark band shimmer in the heat waves across the flat expanse to the west.

Forty-five minutes later, they approached a series of low knolls that gave way to boulder-strewn barren hills.

They made their way to the final and highest hill when Payton saw them. "Men below the ridgeline," he said.

Three armed men stood in a rocky outcrop several feet from the top. A fourth watched their approach through binoculars.

"Aniza Bedouins," Mango said. "Abdul Doka's their leader. He doesn't trust outsiders. I've dealt with him before. He'll speak with me. If your guy's in the border area, Doka will know."

Mango started up. They sank ankle-deep in soft sand. Payton watched the armed men disappear back over the ridge.

They stepped up onto a narrow flat-topped hill and walked to the far side. Below, Payton saw open-sided tents around a campfire pit next to a stream with green foliage-covered banks. Palm trees threw off patches of shade, and camels clustered around a shallow pond beyond the tents.

A cluster of men stared up at them, nine by Payton's quick count and all armed.

Click.

He turned to see five men, each with either an old rifle or AK-47 aimed at them.

"Easy," Mango said, and stepped toward the closest one and spoke with him.

PAYTON WATCHED THE suspicious eyes of their guards. He, Blacknife, and Carl sat on a worn carpet in the shade of two palm trees. Mango was in Doka's spacious tent on the other side of the camp.

"I can take the one with the tennis shoes," Carl said in a low voice.

The guard closest to them was a middle-aged man in tattered dark Nike high-tops with faded red laces. He cradled a rifle in his arms.

Payton shook his head. "Wait," he said.

Fifteen minutes later, Mango rejoined them. "Doka has an idea where they might be. His son took several camels to a salt flat near the border two days ago. When men appeared on a cliff above him, he started back. He was halfway out when a vehicle came from behind and opened fire with a machine gun. They killed his animals. The boy made his way out after midnight. Doka's men on the ridge thought we were the same men. He said he'll show us the way only if he joins us. I tried to talk him out of it, even offered to replace his dead camels, but he insisted."

"We can use the extra guns. When do we leave?" Payton asked.

"Tonight."

"Why the delay? I don't want to lose any more time," Payton said.

"Doka said it's better at night, when we can approach the escarpment without being seen."

THE GUARDS RETURNED their weapons, and women served them pita, hummus, grilled goat meat, and olives in earthen bowls.

After sunset, camels were brought around. Men emerged from their tents with extra ammunition belts across their chests.

Doka, thin and stooped, came out of his tent. His silver-streaked red beard hung to the middle of his chest and he wore a traditional Bedouin turban. He climbed onto his camel and kicked the animal forward.

It was another moonless, star-filled night. They'd traveled several kilometers before Payton saw bluffs and rock-faced cliffs—the perfect place to disappear.

In single file, Doka led them into a narrow-walled gully along a dry creek bed.

Payton estimated they'd traveled a few more kilometers through countless turns when they stopped. Two men dismounted and like black-robed ghosts scrambled up an incline to their left and disappeared.

The man next to Mango pointed to a bright star and said something.

"See the bright one between those rocks?" Mango pointed up over Payton to dozens of stars, to one much brighter than the others. "He said it's called Sadalsuud, luck of lucks. Luck will be with us tonight, *Inshallah*—God willing," Mango said.

"We're way overdue for some luck," Payton said.

Minutes later, one of the men returned and spoke with Doka, who motioned for them to dismount. Once the camels were taken to an open area behind them, they started up. Several hundred feet later, they came to a narrow stone path with a precipitous drop to their immediate right. The path led them around the side of a several-story-high bluff. Once they reached the top, Payton saw Doka's other man at the far edge. They gathered around him, and he pointed to a canyon that spread out below.

Two men with shouldered machine guns stood in front of a massive rock wall. Payton estimated they were the length of three football fields away.

Doka waved his hand. "My camels were killed through there." In the sheer rock face Payton saw the opening. "Saddam's military used salt mines all through here. Now only smugglers," Doka said.

One of the men lit a cigarette. Then a deep mechanical whine echoed around them, and the rock face behind the two moved to expose a lit tunnel. He dropped his cigarette and crushed it with his boot. Another man strolled out and spoke with them for a few minutes, then returned to the tunnel and the wall slid back into place.

"Must be hydraulic," Mango said.

"You and your men go to the boulder pile. I will come down from above and meet you in front of the tunnel," Doka said.

"You'll be too exposed," Payton said.

Doka smiled. "Not if you kill the guards first."

PAYTON PEERED AROUND the wide base of crushed rock and boulders mounded near the canyon's entrance. One of Doka's men was positioned above him with his rifle trained on the guards.

Doka and his men worked their way down the steep slope high above the tunnel entrance in the shadows of several large boulders.

Payton saw his lead man waiting out in the open below the boulders. If one of the guards looked up, he'd be seen.

Doka was almost past the last boulder when a beer-cooler-sized rock careened down and crashed to the canyon floor several feet from the nearest guard. Both men swung their weapons up.

Doka's men froze.

"Get back," Payton said under his breath. Doka's exposed man in the open was on his stomach and didn't move.

A flashlight snapped on, and in long slow movements one of the guards zigzagged the beam up toward the guy in front of the boulders. The two guards had to be taken out. They couldn't risk alerting whoever was in the cave. Payton tapped the foot of Doka's man with the rifle above him.

"Don't shoot," he said, then picked his way around the rocky base and sprinted over to the wall beyond the canyon's entrance. He moved in the shadows along the rock wall. When he passed the cut, he smelled the dead camels.

The light would be on the exposed man with another swing of the flashlight.

Payton took several quick strides and hit the first guard behind the left ear with the Mini Uzi's handle butt. The guard went down.

The other one turned, saw him, and dropped the flashlight. The beam danced away while he fumbled for his machine gun. Payton pointed the Mini Uzi inches from the guard's head and held a finger to his lips and shook his head once. The guard put his weapon on the ground.

When Doka joined them, he asked the guard how to open the tunnel's rock wall entrance. The guy didn't respond. Doka pulled his machete-sized knife and pressed the tip against the guard's throat. The man started to jabber about a lever and pointed to the rock face. Doka went over and pulled an iron bar fitted into an indentation. Payton heard a rumble, then the whine they'd heard before, and the wall separated several feet. Doka called over his teenage son and another of his men, and the two of them disappeared inside.

CHAPTER 45

THE CAVE

THE SON RETURNED by himself and spoke with his father.

Doka said to Payton, "Many smugglers"

"Ever hear of the al-Dulaimis?" Payton asked.

"Before Butros al-Dulaimi's death, my people traded with his family," Doka said.

"How about his sons?"

"Power is all they care about. They cannot be trusted."

"Is this their place?" Mango asked.

"They use many caves."

Doka had his son and two men come forward. His boy removed several grenades from his burlap backpack and lined them on the ground.

Payton saw three flash-bang stun grenades, two smoke grenades, and four vintage World War II fragmentation grenades. He wondered if they still worked.

One of the men, who appeared to be in his seventies, carried a rocket-propelled grenade launcher with three grenades in a frayed canvas haversack slung over his shoulder. The second guy had an old bazooka and a leather satchel with four extra rounds. Payton saw he only had three fingers on his right hand. He hoped he was left handed.

They had a teenage boy and his decades-old grenades, a septuagenarian with an RPG, and a one-handed guy who carried a bazooka. Not good.

Payton tapped Mango. "Let's go take a look."

They jogged into the tunnel, wide enough for a truck to pass through. When they rounded a slight curve, Payton saw Doka's man pressed against the wall at the mouth of the cave. He heard vehicles rumble inside and smelled exhaust.

Payton leaned forward.

The ceiling of the enormous cave soared over four stories high. A dump truck with no rear wheels had been pushed to the far left wall. To his right, on the bed of a bright red Toyota pickup truck, he saw a pile of black duffle bags similar to the ones found in Stanly's ice truck, Titan United's secret warehouse with the kitchen, and under al-Dori's dead hawala broker brother-in-law in the second-floor room where they'd seen Ben.

He felt adrenaline course through his body when he saw the Mercedes next to the Toyota. He'd found the supernotes and, he hoped, Ben Ater.

Beyond the truck and Mercedes were six new white mopeds parked in front of a cargo ship container with open doors faced toward the tunnel opening. In front of the open doors sat a shrink-wrapped pallet of money.

Two men lifted cubes of supernotes off the pallet and with knives slit them open and jammed bundles of bills into duffle bags. Fifteen yards beyond the two guys with knives were several more armed men who loitered around a forklift with a raised pallet of more cubes.

He didn't see Ben, Marco, or Otto. Deeper in the cave he saw mounded rows of crushed rock with more men. Was Ben back there? He scanned over to the Mercedes. Did they leave him in the trunk?

Four men emerged from the mounds and walked toward the forklift group. Payton recognized the Recces from Cliffside who'd tried to intervene when he and Catherine were talking with the accountants. The taller one had a white bandage on his forehead where Payton had planted the beer pitcher. If those two were here, Otto wouldn't be far behind.

Payton motioned to Mango, and they jogged back out.

"We don't have enough men," Mango said.

"My men will fight like a hundred men," Doka said.

"We still need more guns," Mango said.

"Did you find your American?" Doka asked.

"No, but the car they used is here," Payton said.

"The men who killed my camels drove a Toyota pickup," Doka said.

"If it's red, they're inside," Payton said.

"I count at least three dozen. No idea how many more may be in the rear behind those mounds," Mango said.

"We'll go in two groups," Payton said. "I'll head for the container with Blacknife, Carl, and these two. Mango, you, Doka, and the rest go to the dump truck on the left side of the cave. Any men come from the mounds, deal with them."

He motioned over to the geriatric RPG guy and another boy who was younger than Doka's son, who carried a

Lee-Enfield bolt-action rifle looped over his shoulder. The gun appeared bigger than his small frame. Doka nodded, and they stepped next to Payton.

"What're your names?" he asked.

"Umar," the RPG guy said. Ramrod straight with green eyes and one of the only men in Doka's group without a footlong beard. Payton hoped he could use the RPG.

"You can call me Lawrence," the boy said.

"Stay next to me," Payton said to Lawrence.

They hustled through the tunnel. Several yards from the cave entrance, Payton waved them to a stop.

He brought Mango and Blacknife forward who pulled rings from their flash-bang grenades and threw them.

Mango's sailed out into the cave, bounced four times end over end, and rolled under the forklift. Half the men clustered at the machine were knocked down by the concussion. Blacknife's landed near the pallet and exploded. The two men with duffle bags fell between the pallet and the container.

Payton and Lawrence sprinted to the Mercedes. Small arms fire from the mounds thumped into the car. A few men beside the forklift struggled up and fired toward him and Lawrence.

If Ben was still in the trunk, he had to get him out before the car turned into a colander. Payton crawled over and opened the driver's door.

The Mercedes windshield shattered seconds after the passenger-side mirror exploded. He searched for the trunk release near the steering column, then scanned the dashboard next to the door.

The passenger seat headrest disintegrated. He found the release lever on the floor between the door and seat, popped the trunk, and scrambled to the rear.

Empty.

Several rounds punched through the open trunk lid.

He dropped down. Had he led all these men into a fire-fight for nothing?

He scrambled to the driver's side door and peered over the hood. No sign of Ben in the mounds, but he did see the mouth of another smaller tunnel on the far back wall behind the mounds. Possibly another way out?

On his stomach, Lawrence had the Lee-Enfield aimed around the left front tire. He fired, reloaded, and fired again.

Blacknife, bent low, sprinted from the tunnel and joined Payton. He raked the forklift with his M4 machine gun.

"I saw a second tunnel behind those mounds," Payton said. "If Ben's in here, they'd take him out that way."

He touched Lawrence's leg and motioned him to follow. "Cover us," Payton said to Blacknife.

He and the boy sprinted to the money pallet. Blacknife fired a burst at the men behind the forklift.

At the pallet Payton didn't see the smugglers who'd been knocked down by the flash bang.

He heard gunfire from Mango's position. Mango was pinned down behind a heap of discarded equipment in front of the dump truck by several men at the mounds who concentrated their fire toward him.

Behind the dump truck, Doka pointed to Mango, and his bazooka man rushed forward. A man next to Doka fell dead with a bullet to the head.

Doka's man steadied the bazooka on his shoulder, and Mango fed a round into the tube. It coughed. When the shell landed beside the forklift, dirt showered the machine and it tipped sideways on two wheels, then crashed back down. Fingers or no fingers, the guy could shoot a bazooka.

The men at the forklift paused, then started to fire again.

Doka signaled at the tunnel toward Payton's position. Umar and Carl bolted out and ran behind the Toyota. Umar beckoned to Payton with a toothless smile, pointed to the forklift, and gave him thumbs-up.

Payton returned the gesture.

Umar hefted the RPG over the Toyota's rear and fired. The grenade exploded on the forklift's rounded rear end. The heavy machine rotated up and over with the pallet, still on its extended forks, and crashed upside down, followed by a cloud of supernotes. The men there scattered toward the mounds. Lawrence killed one with a shot to the middle of the back.

Doka had his old Winfield rifle up, and shot and killed another man who raced from the forklift. He reloaded and fired again. A second man went down. An arch of bullets punched holes into the dump truck above Doka's head, who didn't flinch while he took aim and winged a third man before he disappeared into the mounds.

Carl sprinted over to Payton with the backpack full of grenades. "Where's Ben?" he asked.

"If he's here, he'll be in the second tunnel behind those mounds," Payton said.

Bullets from automatic machine gunfire came from around the rear of the container and thwacked, thwacked,

thwacked in a straight line along the cubes inches from Payton. It must be the two men next to the container who'd been knocked down by the flash bang.

"Any more flash bangs?" Payton asked.

Carl came up with one from the backpack. Payton pulled the pin and lobbed it over the container. The grenade exploded and silenced the machine guns.

Now bullets from the men who'd scattered among the mounds slammed into the supernotes and popped holes in the container.

A man on a moped shot out from behind the container. He almost made the first row of mounds when Doka's shot exploded the gas tank. The rider burst into flames, flew off, and rolled into the mounds.

Payton and Carl found the other smuggler still unconscious behind the container.

When he looked through the haze, Payton saw a .50 caliber M2 Browning machine gun being set up in the front row of mounds. A .50 would rip them to pieces.

If Ben was in the second tunnel, they'd have to find another way to him. A bazooka round from Mango's position exploded in the open area several yards in front of the .50.

Seconds later, the .50 opened up. Half the supernote-crammed duffle bags on the pickup bed disintegrated. Blacknife and Lawrence hopped up from behind the Mercedes and ran to Payton's position.

Umar, still behind the Toyota, fired his RPG again. Payton watched the grenade slam into the ground too far in front of the .50. The Toyota and Mercedes shook from finger-long .50 caliber bullets.

"We have to take the .50 out," Blacknife said.

On the cave wall behind them Payton saw an iron ladder. He followed it up to a metal catwalk that snaked along the roof to the back of the cave. He had an idea, a low percentage idea, but it might work. "Smoke," he yelled to Carl.

Umar found his range, and his next RPG round exploded in between the first and second mound row.

Sparks and dense white smoke spewed from Carl's grenade when it bounced off the underside of the upended forklift and cartwheeled toward the mounds.

"Cover us," Payton yelled to Carl. "Grab the grenades," Payton said to Blacknife.

Smoke started to rise. Carl handed the backpack to Blacknife, who pulled his arms through the frayed-rope shoulder straps. Payton ran to the ladder.

Fifteen feet from the ceiling, Payton emerged from the smoke.

Ping, to his right. Tiny splinters of dust and rock hit his face. Several rungs below, Blacknife followed. Bullets ricocheted off the ladder below his feet.

If they didn't hurry, his low-percentage idea would soon be a no-percentage idea. He looked down to Blacknife.

"Go," Blacknife said up to him.

Payton tested the metal grated catwalk that hugged the wall. It appeared sturdy enough. The smoke was thinner up here. He saw a metal box the size of a telephone booth twenty-five feet away.

Bullets pinged into the wall above him.

With the flimsy metal rod railing for balance, he moved toward the box. He yanked open the rusted metal door and stepped inside. Blacknife piled in behind him.

The bazooka coughed again, followed a few seconds later by another explosion.

Through the glassless window, he could make out Mango, who tossed another smoke grenade toward the mounds.

The .50 raked Mango's position.

Payton pushed through the box's other door and jogged along the buckled catwalk toward another box where the wall bowed out.

An explosion in front and below ripped a length of the catwalk from its wall anchors. When Payton grabbed for the railing, a section he was about to step onto dropped several feet. The box was now beyond the gap.

Bullets paraded inches over his head, paused, then popped into the wall under them.

They were over the mounds now. Payton could see the .50 being moved back. Then he saw the Recces, the one with the bandage, had an RPG, and his sidekick an AK-47 both pointed up toward them.

The catwalk slipped and the opening got wider. Payton vaulted over the space and was met by a shower of dirt and stone from the Recces AK fire.

"Jump," he said back to Blacknife.

Blacknife leaped but landed short. His legs dangled off the end of the catwalk.

The Recces RPG round exploded below them.

Payton bent down and heaved Blacknife up.

The box they'd come from separated and, with a long piece of grating still attached to it, tore loose and crashed below.

Payton sent a volley from the Mini Uzi toward the South Africans, then stepped into the next box with Blacknife close behind him.

Ping … Ping … Ping … on the floor of the metal box.

"Enough fun for one day. Get the grenades," Payton said.

Blacknife handed over two and kept two.

"Let's hope they still work. Ready?" Payton asked.

Blacknife nodded and they pulled the pins and tossed them.

An explosion above the second tunnel entrance, from either an RPG or a bazooka round, collapsed an avalanche of rock and rubble that blocked the entrance. Then, like giant footsteps, their grenades exploded.

The .50 was abandoned, and men scrambled toward the blocked entrance. Payton watched the Recces race to the back of the cave. Mango with the Bedouins rushed forward.

PAYTON STARTED DOWN another ladder where the walkway turned and went along the back wall. Dozens of rungs later, he hopped down.

Doka's men had several prisoners on the ground with their hands bound behind their backs. Neither the Recces nor Ben was among them.

Payton pointed to the small opening at the top of the rubble. "Where does that lead to?"

Doka kicked one of the prisoners, said something, and motioned to the blocked tunnel. Payton saw the guy's terrified eyes when Doka pushed his head back with the end of his rifle. The prisoner blurted, "Bombs, many, many bombs!"

CHAPTER 46

THE ESCAPE

PAYTON, FOLLOWED BY Carl and Blacknife, climbed over the rubble pile and slid down the back side into the tunnel. He ran down a narrow short passageway to the mouth of another cave.

It was a much smaller cave, with row upon row of munitions. He saw stacks of various colored fifty-five-gallon drums with hazard symbols stenciled on their sides and pallets of mortar shells, boxes of bullets, and RPG rounds. Along the opposite wall were several mid-sized Toyota Hilux pickup trucks with mounted machine guns.

"I guess the WMD inspectors missed these," Carl said.

What Payton didn't see was any sign of Ben, Marco, Otto, or the two Recces. Stabs of frustration cut through him. Was Ben being here another charade like the tea shop?

"Do you think he's still alive?" Carl asked.

"If they intended to kill him, we wouldn't have seen him on the video," Payton said.

"But alive where?" Carl asked.

Blacknife mumbled, "He might be back in Syria."

Several of Doka's men swarmed past them into the cave. One pulled his knife and pried the plywood lid off a box. Long strands of straw fell from a new RPG launcher he lifted out. More knives came out and more lids popped off. Thick plastic wrap around a pallet of cardboard boxes was torn away. A box was ripped open and hand grenades, two and three at a time like apples from a barrel, were passed among the men.

Payton recognized the symbol below Belarus stenciled in yellow on four fifty-five-gallon drums next to the grenade boxes. "Tell your men to keep clear of those. They're chemical weapons," he said.

"Enough," Doka yelled.

His men stopped and moved away. Several carried new RPG launchers with extra rounds and a few had armfuls of grenades.

Doka instructed his son and Umar to search the cave.

When his son walked over to the pickups, he waved back to his father. Payton came over with Doka and saw Umar in front of an emergency exit door-sized opening in the rock wall.

"They escaped through there," Doka's boy said.

Umar stepped into the opening and showed them two sets of dirt bike tracks along with what appeared to be ATV tire tracks. They followed the tracks around a bend and up a rise where the tunnel emptied into a bowl with skyscraper walls.

"The desert is one kilometer through there," Doka said, and pointed to a narrow slit in the other side of the bowl.

———— ✯ ————

NEXT TO THE CONTAINER and mopeds, Carl scooped up a handful of shredded supernotes and let them dribble through his fingers.

"Has to be several hundred million here. Did we stop them in time?" Carl asked.

"We'll know soon enough," Payton said.

"Was our chase after the Mercedes a waste of time?" Blacknife asked.

"Ben was in the trunk when they left the city. I believe they brought him here. When we showed up, their plans changed and he was taken out on one of those dirt bikes," Payton said.

Operator vehicles drove out of the tunnel and rolled to a stop alongside the bullet-riddled Mercedes.

Plum climbed out and came over. One of his men, a medic, attended to the wounded men.

"Did you find your kidnap victim?" Plum asked.

"Not yet," Payton said.

Doka's son said his father wanted to speak with them. Payton and Plum walked over to where Doka stood at the overturned forklift. Several men sat cross-legged next to the line of dead bodies. One of the prisoners stood with Doka.

"He says those three are Iranians. Quds Force fighters." Doka indicated three of the bodies at the end of the line. "His cousin's the barefoot one, and he wouldn't be dead if the Iranians weren't in Iraq. They came on the same truck with the fake money container."

Payton saw the dead cousin beside the Iranians with his open mouth and cigarette-stained teeth.

Cleveland nailed the Quds Force involvement.

"Why're you here?" Payton asked in Arabic to the nearest prisoner on the ground.

He didn't speak. Doka kicked him in the kidney.

"The cave belongs to men my father worked for," the prisoner said.

"The al-Dulaimis?" Doka asked.

He nodded.

"What does your father do for them?" Payton asked.

"We live in Hit, where he's a hawala broker."

Zaki and Marco helped the Iranians with their super-note scheme and at the same time assisted Khleifat. It didn't matter, Payton thought, if the Iranians succeeded or if Khleifat took the election. The brothers win either way. Unless he caught them first.

"Did you see a man in the car trunk?" Payton pointed to the Mercedes.

The man's eyes went to the back of the cave. "They take him to the bomb cave."

Payton's momentary twinge of relief Ben was still alive didn't last. "We found another tunnel and cave where they escaped on an ATV and dirt bikes," Payton said to Plum.

"How long of a lead time do they have?" Plum asked.

"Forty-five minutes, maybe an hour," Mango said.

"Call Major Huff and tell him we need helicopters to search for them," Plum said.

Mango ran to a vehicle, climbed in, and drove back out the main tunnel.

"Once they leave these cliffs, they won't have many places to hide," Plum said.

They left four of Plum's men in the cave to wait for bomb disposal squads dispatched from a marine base outside of Karbala. In three operator vehicles, they sped out of the cave. When they exited the tunnel, Doka directed them toward another narrow cut into a zigzag gully that led onto a sandy dune. In the weak dawn light it took them fifteen minutes to find the churned tracks. Several miles later, they plowed up and over several drifts and saw where tracks cut down the backside of the last one toward a village a few kilometers farther east.

"Bi'r Rah," Doka said. "Much oil there."

CHAPTER 47

TWO OF THE VEHICLES split off and veered to either side of the village to block the single paved road.

Plum and Payton, with Mango behind the wheel, drove the third vehicle into the village and stopped beside an oil rig in the central square.

Mango got out and spoke to a man standing with his wife and children in front of a food store.

"The village elder operates a gun shop the next block over," Mango said back behind the wheel.

He turned into a garbage-strewn alley, past several buildings, and pulled onto a short street. He stopped in front of a squat building with a wooden porch shaded by a frayed awning. An air conditioner unit dripped from the single window.

Payton went into the gun-crammed shop with Plum.

A blubbery man sat on a white plastic garden chair at a cloth-covered round wooden table beside the air conditioner. His suspicious dark eyes moved from Payton to

Plum. He held a cigarette between his third and fourth finger and worked a string of worry beads with his other hand.

"Did men on motorcycles come into your village?" Payton asked.

"Motorcycles?" he asked, and took a contemplative pull on his cigarette. "No motorcycles."

Payton had to hurry the conversation along. He saw a musket mounted among various types of rifles on the wall behind the man. A hundred years ago, the flintlock Kabyle, or camel gun, was the weapon of choice for Arabs.

"How much for the Kabyle?" Payton gestured.

"A magnificent weapon used to kill many men in the Battle of Mulayda." When he tipped back to reach for the flintlock, Payton thought the chair might collapse under his weight. He plopped back down and handed it to Payton.

Payton examined the scarred ivory butt. "The Battle of Mulayda, which started the House of Saud's Kuwaiti exile," Payton said.

"You know your Arab history. One hundred and fifty American dollars."

"These scars will reduce the price," Payton said. He ran his palm over the heavy barrel.

"One hundred and twenty-five," the gun dealer said.

"One hundred," Payton countered.

"One hundred and twenty. Such a small price for a weapon with so much history."

Payton handed the weapon to Plum and lined twenties and fives on the coffee-stained tablecloth.

The gun seller put the bills under his crumpled pack of Marlboros. "Two motorcycles and a desert machine. Five men. One in the back of the machine had his hands bound. They stole a lorry and left east toward Baghdad."

"Describe the lorry?"

"Canvas sides with no back flap."

"How long ago?"

"Less than one hour."

They left the shop. Plum spoke into his radio, and they sped to the east side of the village.

Mango stopped in the middle of the road, where Doka stood with Carl next to the operator vehicle. One of Huff's helicopters landed a hundred yards away.

"Good luck," Plum said.

"Next time I go into Syria, I'll know who to call," Payton said. He handed Doka the Kabyle gun.

"You'll find the men who killed my camels?" Doka asked.

"They won't get away," Payton said.

"Do not waste time with your American justice. Bring them to me. I will deal with them."

Payton knew about Bedouin justice. After being filleted alive, Otto and his Recces would be left in the desert to be picked apart by scavengers. Maybe he'd take Doka up on his offer. He shook Doka's hand and ran to the MH-6 Little Bird helicopter. The pilot handed him a helmet.

When the second helicopter landed, Blacknife and Carl squeezed in.

Minutes later, both helicopters lifted and put their noses down and accelerated toward Baghdad.

"If they're headed into Baghdad, they have two options," the pilot said into his helmet microphone. He pointed to the road they'd landed next to. "That road ends in Hit, northwest of Baghdad. Hop on Highway 10 and you're in the city within an hour. The other option is Highway 8, which criss-crosses Anbar. They won't get far on 10. Traffic's backed up for miles because of those bank riots."

Payton saw a miles-long line of stopped traffic on a strip of highway.

"Highway 8's a parking lot now too."

The horizon was a thick blanket of smog from Baghdad's fires. If the lorry made it into the city, they'd never find them.

Payton had the pilot contact the embassy MSG command center. Several minutes later, Cleveland came on the radio with Rammer. He told them Ben was still alive and about the cave and the dead Quds Force members. "You made the right call with the Iranian supernote connection," Payton said.

"What's Marco and Zaki's angle?" Cleveland asked.

"Play both sides. Help Khleifat get elected, at the same time do whatever the Iranians ask. Either way, they'll be in a position to make a fortune when the dust settles," Payton said.

"Gabe Kuttic's called twice and in his roundabout way asked if we have any idea who did the tea shop," Cleveland said.

"He wants to make sure Yusuf's cover is still solid and to confirm his theory a Sunni militia was behind the shop being blown. Did you tell him about Otto on the roof?"

"Above my paygrade. I'll let you have the pleasure," Cleveland said.

"Why are the Iranians involved with Ben being taken?" Rammer asked.

"Maybe for leverage against our government," Payton said.

"Wouldn't you want to be in Washington to see the blow-back if Ben turns up in Tehran?" Cleveland asked.

The pilot flew beside the traffic. Payton pointed to a truck that looked like it had canvas sides. The pilot turned and zoomed closer. They were metal, not canvas.

Since they'd left the cave, a question ate at Payton. What if the supernotes weren't about stopping the elections? The Iranians might have something else planned.

"The money from the Federal Reserve arrives in two hours. Once it's delivered, any more problems with BUI or the hawala system will be taken care of. Advantage, the United States," Payton said.

"Iraq comes back from the brink," Cleveland said.

"Then what did the supernotes accomplish?" Payton asked. He watched the stalled traffic. What were they missing?

"Besides our military running around in circles?" Rammer asked.

The pilot turned and flew west, close to the road. The other helicopter kept to the east.

"Anything out of the ordinary with the Federal Reserve money being flown in?" Payton asked.

"The delivery date was moved up eight weeks," Rammer said.

"The military's in hurry-up offense mode to get the cash distributed to all the BUI branches," Cleveland said.

"And they doubled the shipment amount to a billion three. All cash," Rammer said.

Had he been so focused on Ben, he'd missed the obvious?

"What's on your mind, Ladd?" Cleveland asked.

"That the supernotes are being used for a different reason other than bringing down the economy."

"Like?" Cleveland asked.

"Create enough chaos, our leaders overcorrect and throw more money at the problem," Payton said.

"You mean overcorrect with more of the billions we've already lost in this quagmire?" Cleveland asked.

"What if the Iranians are after the money?" Payton asked.

"A billion and change goes a long way in Iran. They've been strapped with sanctions for years," Cleveland said.

"How would they get their hands on it?" Rammer asked.

"I'd start with the convoy," Payton said.

"You heard General Qwen, 'you'd need a small army' to take out one of those convoys," Cleveland said.

"They have one with the Quds Force," Payton said. He saw pickups, city trucks, and semicontainer trucks, but no truck matched the gun dealer's description.

"You sure he said canvas sides?" the pilot asked.

"They could've ditched the truck and stolen another vehicle," Payton said.

"Rammer, get over to Mifflin's office and tell her not to transport the money. Leave it at the airport. If she gives you any trouble, call Qwen and lock down her office. How long will it take to get to BGW?" Payton asked.

"Thirty minutes," the pilot said.

"Make it twenty," Payton said.

CHAPTER 48

ARMY MAJOR ADAM BALLARD handed Payton's shield back.

"We move when the money's offloaded, period," he said.

Ballard, who Payton guessed was in his mid-fifties and was maybe all of five foot three, wore his helmet with the chin strap snapped into place. He had weasel brown eyes behind black-rimmed glasses and wore a holstered pearl-handled sidearm on his right hip.

"You may be attacked," Payton said.

"Those are President Timmons's orders. Iraqi Ministry of Finance officials are already at BUI's central branch. They need our cash now," Ballard said.

"Then use helicopters," Payton said. "Don't drive through the city." He'd dealt with Ballard's type before and knew it was useless.

"Anyone comes near my convoy, they're dead." Ballard pointed to two Apache attack helicopters on the tarmac.

Their rotors twirled in slow motion. He stepped over to four of his men next to a Humvee.

"Peckerwood," Blacknife said.

"Cute gun, too," Carl said.

"Every convoy needs a cowboy," Blacknife said.

"Any word about those extra embassy marines?" Payton asked.

"The Green Zone's on high alert. Four more rockets exploded inside the walls in the last three hours. Marines have the embassy locked down. All available military personnel are on duty at the security gate checkpoints," Carl said.

"Those are the first rocket attacks inside the walls in several days," Blacknife said.

"Someone is sending a message," Carl said.

"A message the United States has lost control over the situation," Payton said.

A pinprick of light broke through the cloud cover. The light grew into a Lockheed C-130 Hercules cargo plane.

The behemoth touched down, catapulted to the far side of the airport, turned, and taxied toward them. Two hundred yards in front of the hanger, the four massive propellers slowed and stopped. Five minutes later, a rear cargo door ramp lowered.

If he was wrong, Payton would take the heat for a false alarm, but if he was right and the Federal Reserve money was the target, then Ballard would need twice the number of men who loitered beside the line of vehicles in his convoy.

Several airport workers and a forklift disappeared up the C-130's ramp. A pilot came through a personnel door two and a half stories above the tarmac. She stepped down mobile stairs rolled up to the side of the plane and walked over to Ballard.

Ballard returned her salute and took her clipboard.

"Any trouble?" Payton heard him ask.

"Choppy out of Andrews, otherwise no problems," she said.

"How much tonight?" Ballard asked.

"One point five billion. They brought in another two hundred million at the last minute."

Ballard initialed several forms and handed back the clipboard.

The forklift rolled out and down the ramp with a blue plastic-wrapped pallet and fed it into the rear of a half-bed white panel truck.

Payton went over to Ballard. "You still have time to get more men," he said.

"You want to join the fun, find a spot in the rear," Ballard said. He rested his hand on top of the pearl handle. "If not, your Green Zone bubble's that way." He waved east over his shoulder, then headed toward the first Humvee.

"What a fool," Carl said.

"Why doesn't he use the helicopters?" Blacknife asked.

"Because he wants to be the hero who saves Iraq," Carl said.

"You set with ammo?" Payton asked.

They both nodded.

"I'll take the last vehicle. Both of you get into the Mamba. And keep sharp."

Blacknife and Carl went over to the second-to-last vehicle, a six ton armored South African Mamba personnel carrier.

Payton dialed Cleveland's cell while he went to a Humvee in the back of the line.

"Pinnix," Cleveland answered.

"I'm at BGW with the money convoy. Didn't Rammer tell Mifflin I didn't want the money moved?"

"She wasn't in her office. Her gatekeeper said she stepped out and he doesn't know when she'll be back. Calls to her cell phone go to voicemail."

"We're about to leave. How long before Rammer can have his toy plane in the air?" Payton asked.

"Ten, maybe fifteen minutes."

"Have him follow us. If we're on our way into a debacle, you'll know what to do."

"Didn't you tell the convoy commander he might be attacked?"

"He's a fool."

"See you from above," Cleveland said.

Payton climbed into the Humvee.

"You're our tourist," a young Latino behind the wheel said. He reached over and shook Payton's hand. "Rios."

Rios introduced a hefty black guy in his twenties who stood behind a mounted machine gun. "He's Willie."

Willie bent down and offered Payton his hand.

Payton said his hellos and checked his Mini Uzi. He counted twenty-three men with Ballard's Humvee in the lead, followed by another Humvee, a Stryker, the money truck, two more Humvees, the Mamba, then him, Rios, and Willie.

They sped in single file away from the hanger.

"The guardian angels will be with us all the way," Rios said and pointed to the Apaches.

Payton didn't care if Ballard's orders were to get the money to BUI in short order. He should wait until dark when fewer Iraqis could be hurt from any possible problems they might run into.

"Ballard's not too concerned," Payton said.

"Don't mess with the major, right?" Rios yelled back to Willie.

"Never," Willie said and rotated his gun to the rear.

They blew through BGW's guarded exit and sped along Route Irish toward the city at forty-five miles per hour. The helicopters flew back and forth over the line of vehicles.

They passed only one group of soldiers on Route Irish. A different story from the dozens Payton saw when he had arrived a few days ago.

"Lighter security," Payton said.

"They've been pulled to contain the bank riots," Rios said.

They drove over a rise. Payton saw the spot a few kilometers ahead where Wade was killed and the buildings the bomb disposal unit said were used for cover to trigger IEDs. No security anywhere for miles ahead.

"Put your seat belt on," he said to Rios.

"We don't—"

"Do it," Payton said. Little help a seat belt would do if they were hit by an IED or, worse, an EFP.

Before they came parallel with the buildings, Ballard veered onto an access road. The scorched pavement from Wade's EFP passed to their right.

"Why'd Ballard get off Irish?" Payton asked.

"We sometimes take the airport road deeper into the city, but with the recent IED activity, he was instructed to take an alternative route," Rios said.

Mifflin must've given Ballard new route instructions.

The road they were on fed into a four-lane highway and disappeared into the dense smoky Firdos and Jihad neighborhoods southwest of the city.

In a sharp Tigris River curve, they exited at the Umal Al-Table Square interchange and drove north on Jinub Street through a section of the city called Kindi.

Payton could see they were several blocks from the Damascus Square Green Zone entrance. A million miles away if they needed backup in a hurry.

Rios kept the Mamba ten yards in front of him.

"We've taken Jinub before. It cuts back toward the Green Zone." Rios pointed out Payton's window. "Traffic's lighter, so we won't lose time. One problem, though, we can't travel at any speed. Past Nisur Square, Kindi stacks up with buildings, houses, and parked cars. Trust me, you don't want to get stuck in there. It's a Shiite neighborhood. They hate Americans. We're in luck today because our intel said we have a clean shot all the way to BUI's headquarters."

Five minutes later, the road started to narrow. Drivers pulled over to let them pass.

Residential buildings on either side pressed closer together. Being in such a packed neighborhood, Payton hoped the Mifflin-Ballard brain trust knew what they were doing. He glanced over his shoulder … no vehicles behind them. "I don't hear any radio chatter," he said.

"Major Ballard wants us fast, efficient, and quiet. Willie, be ready," Rios said.

Willie rapped twice on the roof.

Payton watched the Mamba's gunner spin his machine gun forward. Each narrow street they passed was a perfect ambush choke point.

Brake lights came on up and down the convoy, then they started to slow. Buildings crowded along each side of the two-lane road with periodic parked cars.

The odometer needle hovered at thirty mph.

In another half kilometer, cars were parked one after the other on either side of them. Beyond the cars were cinder-block houses and commercial buildings.

One of the helicopters banked hard close overhead.

Payton fingered the Mini Uzi. "Rios, give me the radio," he said.

"Sorry, sir, but Major—"

"Now, Private."

Rios hesitated, then handed over the handset.

"Ballard? Ladd. Get out of here."

"Stay off the radio," Ballard said.

"The country can't afford to lose—"

Click. Ballard was gone.

"Fool," Payton said under his breath and handed the handset back to Rios.

He saw they were down to eighteen mph. "Be ready with your .50," Payton said.

"Always am," Willie said.

Rios drummed the steering wheel several times with his thumbs. "Come on, move, move. Don't slow down," he said.

Parked cars formed a continuous barrier. On their left, beyond the cars, were wooden stalls in front of shuttered retail shops.

"Go, go," Rios said.

Every brake light blazed on. Rios came to a stop.

They idled in silence.

Payton scanned the deserted street. Ballard must be out of his mind to stop.

Willie broke the silence. "What's up?"

"Don't know. The major's never stopped before," Rios said.

Payton peered up the street beside the Mamba but couldn't make out why they'd stopped. He was about to reach over for the radio mic when he saw something sail from the parapet of a shoe store to his right.

A shaving cream-sized can bounced off the hood of their Humvee, ricocheted against a parked minivan, then rolled and wedged behind a Citroën's rear tire several feet away. Red sparks sputtered and dense white smoke poured from the can.

"Smoke, back up now!" Payton yelled. He saw more cans soar from the right-side buildings all along the convoy.

"Where'd it come from?" Rios shouted and threw the Humvee in reverse.

"From the buildings, now move, MOVE," Payton said. More grenades bounced off the road.

Willie swung his gun and unloaded through the thick smoke into the shoe store's parapet. Shell casings, like a stream of jackpot slot-machine quarters, fell at his feet.

Rios looked behind and started to roll back.

The smoke was so thick, Payton couldn't see the rooftops or the Mamba. More convoy machine guns erupted.

Rios jerked to a stop. "I can't see!" he said.

Willie paused and leaned down. "Keep going!"

An explosion slammed Payton against the door and blew the Humvee up over the left-side parked cars onto one of the wooden stalls. He found himself on top of a motionless Rios still strapped into his seat. Willie was gone. A blast rumbled through the smoke from somewhere farther up the convoy, followed by yells and automatic gunfire.

"We can't see you, Spartan 1. Get out of there," one of the helicopter pilots said over the radio.

Payton reached up, shoved his door up and over, and stood with one foot on the side of Rios's seat and the other on the steering column.

"Ballard, you fool," he said.

The Mini Uzi hung by its strap from the emergency brake. He slung it over his shoulder, then reached down and unclipped Rios's seat belt.

The boy moaned.

"Can you move?"

"I … I don't … know," Rios said.

Payton tried to ease Rios out. "Okay?" Payton asked.

He moaned again and gave a slight nod. The rear passenger seat had snapped off its hinges and wedged behind Rios's seat. Payton used his foot to push it out of the way, and Rios's seat settled back several inches.

He coaxed Rios out through the roof frame where Willie had stood behind his .50, which now lay half in and half out of the vehicle.

Payton kicked away splintered two-by-fours from the crushed wooden stall and rested Rios on the cracked sidewalk pavement next to the Humvee.

He found the radio handset stuck under the brake pedal. "Ballard, it's Ladd. We've been hit. I need help back here. Willie's missing and Rios is hurt."

"Stay there, we'll work our way back to you," came a reply. It wasn't Ballard.

Payton reached for his cell phone, but it was gone. The driver's seat gave way when he pushed it forward, and Rios's machine gun and jacket dropped out. Payton set the weapon next to Rios and slid the folded jacket under his head.

Willie limped out of the dense smoke. "One of those stalls broke my fall. How's Rios?" he asked.

"He's injured. I need you to stay with him."

"Will do," Willie said.

"Let's move him to those buildings," Payton said.

They lifted Rios, who moaned again, and picked their way over pieces of wood into a narrow shop vestibule with a secured metal roll-up door.

"I'll be right back," Willie said and disappeared into the smoke.

Payton heard metal scrape against metal, then Willie emerged with Rios's weapon and his .50 along with several belts of bullets.

"Payback time if they come at us," Willie said. He rested the machine gun on a blocky piece of lumber and took aim out the vestibule.

"I'm going ahead. Help will be here soon," Payton said.

Payton picked his way forward through the oppressive smoke. He'd gone several yards to where he thought the Mamba should be, when he heard low voices speaking Afrikaans. The only men he knew who spoke Afrikaans were Otto's Recces. The voices faded.

Bullets ripped into one of the convoy vehicles up ahead.

He moved in the direction of the voices. Two gunshots rang out and vehicle doors slammed.

Through the gloom he saw the red spark glow of more canisters sail overhead. One missed him by inches. A concussion rolled over him from an explosion at the front of the convoy

Back and forth, the two helicopters roamed overhead. The smoke blazed from their powerful searchlights. He heard yells and screams from wounded soldiers.

He thought of Rios and Willie in the vestibule. Anyone came near them, they'd have to get past Willie and the .50. If Blacknife and Carl stayed inside the Mamba, they'd be fine.

A large shape came toward him. It must be the Mamba. He jumped out of the way. He was surprised when he saw the money truck's brake lights flash on, and it stopped, then turned hard right and faded into the smoke.

Payton followed the truck between a gap in the cars and saw the roll-up rear door slip between buildings. He ran and grabbed the door's handle and hopped up onto a metal frame below the bed.

After a short distance down an alley, the truck turned. Gunfire raged behind him.

They wove through a series of short streets. The smoke was still a white haze too thick for the helicopters to see them.

From the sound of gunfire behind them, Payton figured they were a couple of blocks from the ambush site. They came to an abrupt stop. The driver and passenger doors opened and slammed shut.

Payton stepped off and crouched behind a construction dumpster.

One of the helicopters flew close overhead but didn't stop.

With the different routes they could've taken to BUI, why would Mifflin make the decision to go through one of the densest neighborhoods in the city?

Move fast with military precision, blind the helicopters, and hijack the money truck. Simple plan if you had enough people with military skills to pull off such an operation.

The truck inched forward, then disappeared.

Another explosion came from the convoy site.

Payton stepped into a vacant lot between two one-story buildings. He could barely see the wall of another building at the back of the lot. No money truck. He went into the street. One of the buildings on the left had barn-sized wooden doors. Is that where the truck disappeared to? The doors didn't have a handle, only a keyhole. He slid his combat knife blade into the narrow slit between the doors. On his fourth attempt, the metal latch lifted and the doors popped open.

He slipped inside and found himself in a mechanic's garage. A dank oil-tinged smell hung over the place. Buildings were close on either side. At the far end of the dingy space, the money truck idled.

He stood by the double doors and listened. The only sound was the purr of the truck engine. The garage was empty. There must be another door on the other side of the truck.

With the Mini Uzi up, he inched into the space. A helicopter hovered somewhere nearby, then moved away. At the back right tire, he paused. All he heard was the engine. He took a step toward the cab.

"Don't move," a South African voice above him said.

The Recces with the bowling ball head he'd seen in the cave, who Carl took down in Cliffside with his pool cue, had a welder's helmet pushed up off his face and a handgun pointed down at Payton from the roof of the truck.

A cold metal gun barrel tapped behind Payton's right ear. Someone grabbed his knife, Mini Uzi, and Glock.

He turned.

Otto's machine gun was aimed at his chest, and next to him in all her authoritative glory stood Colonel Dara Mifflin.

"I guess I don't have an appointment," he said.

CHAPTER 49

KINDI

"SEARCH HIM AGAIN," Otto said.

Johannes, the lummox with the forehead bandage, pawed over him.

"Those stitches hurt?" Payton asked

Johannes pointed the Mini Uzi under Payton's chin. "When I kill you, I'll use your gun," he said.

"Put the gun down," Mifflin said. "You'll have your turn soon enough."

Of course Mifflin's the key. She'd know the ideal choke points in Kindi where smoke could be used to blind the helicopters.

"They teach Introduction to Treason at Dartmouth?" Payton asked.

She stepped forward and slapped him. "You talk too much," she said.

"Where's Ben?" Payton asked.

"Close by," she said.

From the other side of the truck, men carried white metal panels with "American Red Cross" painted above "HAZARDOUS MEDICAL WASTE." Two of them wore Red Cross uniforms. Another rolled an acetylene torch with a hose connected to a tank on wheels. He handed the metal-tipped end up to the guy on the roof, who popped the torch on and started to weld one of the panels being held against the side of the truck.

Payton nodded to the panels. "Nice touch." Military guards would not want to inspect medical waste trucks. Another angle Mifflin had covered.

"Why wait to kill him?" Otto asked.

"When the money's loaded at the river, you and your men can do what you want with him. Until then, he stays alive," she said.

Johannes yanked Payton's hands behind his back and bound them with a plastic zip tie.

"I guess Vicar and Dale were collateral damage," Payton said.

"Dale was out of his league. Graham …" she looked at Otto and they shared a quick laugh, "had a hard time with instructions."

"Vicar panicked when we discovered the Fallujah supernote operation. His mistake, he called to tell you he was headed to the cave, but you couldn't risk he'd crack under pressure if we caught him. So you sent Otto to kill him."

"Once he was out of his confront zone, Graham was useless," she said.

"I'm curious … Yusuf was the tea shop target, wasn't he?"

"He was a CIA informant al-Dori needed dealt with and the perfect bait we knew you'd fall for."

"Who blew his cover?"

"One of Zaki al-Dulaimi's many sources received a tip Yusuf was being paid by the CIA."

"You were the one who gave him up to al-Dori?"

"Never pass up an opportunity to have an IOU with Nassar al-Dori."

"It was your idea to play up Ben's drug involvement to keep our focus off his work and what he found in Stanly?" Payton asked.

"You being clueless allowed millions of additional super-notes to be put into the financial system," she said.

"Too bad Ben went to Stanly," Payton said.

"His bad luck is now yours. Put him inside"

Johannes prodded Payton with the Mini Uzi. Otto threw up the roll-up door.

"General Riebow will shut down Baghdad until he finds his money truck."

"We'll be long gone," she said.

"You and the brothers?"

She smiled, then said, "Take him."

Another Red Cross panel was lifted by men on ladders to the guy on the roof.

Johannes bound Payton's ankles with another plastic tie. Otto climbed in and pulled him up, while Johannes lifted his feet in. Once inside, they dragged him between two pallets and jammed a red bandanna into his mouth.

"Enjoy the ride," Otto said.

They hopped down, and Payton heard something being fitted into place inside the door.

"Stack the waste containers to the roof. I want the fake wall hidden." He heard Mifflin's muffled voice.

A few minutes later, the door was pulled shut, the truck slipped into reverse, and moved.

CHAPTER 50

THE WHARF

PAYTON TWISTED HIS wrists, which were secured behind his back. The white zip tie bit into his skin. What did she mean, Ben was close?

The truck rattled below him. A foot-long crease from a roof panel weld was his only light.

He pressed his hands back and felt the plastic wrap used to secure the cash onto the pallet give. He pushed harder, and his fingers poked through where the money must've shifted. He ripped through the wrap with his fingers and felt several inches of open space.

He managed to shimmy up a few inches so he could press his rear end into the space, which he thought might give him enough room to bring his knees up. The pallet in front stopped him short.

With another reach, he tore away more plastic and gained an extra few inches. One more heave brought his bound wrists under his feet and in front of him. He pulled the bandanna out and hauled himself up using the top edge of the pallet.

A quick scan didn't turn up anything he could use to get the plastic ties off with. He hobbled between the end pallet and a metal partition fitted into place before the roll-up door was pulled down.

When he came around, he saw a man on the floor. He made his way over to him, using the top of the money for balance.

The man was Ben. One of his eyes was swollen shut, and there was dried blood caked around his nose. Payton checked his pulse. He was still alive, but barely.

On the corner of a pallet near Ben's feet were several exposed nails. Payton brought the wrist tie down hard onto one of them. On his third attempt, the tie snapped off. He used the same nail on the ankle tie and then moved back to Ben.

"Can you hear me?"

Ben turned toward him. The truck slowed and stopped.

Voices came from the rear, and the roll-up door's handle was tossed back. The door slid up through a narrow slit at the top of the partition.

He heard someone ask questions. They must be at a military checkpoint.

"Shh," Payton said and rested his hand on Ben's arm. If they were discovered by military guards now, Mifflin's operation would be over and whoever else was involved would disappear.

"Boxes of surgical waste for the incinerator. All the paperwork's there," a Recces said.

The only incinerator Payton knew of was minutes southeast of the Green Zone, close to the Tamuz Bridge. With a driver in a Red Cross uniform, the guard wouldn't have any reason to doubt the truck was full of medical waste. Mifflin the bureaucrat would make sure every "i" was dotted and "t" crossed on the driver's forms.

Ben moaned.

Payton leaned over. "Easy," he said.

"Close it up," the guard said.

The door slid back and the handle slammed into place. No one wanted to be near medical waste.

The truck started to move.

"Can you hear me?" Payton asked.

Ben gave a slight nod.

"I'll get you out of here."

Ben started to say something, but the truck bounced and his head jostled. He closed his eye in pain.

Payton moved closer and rested Ben's head on his thigh.

"Iranians …" Ben mumbled, then started to hack. Payton heard a gurgle, and blood dripped from the corner of his mouth.

"What about them?" Payton asked.

"Take me to Iran."

Mifflin kept Ben alive to hand him off to the Iranians. The chance to get their hands on Senator Ater's nephew would be a score the Iranians couldn't pass up.

"You're not going anywhere but home," Payton said.

They drove several more minutes, then stopped, and the engine was turned off. The truck shook and went still. Payton heard voices, the handle was thrown back again, and the door slid up.

"Stay still," Payton said.

The decoy boxes were being removed.

Payton knew he'd have one brief opportunity. He moved back in between the pallets and positioned the cut plastic ties around his wrists and ankles.

The partition was pulled out, and an industrial hum filled the truck.

Two men climbed in.

Payton recognized Johannes's voice when he said, "We should kill both of them now."

Another Recces said, "She has a deal with the Iranians for the accountant. Otto gets the guy from the embassy. He might let you do the honors."

"Enjoy your ride?" Johannes asked.

Payton saw that Johannes held his Glock. Tau, the welder with the bull neck, stood beside him.

"Up," Johannes said. He leaned forward and grabbed Payton's right arm.

Payton's hand shot up and, with a handful of the big man's shirt, wrenched him down. By reflex, Johannes brought both hands forward to stop his fall. Before he could react, Payton snatched the Glock and fired twice. Both rounds drilled into the South African's left shoulder.

Johannes spun back into Tau. Payton leaned up and shot Tau in the elbow of his gun hand. The gun clattered to the floor.

Johannes staggered toward Payton, who stood and smashed the Glock handle on the bandage. Johannes crumpled to the floor, blood streaming from the bandage.

Tau squatted and, with his good hand, went to retrieve his weapon under the pallet. Payton smacked the side of his lumpy head with the Glock.

He fished Tau's pistol out, saw it had a full clip, and slid it under his belt behind his back.

He went to Ben and saw more blood had trickled out of his mouth. He needed medical attention now.

Out the open door was a high-ceilinged warehouse full of bulky burlap-wrapped bundles. He jumped down next to the partition that leaned against the truck behind stacks of boxes marked "medical waste." Around the front of the truck, out the open side of the warehouse and across a wide wood-plank wharf, he saw two docked river barges.

The back barge, with a rusted white tower and a metal staircase connected to a second-story walkway, was loaded with the bundles. The front barge didn't have a tower and was empty.

Otto came out of the tower cabin and stood on the metal walkway.

Payton was behind the medical waste boxes, so Otto couldn't see him. He probably wondered where the two inside had disappeared to. He couldn't have heard the gunshots because the incinerator hum was too loud.

He came down the stairs, stepped onto the wharf, unslung his carbine machine gun, and headed toward the truck.

Payton climbed back inside.

"Johannes? Tau?" Otto yelled.

Payton crouched next to the middle pallet opposite the two Recces and Ben.

Otto appeared, with his carbine aimed into the truck, but before he could react, Payton shot him in the right arm. Otto dropped his weapon and fell back.

Payton came out of the truck and stood beside him. "It's only a graze, get up."

Otto was on his back with a hand over the blood-soaked place where the bullet nicked him.

"Move."

Otto hobbled up.

"Get in."

He took small steps to the open rear of the truck. When he was almost there, he pivoted, but Payton was ready and pistol-whipped the back of his bald head. Otto sprawled forward over the truck bed.

Payton heaved his feet up and hurled him in. He slid Otto's belt off and used it to secure his arms behind his back, and with Tau's belt bound his ankles. Once Payton pulled him between the pallets, he stuffed the bandanna into Otto's mouth. Johannes and Tau, both alive, were motionless. Payton used their shoelaces to secure their arms and ankles. They wouldn't bother Ben.

Back in the warehouse, he went to a wooden cart loaded with three bundles. The heavy smell of tobacco hung in the air. Tobacco leaves and stems protruded from a tear in one of the burlap bundles.

He lifted the cart's heavy handle and pushed it onto the wharf toward the barges. The bundles were stacked high enough to block the view of anyone from the cabin who might see him.

At the rear barge, he stepped over the gunwale, climbed the metal stairs, and stopped on the walkway beside the wheelhouse door. With the Glock in one hand, he eased the handle down with his other.

An older, white-haired man leaned over a table next to the control panel and studied a map. Behind him, windows overlooked both barges.

No one else was in the cabin.

Payton slipped inside.

The guy jolted back with his hands up when he saw the Glock pointed his way. Payton put his index finger to his lips and in slow motion moved his head from side to side.

His eyes wide with terror, the man nodded and glanced to an open doorway.

Payton stepped over, saw the spiral stairs, and waved the man over with the gun. Hands still raised, the frightened man came toward him. Payton reached over and opened a narrow closet door beside the doorway. Life preservers and rubber slickers hung on brass hooks.

He gestured toward the closet, and the man stepped into the tight space. Payton shut the door and pushed the dead-bolt into place.

Payton started down one step at a time. At the third turn, he saw the last few steps and dirty beige vinyl hallway floor tiles. The humid air was thick with engine oil and cooked bacon. A low rumble from the diesel engine came from an open door to his right.

He went left and pushed through the first door he came to. An empty galley with bunk beds on either side of an open area and chairs around a table with plates of half-eaten food.

Back in the hallway, he moved to another door, pressed down on the heavy metal handle, and eased it out.

The first row of stacked bundles was ten yards away. He was halfway to them when Colonel Mifflin appeared between two of the stacks and fired once with a small silver handgun. She was gone when his shot thudded into the tobacco where she'd been.

Pain seared through his left side above his hip. He scrambled to the nearest stack.

Three more shots punched into the burlap beside him. Musty tobacco dust puffed out with each shot.

When he looked down, he expected to see a hole in his side but instead saw a long gash.

He edged forward in the few feet of space between the stacks and portside gunwale and quick glanced toward the bow.

No Mifflin.

Had she jumped onto the wharf, or was she still on the barge?

When he stepped toward the bow, several rounds from a machine gun hammered across the deck beside him. He jumped back and through a tiny space between the stacks saw a Recces with Mifflin at the bow behind a mechanical crane used to move cargo.

The Recces fired his AK-47 again. Bullets slammed into the burlap, deck, and gunwale.

He couldn't go forward without being exposed. The cabin's shadow loomed over him, and an idea came to him.

He forced the pain in his side out of his mind and went through the open tower door, back up the stairs, and into the wheelhouse.

When he stole a glance out the cabin's windows, he saw Mifflin and the Recces still behind the crane. The Recces scanned the stacks with his AK.

Next to the closet with the man still inside, he saw what he needed through a round door window. Beyond was a narrow hallway, and another door opened onto the tower's rear walkway a few feet farther back.

In the hallway, he opened the wall-mounted metal cabinet. There was a brass-knobbed fire hose wound around a metal wheel, a white plastic first aid kit, and a canvas bag. He unzipped the bag and saw what he was looking for.

Out on the walkway behind the tower curve, he pulled a stubby flare from the bag and twisted the top off. When the white and red flame popped to life, he heaved the flare over the cabin roof. In quick succession, he twisted and threw three more to the left, middle, and right.

A burst from the AK exploded the cabin's windows, and bullets smashed through the metal roof.

Payton scrambled down a ladder on the back side of the tower. He saw two flares sputter against the port gunwale. The other two landed where he wanted them to among the tobacco bundles. Thick smoke started to rise.

Another burst from the AK sprayed the cabin.

He moved beside the bundles again. Fire raged and smoke engulfed the front half of the barge. He didn't see Mifflin, but the Recces still had his AK aimed up toward the wheelhouse.

Payton glanced around the end stack, and the Recces swung his weapon. Bullets peppered the deck and bundles. When the AK-47 paused, Payton leaned low and fired.

The Glock jammed.

He dropped it and pulled out Tau's pistol. Four of his rounds pinged off the crane base. The fifth found its mark, and the Recces sprawled backward, his machine gun falling from his hands.

"Where is she?" Payton crouched with the pistol aimed at the South African's cauliflower ear. He was Otto's man from the Pizza Hut.

He grunted and held his leg where he'd been hit.

Payton kicked him hard on the hand he held over his leg wound. Pale white, he nodded toward the front barge.

He tossed the AK into the river and checked to see if the Recces had another weapon. He didn't, but Payton didn't have time to deal with him, so he hoisted the guy up and over. Twenty feet below he heard a splash.

Smoke blanketed the deck, but Payton saw a rope and wood walkway stretching to the empty front barge. He went over the flimsy walkway and hopped down onto the buckled metal deck. His side screamed with pain when he landed.

From the rusted gunwale, he saw Mifflin on the wharf sprint toward the money truck. He hauled himself up a short ladder, jumped down, and ran after her.

Off to his left, a black Audi with tinted windows sped toward them from the direction of the incinerator.

Mifflin looked back and fired twice. Both shots went wide.

The Audi slid to a stop between Mifflin and the truck. A guy emerged from the rear passenger seat. She swung her gun toward him, but he was too quick. The gun flew out of her hand when he swatted it away. He picked her up like a doll and stepped back toward the car.

The driver came around and pointed a long-barreled handgun to her head.

"Don't shoot," Payton yelled. He had both arms extended, with Tau's gun aimed at them.

The front passenger door opened. Another man stepped out and said something to the two men, and the guy lowered his gun.

Marco al-Dulaimi walked toward Payton. "Put the gun down, Special Agent. She's coming with me."

"You two have a partner meeting?" Payton lowered the gun a few inches.

"I'm afraid our partnership has ended. She's a thief," Marco said.

"Industrious, isn't she?" Payton said.

"Fifty-eight million American dollars industrious," Marco said.

"Let's say I can make you whole, but she goes with me," Payton said.

"No one steals from an al-Dulaimi and gets away with it."

"She stays, you get your money."

Marco grinned and showed his stained piano key teeth. "Carlo, he wants to write me a check."

The man who held Mifflin snorted a laugh.

Payton nodded. "Take the truck." He knew they wouldn't get far. The truck was too hot.

They stood for several muted seconds. Payton could see Marco do the math. Mifflin let out a squeal and struggled.

Marco said something over his shoulder. His driver ran to the truck.

"The Iranians your new partners?" Payton said, keeping the gun ready.

"They've always wanted Iraq and saw with the American invasion an opportunity not to be wasted."

"You sold out your country to help them?"

"Patriotism, how American. Under Saddam, if you failed to adapt, you were killed. After your army invaded, it was Abu Ghraib or, worse, Guantanamo Bay for those who didn't adjust to the new reality. The Iranians will take control after you leave, and you will leave someday. One must make accommodations."

"With your help they flooded Iraq with supernotes."

"Our Persian neighbors are expert chess players. While Americans plan one or two moves ahead, they have a strategy for the entire game. They knew once the Americans realized the financial system was in trouble, they'd attempt to buy their way out of the problem."

"Fifty-eight million was your cut?"

"A storage fee for use of our cave she hasn't paid. In too big of a hurry to meet the Iranians."

"Your new partners won't have a problem being shorted fifty-eight million?"

"They understand business."

The driver came over, spoke with Marco, then ran back to the truck.

Payton saw something fly out of the smoke and streak toward them. When Marco and Carlo heard the buzz, it was too late. Angel swooped inches above their heads.

In a tight circle she came back at them and fired twice.

The first bullet hit the Audi's back passenger door, the second thumped into the wharf a few feet from Marco. Angel circled and flew into the barge smoke.

"Leave her!" Marco said and rushed back to the car.

Carlo dropped Mifflin.

Marco yelled to the driver.

Angel streaked over the wharf. Payton heard her fire again. The Audi's rear window shattered.

Payton had Mifflin by the collar.

Behind the wheel, with Carlo next to him, Marco jerked to a stop next to the truck. The trunk lid popped open.

Carlo fired several times up at Angel from the open front passenger window.

Several cubes were tossed into the trunk, then the driver hopped down, slammed the truck lid, and climbed back into the car. Carlo took two more shots at Angel. Marco screeched deeper into the warehouse and out a wide cargo door.

"You almost pulled it off," Payton said.

"I should've killed that pig Marco when I had the chance," she said.

"You'll have a long time to mull it over."

A helicopter flew sideways out of the smoke, past the barges, and hovered for several seconds nose down, then flew over the warehouse toward Marco's Audi.

Another helicopter followed and landed on the wharf. Cleveland with MSGs spilled out.

Payton heard faint gunshots from Marco's direction, then a burst from the helicopter's side door Gatling gun. Humvees with more embassy marines rounded the incinerator and came toward them. One peeled off toward the barges.

Blacknife and Carl came out of the first Humvee. Rammer hopped out of the second with Angel's radio. He moved one of the control arms, and she circled over them. Then he set the radio on his seat and came over to Payton with Cleveland.

"Ben's in the truck and needs immediate medical help. Use one of those helicopters to get him to Ibn Sina Hospital. You'll also find Otto with two of his men. Another one's in the river."

Cleveland spoke with Carl, who ran to the truck with several marines.

Payton gave Colonel Mifflin a nudge toward Rammer. "She wanted the money. Let her have it. Put her in the back of the truck."

Rammer handcuffed and hauled her away.

"Not a moment too soon," Payton said and pointed up to Angel.

"She's a doll," Cleveland said.

"We need to hold on to Rammer. He has a future," Payton said.

"A bright one," Cleveland said.

CHAPTER 51

THE EMBASSY

PAYTON AND CLEVELAND stood with Ambassador Rhodes around Cleveland's conference table.

"How's Ben?" Ambassador Rhodes asked.

"In pretty bad shape," Cleveland said.

"His doctors believe they caught the internal bleeding in time," Payton said.

"Why'd they move him all over Iraq?" Rhodes asked.

"When Mifflin's Iranian handlers found out Senator Ater's nephew discovered the supernotes, they wanted him smuggled to Tehran. She had Otto Van Heerden, Titan United's director of operations, send his men to Ben's trailer, where they took him," Payton said.

"How did they get him out of the Green Zone?" Rhodes asked.

"The tunnel we discovered that led into the warehouse with the kitchen," Cleveland said.

"The Quds Force unit in the cave planned to take him back to Iran. When we saw Otto interrogate Ben in the house, he was after whoever else Ben told about the super-notes," Payton said.

"The tea shop business was all part of her plan?" Rhodes asked.

"Mifflin had Otto destroy the building to focus our investigation on what Ben might've been up to in the Red Zone instead of his work. Which gave more time for supernotes to work their way through BUI and the hawala system," Payton said.

"The tea shop and BUI riots were part of their grand scheme to keep us off balance," Cleveland said.

"The Iranians wanted the convoy money?" Rhodes asked.

"The heist of all heists," Cleveland said.

"They knew we'd fly more money over to avert a financial crisis. Mifflin was to barge the cash along with the Quds Force team and Ben to a ship in the Persian Gulf," Payton said.

"Our navy intercepted an Iranian fishing vessel three miles out in the Gulf she was to rendezvous with," Cleveland said.

"Her job put Mifflin in the perfect position to pull off the operation," Payton said.

"The economy flames out, and a billion plus of our money ends up in the mullahs' bank accounts. For the exclamation point, Ben Ater gets taken to Tehran. His uncle is the Iranians' biggest critic. The president has the senator's Iranian sanctions plan on his desk for approval," Rhodes said.

"Imagine the mullahs' joy when his nephew arrives in Tehran," Cleveland said.

"She was a gold mine for the Iranians with her top secret clearance," Payton said.

"Gabe Kuttic will be pleased you found the Green Zone spy," Rhodes said.

"He has a bigger problem with Yusuf being taken out of play," Payton said.

"How did the Iranians turn Mifflin?" Rhodes asked.

"Their Ministry of Intelligence and Security snagged her in a honey trap fifteen years ago and blackmailed her with the video. Once she was promoted to run the contractor program, the mullahs saw their opportunity," Payton said.

"Mifflin brought Otto in, who, with his Recces, handled anyone who got out of line. When Graham Vicar realized what they were up to, she bribed him to keep quiet. His mistake, he lost his nerve so they killed him," Cleveland said.

Rhodes stepped over to the door. "Mexico, now Iraq. Ladd, you're two for two. Every time I'm around you, a country gets saved," Rhodes said and left.

CHAPTER 52

ISLE OF PALMS

PAYTON RAN HARDER through a light mist along the surf's edge where the sand was firm. He'd swum parallel to the shore eight hundred yards and came out of the water almost where the second line of umbrellas and chairs started past the beach bar at Wild Dunes Resort.

Not bad for his first ocean swim in months.

Tomorrow he'd push past twelve hundred yards, and by the end of the week be back to his normal mile swim along the South Carolina shore and run back to his beachfront bungalow.

He took longer strides, rounded the bend, and saw the blue umbrella speck on the wide beach.

The sun was hot on his bare shoulders, and salt air filled his lungs. He ignored the stiffness in his side where the bullet graze was almost healed, and vaulted a water-logged railroad tie washed up by the tide.

Neither he nor Catherine knew if they had a future together, but they decided to try again, one baby step at a time.

He saw her floppy yellow beach hat wave in the breeze under the umbrella, and sprinted the last fifty yards over the softer sand.

She set her open novel against her arm sling and took off her reading glasses. "I lost sight of you," she said.

He ducked under the umbrella, bent down, lifted her hat brim, and gave her a kiss on the cheek.

"I came out at the beach bar."

"You swam all the way down there?"

"By Friday I'll make the inlet."

"What about your side?"

"Can't even feel where the stitches were. How's the shoulder?"

"The pain's gone. Your lunch Lemoncellos did the trick," she said.

He sat on his beach towel. "Those three weeks before your sling comes off will fly by," he said.

He pulled a plastic water bottle from an oversized white and green striped beach bag and took a long drink.

Director Santiago had told her when she was ready, her next assignment would be with Scotland Yard's financial crime unit. Payton had no idea what crisis he'd be off to next. Right now, he didn't care. He only wanted Catherine and their time together.

Her cell phone vibrated and she glanced at the screen.

"Cleveland. Should I answer?" she asked.

He motioned for the phone and pressed speaker.

"You want to make sure we have sunblock?" Payton asked.

"If I know you, Ladd, it'll be sun, sand, and two o'clock cocktails," Cleveland said.

"Only after a nap. How's Baghdad?"

"Delightful. Catherine, you there?"

"Hello, Cleveland," she said.

"Baptism by fire for your replacement. A mortar round from across the river hit the auxiliary building yesterday and knocked out the embassy's HVAC. Won't be back online for a week."

"You'll get danger pay allowance if you have to work without air conditioning," she said and smiled at Payton.

"You mean survival pay. I called to interrupt your beach beauty time to let you two know early voting is under way with hardly any violence. Khleifat's a distant third, and Defense Secretary Ordway's not too happy he won't win."

"Iraqis don't deserve Khleifat," Payton said.

"What's the latest with Ben?" she asked.

"Senator Ater flew him to the Mayo Clinic on a private jet over the objections of his Ibn Sina military doctors. Momma wanted him out of Iraq. The senator's grateful you brought him back alive, but his sister's livid our security was so lax to allow her precious boy to be kidnapped."

"Does she know he sold dope in the Green Zone?" Payton asked.

"Another reason the senator sent him to the Mayo Clinic was for their inpatient rehab program."

"One of these days Ben will run out of free passes," she said.

"Any word on Yusuf?" Payton asked and took another long drink.

"Fisherman found him snagged in their nets several nights ago five miles downriver."

"Too bad for Gabe," she said.

"He's been reassigned to Jamaica, of all places."

"A real hotbed of intrigue," Payton said.

"Zaki al-Dulaimi turned up in Tehran and is now a special adviser to Iran's president. Marco wasn't so fortunate. He was killed by a hit team two days ago while he sat in traffic on a Tigris River bridge. One too many business deals gone bad."

"What about Mifflin?" Catherine asked.

"She's gotten talky with the FBI. A last-ditch effort to shave a few years off what's ahead of her in Leavenworth," Cleveland said.

"She can forget about appointments where she's going," Catherine said.

"Enough of Iraq for one day. You two enjoy your time off. The world can wait."

Cleveland was gone.

Catherine rubbed suntan lotion on her calf. "Now we have to figure out where we'll have dinner," she said.

"Can I do the other one?" he gestured to her other leg.

"Start with my back," she said and handed him the lotion.

"How about oysters?"

"Aren't they an aphrodisiac?" she asked.

"Really?"

ABBREVIATIONS

AMC — Army Materiel Command
ATV — All Terrain Vehicle
BGW — Baghdad International Airport
BUI — Bank of United Iraq
CPA — Coalition Provincial Authority
DIA — Defense Intelligence Agency
DS — Defense Secretary
DoD — Department of Defense
DoS — Department of State
DSS — Diplomatic Security Service
DS/CC — Diplomatic Security Command Center
EFP — Explosively Formed Penetrator
ETA — Estimated Time of Arrival
FOB — Forward Operating Base
IED — Improvised Explosive Device
MSG — Marine Security Guards
MWR — Morale, Welfare and Recreation facility
NGO — Nongovernmental Organization
Recces — South African Special Forces Brigade
RPG — Rocket-propelled Grenade
RSO — Resident Security Officer
SEO — Security Engineering Officer
TDA — Temporary Duty Assignments
WMD — Weapons of Mass Destruction

AFTERWORD

WHILE THE STORY and characters in this novel are fictional, many of the organizations and technologies on which the events are based are real. I made every effort to get the details right in those instances, but if there are errors I humbly beg the reader's pardon, and the pardon of those who live the reality.

Thank you very much for joining Payton and me in this adventure. If you're not one of those folks who writes online reviews, I sincerely hope you enjoyed the book. If you are moved to leave a review, I'm grateful, whether you liked the book or not. Constructive feedback is always welcome.

ABOUT THE AUTHOR

I. James Bertolina is hard at work on his next book. You can find him online at:

ijamesbertolina.com/
facebook.com/IJamesBertolina/